THEATRE SHOES

THEATRE
SHOES

Noel Streatfeild

DELACORTE PRESS/NEW YORK

Published by
Delacorte Press
1 Dag Hammarskjold Plaza
New York, N.Y. 10017

Manufactured in the United States of America
First Delacorte printing

Library of Congress Cataloging in Publication Data
Streatfeild, Noel.
Theatre shoes.

Originally published as: Theater shoes, or other
people's shoes.
Summary: When their father is captured during the war,
three children come to London to live with their grandmother and join all the cousins of their talented
theatrical family in a school for stage training.
[1. Acting—Fiction.   2. England—Fiction]   I. Title.
PZ7.S914Th   1985   [Fic]
ISBN 0-385-29399-2
Library of Congress Catalog Card Number: 84-22937

Chapter 1

TEA WITH THE BISHOP

It is very difficult to look as if you minded the death of a grandfather who, though you may have spent your holidays in his house, seldom remembered that you did. It was like that with the Forbes children. Their mother had died when Holly, the youngest, was quite little. Before the Second World War they had lived in Guernsey with their father. As soon as war was declared, their father, who had retired from the Navy to have time to bring the children up properly, rejoined the Navy, and the children were sent to England and given to their grandfather to look after.

Grandfather was a clergyman; he was vicar of a village called Martins, but Martins, though he did his duty by it, was far less important than a reference book he was writing on animals mentioned in the Bible. He was so absorbed in this reference book that when Sorrel, Mark and Holly first arrived at the vicarage all he said was, "There were four beasts." At the time the children, not knowing about the reference book, thought this both rude and inaccurate, but after a very little while they understood that he honestly did not realise they were there.

Holidays came and went and, except in church, the children hardly ever saw their grandfather. Sometimes they saw him on his bicycle going to visit somebody in the village, but mostly he was shut in his study; he even ate his meals there. Then, two years later, he spoke to them again. He told them about their father. This time he was not so much vague as buttoned-up looking. It was as if he had fastened an extra skin round him as a covering against feeling miserable.

"The telegram says 'missing.'"

"Nothing about 'presumed drowned'?" Sorrel asked.

"Nothing."

"Then he could easily be a prisoner in the hands of the Japs," she persisted.

Grandfather looked at her.

"Quite possibly," he said, and shut his study door. Sorrel was just going to be eleven at that time. Mark was nine and a half and Holly eight and a quarter. The telegram talk had taken place in the hall. Mark swung on the banisters.

"I bet he's a prisoner."

"If he's a prisoner or . . ." Sorrel broke off; she did not believe her father was drowned, so she was not going to say the word. "Who do we belong to? Grandfather?"

Holly smelt something good cooking.

"Let's ask Hannah."

Hannah was what made holidays with Grandfather bearable. She had been looking after him for years and years, and she treated him with a mixture of affection and rudeness, but never with respect.

"I give respect where respect is called for," she would say to Grandfather, "and it's not called for when you wear your suit so long you can see your face in it, and it's green rather than black. And it's not called for when, instead of taking an interest in decent Christian things, you get creating about eagles, lions and the like, which aren't what a person expects to hear about in a vicarage."

Hannah treated Grandfather as if he were a piece of furniture, flicking him over with a duster or a feather mop.

6

"Look at you, looking like something thrown away for salvage! Dust everywhere!"

Perhaps because she had always liked them, or perhaps because she had lived so long in a vicarage, Hannah was a great singer of hymns. All day long snatches of hymn came from her, often with bits that were not hymn stuck on and sung to the same tune, or something like it.

"We plough the fields and scatter, the good seed . . . drat the butcher, that's a wretched piece of meat!"

On the morning when Grandfather had his telegram, Hannah was not singing. She knew what was in the telegram and she was very fond of Mr. Bill, as she called the children's father. All the same, singing or not, she was comforting-looking. She was all curves, a round top piece which was pushed in a little in the middle, only to bulge out enormously down below. Her legs had great calves, which curved only slightly at the ankles before they became feet. She had a curving face finished off with a round bun of hair. Usually her face was red, but that morning it was almost pale.

Sorrel looked at her, and quite suddenly she began to cry, and when she cried the other two did too. Hannah knelt on the floor and made room for them all in her arms.

"Do you think he's drowned, Hannah?" Sorrel hiccoughed.

Hannah hugged them tighter.

"Of course I don't. Nor does them at the top that sent that telegram. Gentlemen of few words they are in the Navy. If they mean drowned, they say drowned; if they mean missing, they say missing. Why, we're used to your father being missing. We're always missing him."

After that the children felt better. Hannah said worrying made you cold inside and she gave them all cups of cocoa and, as if there were no such thing as rationing,

7

two spoons of sugar in each cup. While they were drinking their cocoa Sorrel asked Hannah what was going to happen to them. Hannah did not see at first what she was worrying about, and when she did she gave a big laugh.

"You never thought your father didn't arrange for something like this; of course he did. You'll go on just the same until he comes back. You and Holly at Ferntree School for Girls, and Mark at Wilton House."

Mark frowned when he was puzzled.

"But who pays for us if Daddy can't?"

"Who says your father can't? Of course he's provided for you, and, as a matter of fact, your grandfather pays your school bills, and always has."

Mark took a big swallow of cocoa.

"Why?"

Hannah was cooking the lunch. She looked over her shoulder at him.

"What a boy for questions! Your father lost money when the Germans took the Channel Islands, but your grandfather had enough, so that was all right."

Sorrel had two plaits. She fiddled with them when she was worried. She was fiddling now.

"He doesn't seem to get much for it. I mean, we aren't what you'd call a pleasure to him."

"I wouldn't say that," said Hannah. "There's pleasure comes from knowing you're doing your duty. When he takes his mind away from his lions and snakes and that, he knows you're safe here or safe at school and he can go back to his work feeling there's nothing more he can do."

In August Grandfather died. He finished writing his reference book, and it was as if that was what he was waiting for, because he just ruled a neat little line under the last animal's name, and then he was dead.

"If only we had the coupons for decent black; you couldn't want anything more seemly," said Hannah.

The people who lived in the parish were always very

8

nice to the children, and when Grandfather died they were nicer than ever, asking them to so many meals that they could have had two or three lunches and teas every day. The children did not go to the funeral, but after it they had tea with the Bishop, who took it. Hannah had been so pleased that the Bishop was taking the funeral, and so sure that the furniture ought to be given an extra polish because he was coming, that the children were prepared for somebody they would simply hate, but he was not at all hateable. They had tea in the dining-room with cucumber sandwiches and a jam sponge, and he was just as openly pleased about the sandwiches and the jam sponge as they were. It was when the last sandwich was eaten that he began to talk about the future.

"I suppose you three have got on to the fact that you won't be living here anymore."

They had, of course, realised that a new vicar must be coming. Mark said so.

"Hannah thought I was the person to tell you about your future. Hannah has a very great respect for gaiters. She thinks where there are gaiters there must be great intellect. It's not correct, of course. I'm just an ordinary person that you can ask ordinary questions from. So stop me if I tell you something stupidly and you don't understand what I'm saying. How much do you know about your mother?"

The children thought.

"I can remember a little, I think," said Sorrel. "I'm not certain though; I may just think that I do."

"Did your father never talk to you about her?"

"Oh, yes, of course," said Holly. "She was so beautiful that people used to turn and stare in the streets."

Mark leant forward.

"She was very gay. When she was in the house it was as if the sun was always shining."

Sorrel flicked back a plait which had fallen forward.

"In Guernsey everything lovely in the house she chose and Daddy never would have anything moved from where she had put it."

The Bishop nodded.

"Very lucky children to have had such a mother, but she was even more interesting than you know. She was a Warren. Adeline Warren."

He said Adeline Warren as if it were something that tasted good.

Holly said: "We knew her name was Adeline. Daddy called her 'Addie.'"

"But you didn't know she was a Warren, or what the name Warren means. The Warrens are one of the oldest and one of the most distinguished theatrical families in this country."

The children were so surprised that for a moment they said nothing. Never once had their father said anything about the theatre.

"Do you mean our mother's father was an actor?" Sorrel asked.

"Her father was an actor, her mother was, and still is, an actress. Her brothers and sisters are all on the stage. So were her grandparents and great-grandparents. So was she for just one year. Lovely Adeline Warren! I had the good fortune to see her."

Mark liked his facts clear.

"Did she stop acting because she married?"

The Bishop looked at each of them in turn to be sure they were attending.

"She was eighteen, and your grandmother was very proud of her, so proud that she thought she ought to have the very best of everything, especially husbands."

"And she chose Daddy," said Holly.

"No. She chose somebody else. A very important man. Your mother was very young and perhaps a little afraid of your grandmother, and she did not say 'I won't marry

10

him, I love somebody else,' so preparations for an enormous wedding went on, and then, when everybody was in the church, including the bridegroom, a message came to say that she was sorry, she was not going to be married that day, and never to that bridegroom. She was going to marry your father."

"And so she did," said Holly.

"Yes, but it wasn't as easy as all that. Your grandmother was very angry, and she never saw your mother again."

"What, because she married Daddy?" said Mark. "I should think she ought to have been jolly pleased to have Daddy in the family."

"I know, perhaps she should. Perhaps she's sorry now, but at that time she felt she'd been made to look foolish, and she lost her temper. Very understandable, you know."

"I don't think it was very understandable," said Sorrel. "To be angry at the time was all right, but fancy never seeing our mother again!"

"The Channel Islands are a long way off. Your mother only lived four years after she married your father. I expect your grandmother was heartbroken when she died. I feel sure she was."

Sorrel eyed the Bishop suspiciously.

"Why do you want us to like our grandmother?"

There was quite a pause before he answered.

"Because we have been writing to her. You are going to live with her."

Questions burst from them all.

"Where does she live?"

"Does she act now?"

"When are we going?"

"I don't think she is acting in anything at the moment. You are going next week. She lives in London."

Chapter 2

IN THE TRAIN

It was when they were in the train traveling to London
that Hannah broke the news. The train was an inconve-
nient place to talk in because there were fourteen people
in their carriage. Ten quite sitting, two partly sitting and
two standing up. Sorrel and Mark were on the same side;
Sorrel was a quite sitter and Mark a part sitter. Hannah
and Holly faced them. Both Hannah and Holly would
have been quite sitters if it were not for Hannah's curves,
which took up nearly two seats. On the non-Holly side of
Hannah there was a thin woman, who looked as if she
were wearing tin underclothes, she was so stiff and held-
in looking. She was clearly a woman who knew her rights,
and her most immediate right was, having paid for a seat,
to have the proper space for one person to sit on. She
fought so hard to prevent even a quarter of an inch of
Hannah bulging into her piece of seat that she dare not
open a book or take out a piece of knitting for fear she
should relax and Hannah's curves win. Because of this
woman Holly had to do all the giving way to Hannah's
curves, and she had less than a quarter of a seat and was
pushed so far foward that she was almost in the middle of
the carriage.

The train had been bumbling along for about half an
hour when Hannah, taking a deep breath as if she were
going to blow up a balloon, said:

"You aren't any of you going back to school."

They were all so surprised that for a moment they did not speak. After all, it was almost term time, and up to that minute it was as certain they were going back as it was certain that Christmas was coming. It was all kinds of stupid things which did not matter at all which struck them first.

"But we've got the uniform," said Sorrel, "and we haven't the coupons for anything else."

Mark was frowning.

"I left a pencil case in the bootroom."

Holly was gazing up at Hannah.

"We'll have to go back. They're expecting us. Matron said so when she kissed me good-bye."

"That's for your granny to decide."

Hannah spoke firmly because inside she thought the children's grandmother was making a mistake, and she knew that the Bishop thought the same thing. When the letter came asking had notice been given the schools that the children were not returning, and if not please would somebody do it at once, the Bishop had written to Grandmother. He pointed out that the children were happy at their schools and too many changes at once were upsetting. He wrote very nicely, of course, saying it was not his business to interfere, and he only dared as an old friend of the children's father's family. Grandmother had written back also very nicely, but also a very dignified letter. It was good of the Bishop to trouble himself, but she was arranging to have the children educated in London.

"Where are we going to school, then?" Sorrel asked.

Hannah did her very best to sound as if she approved.

"Your granny's having you educated in London."

"But where?" Sorrel persisted.

"Now, how should I know?" Hannah sounded cross. "We'll learn soon enough when we get there."

13

Sorrel said no more. She stared out of the window. It was, of course, nice to be going to see London. It was exciting in a way to be going to meet her grandmother, but on the whole, everything was pretty dismal. She liked Ferntree. Since Grandfather had died and they had heard about London she had felt a sinking-lift feeling inside, not all the time, of course, but quite often, and the cure for the lift feeling was thinking of Ferntree. When she and Holly got back there everything would be ordinary again. Of course there would still be no vicarage, and only Grandmother to go to in the holidays, but it would be easier to sort things out at Ferntree. It did not, Sorrel decided, matter very much if bits of your life became peculiar as long as there was something somewhere that stayed itself. Up till this minute Ferntree had been the something somewhere. To her horror, thinking about no more Ferntree made her eyes suddenly full of tears. She was horribly ashamed. Crying in a train! What would people think of a girl of eleven crying in a train! She sniffed, pushed up her chin, threw back her plaits and, as a way of getting rid of the tears, shook her head; then she muttered, "Smut in my eyes," and turned to Mark.

Mark was making awful faces at his shoes. It was the only way to stop himself from crying. Not going back to Wilton House! He thought of his friends, of his chances for the second football team, of how one of the boys had said he would bring him back a forked bit of wood off a special sort of tree which only grew in the woods near his home and made a simply super catapult.

"I daresay," Sorrel said to him in a wobbly voice, "schools are all right in London."

Mark gulped and made even worse faces.

"Pretty sickening it being this term. I was going to have a special do for my birthday."

Sorrel's voice wobbled more than ever.

"I expect we wouldn't mind so much if it wasn't there's been such a lot of changes. I mean, our coming to Grandfather and then the Germans landing at home so we couldn't go back there even for a holiday."

Mark tried so hard that a woman with a baby in the corner looked at him and nudged her husband.

"Shocking faces that kid makes."

"Then Dad . . ." said Mark.

Sorrel knew that their father was the last person they dared think of, so she scuttled on, stammering she spoke so fast.

"Then Grandfather dying and us having to leave the vicarage."

Mark's tears were gaining.

"And now not going back to school."

Hannah could not lean forward because the thin woman with her rights kept her wedged; instead she pressed Sorrel's toe with her foot.

"What about us having a nice bit of something to eat. You'll none of you guess what I've got in our basket."

The basket was on the rack. Neither Sorrel nor Mark felt like eating, but they were glad of something to do.

"If Holly gets up," said Mark in a sniffy voice, "I can climb on her bit of seat and get the basket down."

An American soldier was standing by the window chewing gum. He gave a slow smile.

"All right, son, I'll pass it."

He took the basket off the rack and put it half on Hannah's knees and half on the skinny knees of the woman with her rights. It would have seemed an accident, only as he turned away to loll back against the window he gave Sorrel and Mark a very meaningful wink.

That wink somehow cheered things up. A world where grown-up people could do funny things like that could not be as depressing as it had looked a few minutes ago.

15

Hannah, quite disregarding her next-door neighbour, opened the basket. The woman with her rights spoke as if each word were a cherry-stone she was spitting out.

"Do you mind moving that basket on to your own knees."

Hannah beamed at her as if she were being nice.

"I'm sorry, I'm sure, but fixed like we are it's hard to know whose knee is whose." The rest of the people in the carriage, because of too little space and too much tobacco smoke, had been half asleep. Now, as if Hannah's voice was the breakfast gong, they all sat up and looked interested. Hannah was pleased; she liked conversation to be general. She drew everybody in with a glance. "We had an early breakfast and we're a bit low-spirited. Nothing like something to eat as a cure for that."

In her basket Hannah had egg and cress sandwiches, and in a little box some chocolate biscuits. Eggs were not a surprise because at the vicarage they had kept hens, but chocolate biscuits!

The sight of real egg and chocolate biscuits both at the same minute excited the other passengers so much that in no time they were talking like old friends. Of course the conversation was mostly food, but food was what grown-up people liked talking about, so that was all right; anyway, the general buzz made a cheerful atmosphere, and that, together with eating, made Sorrel and Mark feel a lot better, and the finish to feeling better was put by the American soldier. Like a conjurer pulling a rabbit out of a hat, he suddenly produced three enormous sweets out of his pocket and gave them one each. Sorrel was worried about taking them.

"Are you sure you can spare them?" she asked anxiously. "I mean, as big as this they must be a lot of your ration."

The soldier did not seem to be a man who said a lot.

16

"Forget it."

It was when the American's sweet was in their mouths and they could not speak that Hannah had her talk with a nice-looking woman in tweeds. It began by the woman asking where they were going, and Hannah not only told her, but told her all the other things, starting with their mother and going through the Channel Islands, their father and then Grandfather, finishing with who their grandmother was. The woman was interested and asked about schools. Hannah explained about Ferntree and Wilton House. The woman shook her head and said "bad luck," and then she said:

"Changing about is a nuisance, especially if there was any thought of scholarships later on."

"I never heard talk of that," said Hannah.

The tweed woman leant forward and smiled at Sorrel and Mark.

"Just as well. It's so easy to miss a chance by shifting about at the wrong age."

The conversation about education finished there and shifted to the baby of the woman in the corner, but it did not finish in Sorrel's mind. "It's so easy to miss a chance." Did Grandmother know that Mark was going into the Navy? Mr. Pinker, headmaster of Wilton House, had known. Had he been teaching Mark thinking of his entrance exam? Of course Mark would not be the right age to go in for his examinations yet, but how awful if he ought to be being specially prepared. Daddy had written to Mr. Pinker, and he knew all about it, but would the new London school? Sorrel looked at Mark and saw he had either not listened to the tweed woman or was not interested; he was placidly sucking and playing with an indiarubber band. She looked at Holly, but of course Holly was not bothering, she was far too young; in fact, in spite of the smallness of her piece of seat, she seemed to

17

be nearly asleep, though she was still enough awake to suck at her sweet. Sorrel looked at Hannah. Hannah was an angel, but not the person to understand about examinations. She looked on education in the same way as she looked upon food rationing, something the government insisted on and therefore you had to do, but she personally did not think education was important except perhaps reading, writing and being able to add and, if put to it, subtract.

It is queer how all in a minute you can understand what growing up means. Sorrel did not look very grown-up, she was small for her age. She was wearing a rather short cotton frock. She usually had bare legs, but to travel in she was wearing white socks and her brown school walking shoes. Looking at her you might have made a guess that she was ten and not a person who was going to be twelve in April. But at that minute inside she was far more than her age. Grandfather was dead, Daddy was a prisoner in the hands of the Japs, at least that was what she was going to believe; Hannah was grand for most things, but not everything, and Mark and Holly were still too young to feel responsible. It was up to her to take a little of her father's place. Of course Grandmother might be absolutely perfect, one of those sort of grown-up people who always did sensible things without any fuss, but then she might not. She pushed her sweet into her cheek and turned to Mark.

"When we get to Grandmother's, if you and Holly don't like things awfully, you will tell me, won't you?"

Mark had been thinking of catapults; he came back to the train with a jump. Sorrel had to repeat what she had said. He fixed puzzled eyes on her.

"What sort of things?"

Sorrel wished she had not said anything, it was so difficult to explain.

"Just things. I mean, I want you to know I'm there."

Mark thought she was being idiotic.

"Of course you'll be there; where else would you be?"
He went back to thinking about catapults.

Chapter 3
NUMBER 14

They drove to Grandmother's in a taxi. The children stared out of the windows. After Martins London seemed a busy place. Buses dashing everywhere and crowds of people on the pavements. They asked Hannah every sort of question because she had once been to London for the day and so they thought she ought to know all about it. Where was Madame Tussaud's? Where was The Tower? Where was Westminster Abbey? Where was the Zoo? Hannah had no idea where any of these places were, but neither had she any intention of admitting it. She looked out of the window with a thoughtful, pulling-things-out-of-her-memory expression, and said: "We're not so far now." As the station they had arrived at was Paddington, and they were making for a square near Sloane Street, they never went anywhere near any of the places, but by the time the taxi stopped they were all too full of interest in what they were seeing to remember what they had not seen.

No. 14, Ponsonby Square, London, S.W.1, was the address. Ponsonby Square was not a square really, only three sides of one. Tall grey houses all attached to each other, all alike, all built in the reign of Queen Victoria, when houses were long and thin and people expected their servants to live underground in basements, and not to mind carrying water and coals and other heavy things up five flights of stairs. Number 14 looked as if it was the only house in its bit of the square that was being lived in. Number 11 had been blown away by a bomb and nothing was left of it but different-coloured walls and some mantelpieces, which were part of the wall of Number 10, and some more wallpaper and a piece of staircase and a door, which were part of the wall of Number 12. The other houses within sight looked rather battered, and some had lost bits of themselves and it was clear no one lived in them, for they had large E's painted on the doors. Even if the children had not guessed that meant empty, the rusty petrol tins of emergency water on the doorsteps would have told them, for nobody surely would live in a house with a petrol tin standing just where you were bound to fall over it every time you came out.

The children's schools were in the country, and they had only been in little towns and had not seen much bomb damage before, and never deserted houses which people had been forced to leave in a hurry. Hannah was busy with the taxi-driver, and they had not for a moment her sensible, comforting way of looking at things to help them. They stood staring round with horror written all over their faces.

"People can't live here," said Mark. "It's much too nasty."

Sorrel had her eyes on the space which had been Number 11.

"How queer to think that it once had a door and windows and people coming in and out."

Holly began to cry.

"I don't like it. I want to go back to Martins. It's all so dirty here."

Hannah swung round from the pile of luggage she and the driver were counting.

"What's all this about?" She glanced at Number 14 and

along the square. If, to her country eyes, it seemed as depressing as it did to the children, not a sign of it showed on her face. She beamed as if the houses were old friends. "Proper old-fashioned, isn't it? Go on, Mark, ring the bell; I can do with a nice cup of tea if you can't."

It was queer how Hannah changed things. As she said "proper old-fashioned" the square seemed different. It was just as shabby, the petrol tins were just as rusty, the white-painted E's on the doors just as queer, but instead of it all seeming rather sinister it became curious.

It was when Mark was on the steps ringing the bell that he noticed the garden.

"Look," he said, "a garden!"

Sorrel was mopping and tidying Holly's face, so she did not turn at once, but when she did she felt a shiver of pleasure run all through her. The garden had once been shut in with railings, but the railings had been taken away to make munitions, and the trees of the garden were sticking out over the pavement and, though there was a proper gate and path a little way down the square, it was clear you could push in anywhere. Through the trees there were patches of colour, the mauves and purples of Michaelmas daisies, the pinks and reds of roses.

"Look, Holly," she said, "a proper garden. Now there's nothing to cry about, is there?"

The taxi-driver, who was unstrapping their big box, looked at Sorrel over his shoulder.

"You're right there, it's a proper garden. Me and my mate we often slips in there for a smoke after our dinner. Lovely it is inside. Flowers and all. Ought to see it in the spring, proper picture it is."

"Who does it belong to?" Sorrel asked.

The taxi-driver laughed.

"Well, the people in this square rightly, I suppose. I hear they pays to keep it up, but they aren't here and the

22

rails is gone, so there's no 'arm done when you has a nice sit down and a smoke."

Sorrel looked at the others.

"The people in the square! That's us. Fancy us having a garden in London!"

They heard steps inside the house. Hannah, who had just brought up two of the suitcases, looked in a nervous way at each of the children.

"Sorrel, keep hold of Holly's hand. You all look as if you'd come off a train, but I daresay your granny will understand you started out looking nice."

There was the sound of a rusty key being turned and the clank of a heavy chain, and the door was thrown open. In the doorway stood a little thin grey-haired woman with the biggest smile any of them had ever seen.

Mark remembered his manners. He lifted his cap.

"How do you do? Are you our grandmother?"

The woman laughed. Not a gentle laugh to fit her size but a great rolling sound as if she enjoyed it so much she did not care if it tore her to bits.

"Your granny! No. Bless the boy, you'll be the death of me! Your granny! No, indeed, I'm Alice. Buckingham Palace to you."

Sorrel held out her right hand.

"How d'you do? I'm Sorrel."

Alice took her hand and pulled her into the hall; then she turned her to face the light. She gave her a kiss.

"So you're Sorrel. Why, you're the living image of Miss Addie."

Mark was shocked.

"Do you mean our mother? Sorrel can't be, our mother was a great beauty."

Alice kissed him.

"Not always she wasn't. Not when she was your sister's age and popping in and out of our dressing-room, driv-

23

ing us mad with her tricks; she was the spitting image of Sorrel then." She knelt down by Holly and hugged her and then turned her to the light. "I don't know who you're like. Maybe there's something of your granny, but she never had curls. Hair like a pikestaff we've always had." She caught hold of one of Mark's hands and drew him to her. "Well, there's no doubt what family you belong to. You're the spitting image of your uncle Henry, and he's the spitting image of old Sir Joshua, if the portrait of the old man doesn't lie."

Mark's eyes screwed up at the corners when he was cross. He drew himself up to look as tall as possible.

"If you are at all interested, I'm exactly like my father, and he was exactly like his grandfather, who was an admiral. We know that he was an admiral because there was a picture of him in the dining-room in the vicarage."

Alice rolled out another laugh.

"Well, I'm not going to quarrel, but you have a look at the picture of Sir Joshua sometime, and one afternoon we'll go and see your uncle at the pictures, and then we'll see who's right."

Sorrel had wandered up the passage having a look round. She came hurrying back at Alice's last words.

"Have we an uncle in the pictures?"

Alice seemed startled. She opened her mouth and then closed it, and then opened it again.

"Didn't you know Henry Warren was your uncle?"

Sorrel could see that Alice thought they must have heard of Henry Warren; she spoke gently, as she did not want to seem rude to her uncle.

"We didn't know we had an uncle Henry, so of course we didn't know if he acted for the films. As a matter of fact we haven't been to any films since the war. Except 'Pinocchio' when Daddy had leave."

"And that 'Wizard of Oz,' Mark reminded her.

"We don't go to films at school," Sorrel explained, "because of infection, and there wasn't a cinema in Martins."

Hannah and the taxi-driver had the luggage in the hall. Alice examined it. She looked in a friendly way at Hannah. "You and I can manage that. If the box is too heavy, you can unpack it down here." She waited while Hannah paid the driver, then she took Holly's hand. "Come on, follow us up the old apples and pears." She saw Holly's face was puzzled. "Stairs to you. You'll get used to me in time."

It was a queer house, grand in a way, but shabby. There was a thick purple carpet all up the stairs, but it was getting very worn in places. Half-way up to the first floor there was an alcove with plants in it; this had stiff yellow satin curtains in front of it, but the satin was full of dust and in places was torn. All up the stairs were framed advertisements of old plays, yellow and queerly printed. Some of them had their glass cracked. In the top passage, where were their bedrooms, there was an enormous velvet sofa with a piece of brocade thrown over it. Alice kept up a running commentary on what they were passing.

"Those curtains were in the drawing-room set of ever so comic a comedy. This carpet was used in the front of the house when Sir Joshua had the Georgian Theatre. They're going off a bit now, of course, but they must have been ever so nice in his day. Some of these play bills were cracked when the bomb got Number 11. This sofa was in a season we did of that Ibsen. Proper old whited sepulchre it is now. Got a hole in the velvet you could put a big drum in. That's why I keep the brocade there; that brocade was a bit of our third-act dress in a play by Somerset Maugham." She opened a door and her voice softened. "This room is for Sorrel. It was Miss Addie's."

Sorrel went in first. It was the queerest feeling. "It was Miss Addie's." Her mother's room. Somehow, although her father was always talking about their mother, she had never come as alive before. In Guernsey everything had been as she had planned it, but it was grown-up planning. This room was the room of a girl, someone of about the same age as herself. Sorrel walked round. Unconsciously she walked on tiptoe. It was a pretty room. A white wooden bed with a powder-blue eiderdown. Tied to the bed head was a felt doll with wide skirts and silk thread plaits. Lying on the eiderdown was a pillowcase made like a large white cat. There were blue shiny chintz curtains and the dressing-table had the same chintz frilled round it. On the dressing-table there were silver dressing-table things with "Addie" written on the backs. There was a white chest of drawers and a white cupboard. The carpet was blue, with pink flowers. By the bed on a white table was a white bedside lamp and, propped against it, a green frog. On the mantelpiece were fourteen wooden bears, ranging from a very big bear to a tiny one. There was only one picture; it was of a cornfield. In the corner there was a bookcase. Sorrel knelt down by it. Three whole rows of plays. A Bible. A dictionary. There were a lot of books Sorrel had never heard of, but, as well, there were several old favourites, "Little Women," "Little Lord Fauntleroy," "David Copperfield," a very nice "Alice in Wonderland," and, as well, some baby books, all the Beatrix Potters and Little Black Sambo. Hannah and Alice were talking in the doorway. Sorrel waited for a pause and then broke in.

"This is just as if my mother had only just left it."

Alice came to the top of the bed.

"So it is very near. We sent her clothes on, of course, and we sent her toilet things. That lot there are what she had as a child. Of course, when she was here you could hardly see the walls for photographs; you know what theatricals are."

"What happened to the photographs?" Mark asked.

Alice seemed flustered by the question. She tried twice to answer it, and then she spoke more to Hannah than to the children.

"We acted very foolish, no saying we didn't. Destroyed a lot of things when we lost our temper."

Hannah seemed to be tired of the subject of photographs. Her voice was brisk.

"Well, Sorrel isn't the only one who has to sleep tonight; where're the rest of us going?"

There was a large linoleum-floored room, which had been the nursery, for Hannah and Holly and a small room at the end of the passage for Mark. Neither room was in at all good condition; the walls looked dirty and such furniture as there was badly needed paint. Alice was apologetic.

"Looks a bit off, but I had to scratch round and find what I could."

Mark was not fussy, but he was hurt that so little preparation had been made for his coming.

The bed was iron, and instead of an eiderdown there was a plaid rug. It had once had J.W. embroidered on it, but the embroidery threads had broken with age and half the stitching was gone. There was no proper cupboard, only a curtain which had once had a silky pattern on it, but with use almost all the silk pattern was gone and only the cotton threads which had held the design were left. There were no books and no pictures. The only curtains were the blackout ones. Mark went to the window. It looked out on a narrow street at the back of the house. It was one of those streets you find in towns which seem to have nothing in them but the backs of places and storehouses. This street, too, was very battered looking. A black cat was the only living thing to be seen. Mark turned his face entirely to the street and made fearful faces at the cat.

Hannah glanced at Sorrel; they both knew how Mark

27

was feeling, but they knew, too, that since they could not alter things it was not much good saying anything. Instead Hannah turned to Alice.

"When are they seeing their granny?"

Alice too had her eyes on Mark; she seemed glad to be interrupted, for she pounced on the question and answered it in an unnaturally gay voice.

"As soon as we've had a drop of rosy." Hannah looked enquiring. "Lee. Tea. You'll soon get used to old Alice."

"I'll get some things up, then." Hannah struggled hard to sound as bright as Alice, but her eyes kept turning to Mark, and as well she was thinking of the old nursery. She did not mind the linoleum, but in the nursery too there were no real curtains, only black-out, and though there was a cupboard, it was meant for toys and there was nowhere to hang anything. She knew she had not sounded as cheerful as she had intended to, so she added, "Come on, Holly dear, you come and help Hannah," and then, to make sure nobody thought her spirits were low, she went along the passage singing "Pleasant are thy courts above," only she sang it properly, without adding any words of her own, which was so unlike her that anybody who knew her would have guessed there was something wrong.

Sorrel scratched one leg with the top of her shoe. She was so sorry for Mark that it hurt inside, but she knew he would not like his misery pried on, especially as he was doing his best not to show he was miserable. She spoke as if she were only that minute noticing the room.

"This room looks pretty drab. I'll get that eiderdown from mine; it'll cheer it up a bit."

Mark sounded as if he were being strangled.

"No."

"It's not fair I should have such a nice room when you've got a foul one." She saw she was doing no good and that the only thing that could possibly help was to

28

find something to admire in the room as it was. It was then she noticed the rug. "I say, I wonder whose rug this was? The W will be Warren, of course, but who was J? Alice said our uncle was called Henry. Oh, I say, when she was talking about who we were like, she said there was a Sir Joshua. I wonder if it was his rug. I bet it was. I say, you are honoured."

Mark was not to be fooled by a tale like that, but Sorrel mentioning Sir Joshua did him good. One emotion can cancel another, and all in a flash Mark stopped feeling miserable and was angry instead. He turned round, his face pink.

"That old Sir Joshua! I'd rather have nothing on my bed than anything of his. I'm like our father, I don't want there to be anything Warrenish about me. Mean sort of stuffy people."

Sorrel nodded.

"Never to see our mother because she had the sense to marry Father."

"And when she does see us to put us into rooms that would be much too shabby to give to a dog that had distemper." Mark hung on the other end of the bed and looked across at Sorrel. "Do you know what I think? I'm going to hate our grandmother. Hate, hate, hate her!"

Alice hurried up the passage. She had a comb in her hand.

"Come on, dears, you're not having your rosy yet; you're to go down straight away."

Sorrel straightened up.

"Where to?"

Hannah began unplaiting Sorrel's hair.

"Where to? Where do you expect? Down the old apples and pears to be received by the great actress Margaret Shaw. In other words, your granny."

Chapter 4
GRANDMOTHER

The whole of the first floor was one big room. There were sliding doors to turn it into two rooms, but when the children first saw the drawing-room the doors were open. Because it was summer-time and there were windows both ends of the room, there was a lot of light streaming in, but somehow, in spite of this, the effect was dim, like the inside of a cathedral. It was in a way the grandest room the children had ever seen. Two great chandeliers hung from the ceiling. The curtains were crimson silk. There were three large statues that looked as if they ought to be in a park. The sofa was piled with violent-coloured cushions and, as well, a gay embroidered piece of Chinese silk. There was a great deal of furniture, all different and all rather big. There were several portraits on the walls. On every table and shelf, and behind glass in two cupboards, were ornaments—silver, gold, porcelain, jade—enough to stock the window of one of those sort of shops which says that it specialises in gifts. As well, on every table, there were photographs in silver frames. On the floor and over some of the chairs were thrown fur rugs. In spite of the amount of things about and the rich colours the drawing-room, just like the rest of the house, looked shabby. The curtains were dusty and threadbare.

The carpet had places where it was wearing thin. A spider had made a web across the frame of one of the portraits. The room had the smell of very old books which have got a little damp.

Of course the children did not see all the things in the room straight away. Each of them saw bits; they all smelt the old-book smell, and they were all impressed with the grandeur, and Sorrel and Mark as well saw some of the shabbiness. It was that quick seeing things and feeling things which comes in the first second in a new place, for there was no time to stare about, for under the window was a chaise-longue, and lying on it was Grandmother.

The children had not before seen a grandmother of their own. Their Forbes grandmother had died before they were born. If they had imagined their mother's mother at all, it was just to suppose she would be bent and grey like Grandfather. What they saw was so different from this picture that for a second they lost their manners and just gaped.

To begin with, Grandmother did not look old. She had dark hair piled up in curls on the top of her head, held in place with combs. She had bright sparkling dark eyes. She was wearing somthing made of mauve velvet that might have been a dress with loose sleeves, or a dressing-gown of a grand sort. She was sitting upright against a jade-green brocade cushion; she had thrown across her knees a Spanish shawl with crimson and orange-coloured flowers embroidered on a white background. Perhaps because the drawing-room lighting was dim, or perhaps because of all the colour on and around Grandmother, it was as if she were a tree with flaming leaves in a wood where all the other trees were dark green.

Grandmother held out a hand.

"Come here, children." Sorrel had to nudge Mark and

pull Holly by the hand. They came slowly up to the couch. All the time they were walking Grandmother's eyes darted from one child to the other. When they were within touching distance she gave a nod. "That's better, now I can see you." She fixed her eyes on Sorrel. "You are very much like your mother."

Sorrel swallowed nervously.

"So Alice said."

Grandmother was examining Mark.

"Alice is a good creature, but she talks too much. Good gracious, boy, you are pure Warren! Extraordinary! Sir Joshua must have been the image of you when he was a child."

Sorrel could see Mark getting red. She nudged him with her elbow. The nudge was meant to say, "Please, please don't argue," but you cannot do much with an elbow. In any case Mark was past nudges. He was scowling horribly.

"As a matter of fact, if you are interested to know, I'm the absolute exact image of my father, and he was the absolute exact image of my great-grandfather, who was an admiral, not just an actor."

There was silence for a moment. Sorrel, twisting her hands nervously, stared at Grandmother wondering what she would do. Mark, still scowling but with his chin in the air, looked as if what he hoped was coming was a further fight. Holly had seen a green-jade horse-like animal on a little table and was thinking how she would like to have it to play with.

Grandmother's face expressed nothing. Her dark eyes bored into Mark, but it was impossible to judge if she was angry. Then suddenly, with one big sweeping movement, she tossed aside the Spanish shawl and got off the chaise-longue.

GRANDMOTHER

"Come with me," As she spoke she propelled Mark across the room. Sorrel and Holly followed behind.

The portrait hung at the far end of the room. It had special electric lights in the frame to show it up. Sir Joshua had been painted as King Henry the Fifth in Shakespeare's play. He stood sideways, his head lifted, a light on his face, his armour gleaming against darkness. His head was uncovered and his dark hair somehow faded into the night background.

The last thing Sorrel meant to do was to take sides with Grandmother against Mark, but she had spoken before she could stop herself.

"It is just like Mark."

Grandmother flung out her arms, her velvet sleeves hung down like banners.

> "A largess universal, like the sun
>   His liberal eye doth give to everyone
>   Thawing cold fear."

She used a big, magnificent sort of rolling voice. Holly, who had not before seen anyone recite with gestures except in a classroom, thought Grandmother was being funny. She laughed. She had a nice laugh, it had a gayness about it which made other people laugh too. It did not make Grandmother laugh, but it stopped her reciting. She fixed her whole attention on Holly.

"Come here, child." Holly came to Grandmother and looked up at her hopefully in case she was going to be funny again. "That's a beautiful laugh. Study it. Keep it. It will be invaluable to you."

Sorrel looked despairingly at Mark. Had he understood what Grandmother meant? Holly had not bothered to try and understand. She caught hold of one of Grandmother's hands.

33

"Could I play with that green horse over there?"

The green horse seemed to bring Grandmother back to ordinary things. She gave Holly permission, flicked off the lights round Sir Joshua's portrait and went back to her chaise-longue. She pulled the Spanish shawl over her and smiled at Sorrel and Mark.

"Wouldn't you like to sit? Now, tell me, is everything upstairs exactly as you like it?"

Sorrel wanted to laugh. It was such sauce to talk like that, seeing what two of the bedrooms were like. She managed to hold her laugh back by turning away and pulling up a chair. Mark was not a boy who let anything pass very easily, and he certainly was not going to let Grandmother suppose he was pleased. He was by the foot of the chaise-longue. He played with a bit of the fringe of the shawl.

"Do you think mine's a nice room?"

Grandmother leant over to a box on the table beside her and took out and lit a cigarette. Then she leant back, waving her cigarette in the air, and quoted in her grand way:

"Two old chairs, and half a candle,
One old jug without a handle."

They knew their Edward Lear, but this quotation so exactly described what Sorrel and Mark thought of his room, and at the same time was so much ruder about it than they would ever have dared to be, that they were speechless. Holly was lying on her face pushing the jade horse across the carpet. She did not mean to be rude, but she just spoke out loud what she was thinking.

"But Mark doesn't live in a wood, nor he isn't a Yonghy-Bonghy-Bo."

Grandmother did not seem to have heard her.

34

"It shall be altered, dear boy. Just give shape to your wishes. Carpets from Persia. Hangings from China. The bed on which a Borgia slept."

Sorrel tried to help Mark.

"It is not those sort of things, though of course the carpet from Persia would be nice; there isn't one, you know."

"No carpet! Extraordinary! Tomorrow everything shall be altered." She broke off, remembering something. "Has Alice told you about tomorrow?" She looked at Sorrel but Mark answered.

"No."

Grandmother took a deep breath of cigarette smoke.

"Tomorrow you are being seen by one of the finest teachers this world has ever produced."

"What does she teach?" Sorrel asked.

"Everything. Voice control. Poise. Diction. Dancing."

Sorrel gaped.

"And arithmetic and grammar and Latin?"

Grandmother waved a hand as if arithmetic and grammar and Latin were made of smoke and could be blown away.

"Those too, I believe."

Sorrel had an awful feeling that Grandmother was not quite real, or at least that she was living apart from real things.

"Is it a school?"

"Certainly it's a school. The best school. I shouldn't dream of allowing my grandchildren to attend any other."

"Does Mark go with us, or is his different? I mean, diction and dancing aren't so usual at a boy's school, are they?"

"Certainly Mark goes. Mark more than anyone. Sir Joshua may live again."

Sorrel tried not to sound desperate but she did not succeed.

35

"What's this school called?"

Grandmother took a deep breath. The words came out of her mouth as if they were beautiful in themselves, which to Sorrel and Mark they certainly were not.

"You are going to Madame Fidolia's Children's Academy of Dancing and Stage Training." She stubbed out her cigarette and waved a dismissing hand. "Take them upstairs, Sorrel dear. I shall see nobody else today." To prove this she shut her eyes and pulled the Spanish shawl over her face.

Chapter 5

BEES AND HONEY

The children ran up the stairs. As soon as they were out of reach of a whisper being heard they stopped.

"If the school's for stage training, do you think it means we're going to be taught to be actresses and you an actor?" Sorrel asked Mark.

Mark scratched at a hole in the carpet with his toe.

"They can teach me what they like, but if they think I'm going to be like that awful Sir Joshua, they couldn't be wronger."

Sorrel leant on the banisters.

"I don't think you can go to a stage school. You're going to be a sailor." She glanced down at Holly, who had seated herself on a step of the stairs. "Oh, Holly, you've taken that horse!"

Mark kicked more violently at the hole.

"A jolly good thing, too, I should say. Sitting in there with so much of everything that she simply can't breathe while people like us haven't even a carpet."

"She said you could have one tomorrow," Sorrel reminded him.

"Hullo there, coming up for your rosy?"

There was no doubt that having Alice about was a help. Everything seemed more ordinary with her around. They hurried up to her. Sorrel got there first.

"Did you know we were going to a stage school?"

"At least that's what she thinks," said Mark.

Alice looked severe.

"'She' is the cat's mother; didn't anyone tell you that?"

Holly held out her horse.

"Look!"

Alice clicked her tongue against her teeth.

"Oh, dear, we won't half make a scene when we find that's gone. Give it to Alice, ducks; I'll just slip it back before it's missed." She saw that Holly looked as if she might cry. "You run up and see what we've got for tea. Something Hannah says is a treat you haven't had since ever so long."

Hannah was laying the tea on a round table in the nursery. They knew what the surprise was before they saw her because she was singing, "Come, let us gather at the river. The beautiful, the beautiful river. What sh-a-a-all I put the shrimps on?"

There is something about shrimps for tea. You can't really feel miserable taking the heads and tails off shrimps, especially when for years you have never seen the sea, let alone a shrimp. They started heading and tailing right away and were talking hard when Alice came back from returning the horse to Grandmother.

"Did you get it back without her noticing?" Sorrel asked.

Alice sat down. There was rather a funny expression on her face.

"Practice makes perfect. Anyway, we had the shawl over our meat pies."

Mark bounced in his chair.

"Eyes! Meat pies means eyes; is that right?"

"You be careful," said Alice; "get much sharper and you'll cut yourself."

Hannah passed Alice a cup of tea.

"Is that right what the children are saying, they are going 'on the stage'?"

Alice laughed.

"Chance is a good thing! They're starting their training tomorrow; that's right. At least that's what was planned, but what we're going to do for bees and honey I don't know." She looked at Mark. "I'll tell you that one, son, because it's a funny day you don't hear me talk about it. Bees and honey means money."

Sorrel looked up from her shrimps.

"But we've always been at schools; I suppose they all cost about the same, don't they?"

Hannah broke in quietly.

"We don't want to spoil our shrimps talking about things like that." She watched Mark help himself to margarine. "That's your grandmother's and Alice's ration, so go carefully now." She turned in a person-at-a-party way to Alice. "I've got what's left of our week's rations in the box I'll give you afterwards. I must go to the Food Office about our change of address tomorrow."

Hannah and Alice began one of those conversations about food that grown-up people enjoy, but Sorrel could feel that Hannah was not having this one because she was enjoying it, but to keep Alice from talking about something else, and she had a frightening thought that the something else was what Alice called bees and honey. What did Alice mean by saying "What they were going to do for bees and honey she didn't know"? There always had seemed to be money. You couldn't suddenly have none, could you, even when your grandfather died? Besides, how could there be none when they had a grandmother who had a big house in the middle of London?

Hannah and Alice had shifted from food to clothes.

"What have you got they can wear tomorrow?" Alice asked. "Have the girls got any of those shorts?"

Hannah was puzzled.

"Yes, they had them for games at their school, but you only put them on for games, didn't you, dears? You didn't wear them regular?"

Holly brushed her hair off her face and left some shrimp whiskers hanging on a curl.

"And we wore them for gymnasium and dancing."

Hannah's face was always red, but now it was going peony-coloured. Her eyes were fixed on Alice and they were anxious as are a dog's who is afraid he is not going to be taken out with his family.

"I've never got to take the children to a theatre school, have I?"

Alice did not understand what Hannah was worrying about.

"I'll tell you how to go."

Hannah looked more anxious than ever; she was so worried she forgot to resent the suggestion that she could not find her way about London.

"It's not that. Church now, or a parish concert, or out to tea however big the house, I've taken the children to them all, but a stage school! I'd feel awkward."

Alice laughed.

"You'd think it was you had to have an audition."

Mark tore the head off a shrimp as if he were tearing the word at the same time.

"What's an audition?"

Alice shook her head at him.

"You'll see, Master Scornful."

Sorrel tried to make up for Mark's rude voice.

"Please tell us, Alice dear."

Alice loved talking about anything to do with the theatre. She took a gulp of tea as if to get her voice in order.

40

"Well, of course, an audition at a school isn't the same as in a theatre, but it's near enough to give you a taste of the real thing. Madame Fidolia will want to see what you can do. Of course, in a theatre audition you do whatever it is right off. Singing, reciting, high kicks and all, but I should think in a school like that different teachers would try you out for each thing separately."

The children's eyes were round with horror.

"But we don't do any of those things," Sorrel gasped.

Mark leant on the table, his voice was ferocious.

"Nor am I going to."

"I did basket ball at our school," Holly explained, "and you aren't allowed to kick at it."

Alice looked from one face to the other; you could see an idea dawning.

"Don't you want to go on the stage?"

Her voice was bewildered and, with equal bewilderment, the children answered.

"Why should we?"

"I should jolly well think we don't."

"I want to go back to Ferntree, Matron's expecting us."

Alice hesitated. It was clear she had a lot to say, but before she could speak Hannah broke in.

"Maybe we could talk about all this later." She looked round at their plates. "You get on with your shrimps now, I've all the unpacking to see to before bedtime."

Alice, having run down to see that Grandmother wanted nothing, helped Hannah unpack. They shut themselves in the nursery to do it and they talked hard in low voices. Sorrel thought Hannah talking to Alice was a good idea. Hannah knew they had been happy at their boarding schools and perhaps Alice could explain that to Grandmother, and all this idea about the stage would be dropped. She invited Mark and Holly into her bedroom.

It was queer how different Sorrel's bedroom was from

41

the rest of the house. It was not only that it was pretty and not torn or dusty, it was something about it. Mark, prowling round, got somewhere near explaining this.

"I bet our mother didn't care what that old Sir Joshua did."

Sorrel was kneeling by the bookcase; she turned round, her eyes shining.

"Do you know, as you said that I could almost see her. She must have knelt by this bookcase just as I am now. I wonder what her hair was like. I wish there was a picture of her. Not grown-up, I mean, like the ones we had at home, but when she was my age."

Holly climbed on to the bed and patted the felt doll. "Can I untie this doll and play with her?"

Sorrel said "no" with a snap before she had time to bite it back. Then she was sorry.

"I didn't mean to bite at you, but I do want to leave this room just like she had it, for a bit anyway."

Mark joined Holly on the bed; he stroked the pillow-case cat. "You know the Bishop said he saw her act. I expect Grandmother made her. I bet she didn't do it because she wanted to."

Sorrel was taking the books out of the shelves and opening them.

"I'm not sure. All these plays are rubbed with reading, just like Babar got when Holly was first given it and would read it every day."

Mark laid his cheek on the cat's back.

"I expect that was lessons."

Sorrel shook her head.

"I don't believe it. These ones are Shakespeare. This is 'Romeo and Juliet.' Nobody who has to read 'Romeo and Juliet' as a lesson as much as this has been read would keep it in their bedroom; they'd keep it wherever they did their lessons. What I believe is, our mother liked reading Shakespeare."

Mark sat up.

"She couldn't. Nobody could. That awful 'Twelfth Night.'"

Sorrel put "Romeo and Juliet" back on the shelf.

"Shakespeare can be nice. I liked it when I was Shylock last Christmas; it wasn't like lessons then."

Holly was tugging at the cat, so Mark, to save a fuss, let her have it. He got off the bed and went over to the mantelpiece to have a look at the fourteen bears.

"That was because you dressed up and had a beard."

"Partly," Sorrel agreed, "but not only. When we all knew it and nobody forgot their words, then it was exciting. I felt cruel, and as if I really meant to have a pound of flesh."

Mark rearranged the bears in a crocodile, two and two, the small ones leading.

"Then you'd like to go to this awful stage school?"

Sorrel got up and pulled down her frock.

"I don't know. I shouldn't think so. We'd probably look awful fools." She joined Mark and picked up the smallest bear. "It's you. You simply can't go to a stage school, you'll never get into the Navy from there; at least it doesn't sound right. Sailors don't learn dancing and diction."

Mark stood the biggest bear on its hind legs.

"I never did mean to go. Not because of the Navy, there's heaps of time to mug for that, but because I won't be turned into a Warren when I'm all Forbes."

Hannah opened the door.

"Come on, Holly dear. The water's not too hot, but you must have a bath. You make a start too, Mark."

Holly looked pleadingly at Sorrel.

43

"Could I, oh, could I take this cat to bed?"

Sorrel did not at all want her mother's things to leave her room, but the old nursery was so dreary and her own room so perfect she could not be so mean as to say no. She was rewarded by Holly's ecstatic hug and seeing her skip out of the room.

Mark hung about. Now that he was actually faced with sleeping in it his room seemed worse than ever. Sorrel, watching his face, felt swollen with being sorry for him. She nodded at the bears.

"Would you like to take those along with you? You've got a mantelpiece."

Mark smiled properly for the first time since they had come to the house. He collected the bears quickly in case she should change her mind.

"Thanks awfully. I think their name is Tomkins. This is Mr. Tomkins and that's Mrs. Tomkins. I'll christen all the others later on; you don't mind, do you?"

Sorrel did mind. She minded the mantelpiece not having her mother's bears on it, but she was glad she had let Mark have them because his room really was horrible, and now that he had the bears he whistled as he went up the passage, which showed he must be minding less.

Alice came in. She closed the door behind her in a purposeful way.

"Sorrel, dear, I've been having a talk with Hannah. She says that I had better speak right out to you."

Sorrel felt as if somebody had taken hold of her in front and was squeezing hard. It was so certain that Alice was not going to say anything nice.

"Yes?"

"Your granny won't tell you, so I must. There's no bees and honey in this house."

Sorrel screwed up her eyes, she was thinking so hard.

"You mean Grandmother hasn't any money? But we

44

have. There's some that comes from the Admiralty because of Daddy."

"Right enough."

"But most came from our grandfather, and as he's
dead and doesn't need it, I expect we can have it. He
used to pay for our schools."

Alice sat on the bed.

"We've earned a packet of bees and honey in our time,
but stage people are all the same, easy come, easy go."

"You mean it's been spent. Can't Grandmother earn
some more?"

"Chance is a good thing. She'll tell you we've had heaps
of plays offered us and we didn't fancy them. That's not
true. Your grandfather, John Warren, wasn't much of an
actor, but he was the cat's whiskers at producing. While
he was alive he hardly had a failure and he picked plays
to star your grandmother. Since he's been gone we've
hardly had a success. Difficult to cast, and we're a bit of a
madam too. Must be the only fish in the pond."

Sorrel did not understand all this but enough to grasp
what Alice meant.

"If she hasn't any money why does she live in this big
house?"

"First, it's our own, and secondly, have you had a good
look at the house? Old Mother Hubbard's cupboard was
crowded out compared to most of the rooms here."

"Where's it gone?"

"Sold. Things fetch good prices today. But don't you
tell your granny."

"But she must know if she's sold things."

Alice laughed.

"She didn't. I did. Tradespeople must be paid, so must
the gas bill and the electric light and the telephone."

Sorrel was taking in so many things at once that her
head spun.

"Are we to be trained to be actresses and an actor because of the money?"

Alice's expression was approving.

"Clear spoken and sensible. I knew it the moment I set eyes on you. Now look, you don't like the idea? Well, maybe you won't have to stick to it. You can't be licensed for the stage until you are twelve, and that's not until next April. Meanwhile, there's something called probate to do with lawyers going on about your grandfather's money. When that how-de-do's settled you may all be rolling for all we know."

Sorrel sat on the bed by Alice, hugging her knees.

"It's not me or Holly, it's Mark. Daddy meant him to be a sailor, and he ought to go to a school to teach him the right things."

Alice put an arm round Sorrel.

"Don't let's worry about that, duckie, yet. Mark's just about ten, isn't he? Well, two or three months won't make all that difference at his age."

"But he ought to be at a proper school by the time he's eleven anyway."

"So he shall. Don't you worry." Alice gave Sorrel's shoulders a squeeze. "I've spoken plain to you, ducks, because I want you to get the others to try tomorrow. This Madame Fidolia has known your granny all her life, and, though none of you seem to appreciate it, the name of Warren counts for a lot. If you show even a scrap of talent she'll take you for next to nothing. You see, you've got to be educated, that's the law. In her school you do all the usual things and your training as well. I daresay you won't need to go on the stage when the time comes, but it's good to have galoshes by you, there's no knowing when the road will be wet. Will you have a talk to the others?"

Sorrel felt very grand and eldest of the family.

"Yes, if you'll give me a promise. Holly doesn't matter, she'll do what she's told anyway. It's Mark. I'll have to work on him. If I do will you swear that you'll help me to see he's sent to a proper school next term, if possible."

Alice raised her hand and put it on her head.

"I swear by my loaf of bread."

Your head seemed a funny thing to swear by. Sorrel preferred "see this wet, see this dry," or "my hand on my Bible," which was what Hannah always said, but she could see that to Alice it was the most important swear that she could make and that she meant to keep it.

Sorrel waited till Mark was in bed. He was sitting up with his face very clean from the bath and his hair wet and, therefore, unusually neat. The room faced west and the sun was shining in and made the bare boards and the shabby curtain over the clothes and the battered iron bed look worse than ever. It was a warm evening and Mark had thrown back the rug and the blanket and had only the sheet over him. He had stretched this flat across his knees and on it, in a circle, he had stood the bears. As there was nowhere else to sit Sorrel sat on the edge of the bed and promptly eight bears fell over. Mark looked up at her reproachfully.

"You have interrupted the christening. These bears have trekked for miles into the Antarctic for the ceremony."

Sorrel helped stand the bears up again, and while she was doing it she was turning over in her mind the best way to bring up the subject of tomorrow.

"Could you leave the christening for a moment? There's something rather important I've got to explain. Did you know that when people died other people don't get their money at once? I mean, we haven't got Grandfather's yet."

"Do we get it ever?" Mark asked, moving the bear that was to be christened into the centre of the ring.

47

"I think so, or at least Daddy does, and then we can have it to educate us. Anyway, at the moment there isn't any except what we get from the Admiralty, and that, I suppose, is just enough for clothes and food and things. Grandmother hasn't any. When they want money Alice sells something. That's why the house is empty. Alice wants us to try very hard when we go to that school tomorrow, because then she thinks they won't charge much to take us. Alice doesn't think we'll ever have to be actresses or an actor really. She thinks Grandfather's money will have come before then and, anyway, I've made her swear that you shall go to a proper school for the Navy by the time you are eleven."

Mark swept all the bears into a hollow that he had made between his knees.

"If you think I'm going to shout poetry like Grandmother so that everybody thinks I'm like that Sir Joshua, you're wrong."

Sorrel made little pleats in Sir Joshua's rug.

"I absolutely see how you feel about Grandmother, but I don't believe that it's Grandmother who's going to worry about the school. It seems to me it's Alice, and I like her."

Mark stared at her.

"But why should Alice? She's not a relation or anything, is she?"

"Why should Hannah? But she does."

Mark picked up the bears again and once more arranged them in a circle. He took the largest and a medium one and put them in the middle. He made a growling sound.

"That's the christening call ringing across the ice." He pulled forward the smallest bear and spoke in a squeak. "What names do you give these bears?" He turned to Sorrel. "A sea lion's taking the christening." He barked, with

his hand on the largest bear. "I name thee Hannah."
Then he touched the other bear. "I name thee Alice."
Then he made a lot more growling noises. "That's the
bears growling 'amen.'"

Sorrel thought Mark christening one of the bears Alice
was a good sign.

"If it's to help Alice, would you try tomorrow?"

Mark did not answer for a moment because he was collecting the bears to put them on the mantelpiece for the
night.

"All right. Just for her I will, though I should think
we'd all look the most awful fools."

Sorrel kissed him good-night.

"I should think that's certain. I wish tomorrow was
over."

Chapter 6

THE ACADEMY

The Children's Academy of Dancing and Stage Training was in Bloomsbury. Hannah tried very hard to persuade Alice to take the children.

"The very word 'stage' turns me over. I was brought up strict and though I daresay some of these actresses live just as nicely as the rest of us, I can't get over the way I was raised!"

Alice would have loved to have taken the children. It would have been a day out for her, but she had to say no.

"I wish I could oblige but we take a terrible lot of getting up in the morning. Our hair alone takes us half an hour, what with the brushing and fixing the combs and that. And we have our ways; you'll get used to us in time, but right away the first morning wouldn't do. And we've got an artistic temperament. We've been known to throw things when we weren't pleased. We don't want any of that." She gave Hannah a friendly pat. "Cheer up now, there are worse troubles at sea."

Neither Hannah nor Sorrel thought that shorts were at all suitable wear for London. London was a place for best clothes and even for gloves. But Alice was firm, and so it was in their school cotton blouses and grey flannel shorts that Sorrel and Holly dressed. Mark had on his school grey flannel suit and his school tie and turn-over stockings with the school colours.

They went to the Academy by tube, getting in at Knightsbridge and getting out at Russell Square. It made a good beginning to the day because of the escalator at Knightsbridge. None of them had ever been on a moving staircase before and they thought it too thrilling for words. Hannah loathed the escalator. She stood at the top putting out a foot and pulling it back, afraid to get on, and she was only got on to it by Sorrel dragging her on one side and Mark on the other. Even when she reached the bottom she was still what she called "all of a shake" and she sat in the tube in a kind of heap, taking up more room even than usual, saying in an angry whisper at intervals, "It's not a Christian way to get about. It was never meant."

The Academy was three large houses joined inside by passages. Across the front had been written in large gold letters "Children's Academy of Dancing and Stage Training." The words were divided between the three houses, but a bomb across the square had blown some of the letters away altogether, and others upside down. On the first house was written *Ch* and then a space, and then *e* upside down, and then *s*, and then another space and *cad*. On the second house was *emy* and then a space, and then *D* upside down. On the third house there was a *d* and then *Stag*, and then a space and then *ing*. Sorrel, Holly and Mark stood in the road puzzling what it all meant. It was Mark who worked it out and Sorrel who noticed the static water tank in the corner and guessed it had once been a house and that was how the letters had got blown away.

Grandmother had made an appointment for the children to see Madame Fidolia at eleven o'clock. Hannah had been so afraid they would be late that it was only a quarter to eleven when they arrived, so they were shown into a waiting-room. It was a large, rather bare room with green walls. All round the walls were benches. Hannah sat down in the corner farthest from the door. The children walked round looking at the photographs, which were interesting. They were of children dressed in ballet skirts, and each child was standing on its points, but best of all, each child had signed its name. There were some funny old ones which were getting faded, with names like Little Doris, and Babsy, and Baby Cora to Dear Madame, written on them. But the newer ones, and much the best photographs, had quite sensible names, like Janet and Ann. As well there were large groups of pantomimes and these the children liked much the best, because it was fun trying to work out which pantomime they were meant to be. Mark amused himself by giving imaginary prizes for handwriting to the different children. The somebody called "Little Doris" was winning. It was a very old photograph but it had got almost first prize when Sorrel called the others over to look at a picture of the prettiest girl they had ever seen. She was dressed as Alice in Wonderland, except that instead of Alice's shoes she wore black ballet shoes and was standing on her points. Across this picture was written, "With much love to dear Madame. Pauline."

"I call that a lovely little handwriting," said Sorrel.

Holly climbed on to the bench to see better.

"There's a picture of that girl over here." She dragged at Sorrel to make her come and look, "only she's dressed as a boy."

Holly, when she wanted you to look at something, kept on bothering till you did, so Sorrel and Mark came and looked. It was an enormous group, almost all of children. In the middle was the same girl who was Alice in Wonderland, only her hair was turned underneath to look like a boy's. She was dressed in knickers and a coat that seemed to be made of satin, and holding her hand was a little dark girl dressed as Red Riding Hood.

52

"Now I wonder what pantomine that is," said Mark. "Look, there's a cat! Do you think it's 'Puss in Boots'?"

"It couldn't be," Holly objected. "That cat hasn't got no boots on."

"And anyway there's a dog too," Sorrel pointed out. "You couldn't have a dog in 'Puss in Boots.'"

Mark dashed across to Hannah. He was so excited his words fell over each other.

"Do you suppose you could earn money as an actor, being a cat or a dog?"

Hannah was still breathless from the escalator. She spoke in a puffy sort of voice.

"I should hope not indeed. Making fun of poor dumb creatures! They know it isn't right to be made a show of even if we don't."

Mark bounced back to Sorrel.

"Do you think I could be a cat or a dog, or, best of all, a bear? If I could be a bear I wouldn't mind a bit about going on the stage."

"But you've got to mind," said Sorrel anxiously. "You know what I told you last night. It's only till you're eleven. Oh, Mark, you won't get liking it, will you? It will be simply frightful for Daddy when he comes back if he finds you aren't going into the Navy."

Holly was still examining the picture.

"You said that I couldn't be an actress like Grandmother until I was twelve. But these little girls aren't twelve. Lots of them are only about six."

Sorrel and Mark knelt on the bench and had another look at the picture.

"It's absolutely true," Sorrel agreed. She laid a finger first on one child's portrait and then on another's. "This one is tiny and so is this one and so's this."

They were startled to feel hands on their shoulders.

They turned round and found themselves looking at an oldish lady.

Madame Fidolia was, the children thought, a queer-looking lady. She had hair that had once been black but was now mostly grey, parted in the middle and dragged very smoothly into a bun on the nape of her neck. She was wearing a black silk dress that looked as though it came out of a history book, for it had a tight stiff bodice and full skirts. Round her shoulders was a cerise shawl. She leant on a tall black stick. But the oddest thing about her was the way she finished off, as it were, for on her feet were pink ballet shoes, which are the last things you expect to see on the feet of an oldish lady. She gave a gesture with one hand, which, without words, said clearly, "Stand up." The children slid off the bench and stood in front of her. Her voice was deep, with a slightly foreign accent.

"How do you do? So you are the Warren children."

Mark's head shot up.

"No, we're not. Our name is Forbes."

Madame Fidolia looked at Mark with interest.

"You don't wish to be a Warren. Most children would envy you."

Sorrel was afraid Mark might be rude, so she answered for him.

"Our father is a sailor. Our great-grandfather was an admiral, and Mark's going to be an admiral too. At least, we hope he is, but, of course, it's not easy to be an admiral."

Madame Fidolia was looking at the picture behind them.

"You three remind me of three little pupils that came to me many years ago. This picture you were looking at was the first play in which they appeared. It was a special

54

matinée of 'The Blue Bird.' You've read 'The Blue Bird,' I suppose?"

Sorrel could tell from Madame Fidolia's voice that they ought to have read it, so she answered apologetically:

"I'm afraid we haven't. It wasn't in our grandfather's house."

Madame Fidolia laid a finger over the picture of the boy in the satin suit.

"This is Pauline." She touched the portrait of the child dressed as Red Riding Hood. "And this Petrova." Her fingers searched amongst the small children and came to a stop against a tiny girl with her head all over curls. Her voice warmed. "And this is Posy."

The children knelt up on the bench to look again at the picture.

"Are they sisters?" Sorrel asked.

Madame smiled.

"Not exactly. Adopted sisters, brought up by a guardian. You've seen Pauline, I expect, lots of times. Pauline Fossil."

She said Pauline Fossil in exactly the same voice as Alice had said "Didn't you know Henry Warren was your uncle?" so Sorrel hurried to explain their ignorance.

"I'm afraid we haven't. We've spent our holidays in the vicarage, and in a vicarage you don't see stage people much."

Hannah gave a snort.

"Brought up very decently, they've been."

Madame Fidolia gave her a lovely smile and came across to her, holding out her hand.

"I'm sure they have. Mrs. . . . . ?"

"Miss Fothergill," said Hannah firmly. "Looked after the children's grandfather, I did, and there's nothing about vicarages anyone can teach me."

"But nobody calls her Miss Fothergill," said Holly.
"Everybody calls her Hannah."

Madame Fidolia was shaking Hannah's hand.

"And may I call you Hannah too? Now, if you'll come
with me, I'm going to take the children to a classroom; we
must see what they can do." She was leading the way out
of the room when she thought of something. "You children will call me Madame, and when you first meet me in
the morning and last thing at night, and before and after
a class, or any time when we meet, you make a deep
curtsey and say 'Madame.' And you, Mark, lay one hand
on your heart and bow."

None of the children dared look at each other, because
they all wanted to giggle, and obviously Madame was not
the sort of person that you giggled in front of.

"Now let me see you do it," said Madame firmly. She
looked at Sorrel. "You start."

Sorrel and Holly had learnt dancing at Ferntree School,
but curtseying had not been part of it. Sorrel, crimson in
the face, did the best she could. She bowed both knees a
little and muttered "Madame" while she did it. Madame
Fidolia shook her head. She gave Mark her stick.

"You hold this. I've had a little trouble with rheumatism in my knees, but I can still show you." She moved
one foot sideways, put the other leg behind it, held out
her skirts and swept the most beautiful curtsey down to
the ground, saying politely, "Madame." Then she stood
up, took her stick back from Mark and nodded at Sorrel.
"Now, child, try again."

Shorts are the most idiotic things to curtsey in, but Sorrel was quick and did her very best. Madame seemed
quite pleased. Then she looked at Holly.

"Now you."

Holly had been charmed by the way Madame's skirts
billowed round her and it was no trouble at all to pretend

56

that she had skirts too, so instead of holding out her shorts as Sorrel had done, she lifted her hands as if she were holding up silk, and swept down to the floor. "Madame," she said politely, and then added as she got up, "I'm wearing pale blue with little stars all over it."

Madame laughed.

"I could see you were wearing something very grand. Now Mark."

Sorrel prayed inside her, "Oh, please God, don't let Mark argue." But Mark, oddly enough, did not seem even to mind being made to bow. He swept a really grand bow. "Madame." The only thing he did not do very well was saying her name. He spoke it in a low deep growl. Madame's eyes twinkled. She took Mark's chin in her hand.

"And what had you got on when you bowed to me?" Mark wriggled, but she smiled down at him, holding him firmly. "Tell me."

Mark looked cross for a moment and then something in Madame Fidolia's face made him feel friendly.

"I was wearing a bearskin. I was a bear in the Antarctic who's travelled miles to call on the Queen there."

Hannah was thoroughly ashamed.

"Really, Mark, what a way to talk!"

But Madame did not seem to mind at all. She took Mark's hand in hers.

"And a very nice thing to be," she said cheerfully. "We'll lead the way, shall we?"

In a long room a lot of small girls and boys were doing dancing exercises. A tall, ugly girl with a clever, interesting face was teaching them. She had on a practice dress, a very short black tunic, worn over black tights. The tights finished at the ankle, and she had on white socks and black ballet shoes. As the door opened this girl and all the children stopped work and bowed or curtseyed, saying "Madame." Madame beckoned to the girl.

"This is Winifred, children, who teaches dancing. We're very short of teachers now, but we're allowed Winifred because she teaches you lessons as well. Winifred came to me as a pupil when she was younger than you, Holly." She turned to Winifred. "These are the Warren children." She smiled at Mark. "Their name is really Forbes, and Mark, at any rate, wants to be called Forbes. This is Sorrel, this is Holly, and this is Mark. You might try them out and see what they know, but I imagine, with their tradition, acting is more in their line." She turned to the rest of the class. "Sit, children." The children, without a word, ran to the side of the room and sat cross-legged on the floor.

There was a piano at the far end of the room on which a fat woman in a red blouse had been playing. Winifred went over to her.

"You might play that Baby Polka, Mrs. Blondin." She came back to the middle of the room. The piano struck up a gay little polka and she began to dance. It was only one, two, three, hop, but she did it so well that it seemed quite important kind of dancing. As she danced she held out her hand. "Come on, children, you do it too."

Sorrel felt the most awful fool. She could not forget the eyes of all the children sitting cross-legged on the floor watching her. What must they think she looked like! Prancing about in her shorts. She was so conscious of the eyes that she danced worse than she need have done, and twice she fell over her feet.

Mark put on his proudest face and folded his hands behind his back while he danced. He did not pick up his feet very much, but slithered from one step to the other, and Sorrel, watching him out of the corner of her eye, could see that he was not minding dancing because he

58

was not a boy dancing in a room full of children, but a bear skating in the Antarctic.

Holly had learnt the Baby Polka at school and she liked dancing, so she held out imaginary skirts and pranced round the room, only stopping in front of Madame for a moment to say, "I've changed now and I'm in white satin with blue bows."

Winifred suddenly called out "Stop." She came over to the children and one by one lifted first their right legs and then their left legs. Then she went to Madame and curtseyed.

"Elementary."

Madame nodded.

"But watch Holly, Winifred, you never know. I thought there might be something."

Winifred gave Madame a respectful but affectionate smile.

"Another Posy?"

Madame shook her head.

"One can't expect to find two Posys in a lifetime, but I shall always go on looking. Come along, children."

She stood in the door and Winifred and all the children curtseyed and said "Madame." The fat woman at the piano just sat and stared. "I suppose she either doesn't quite belong," Sorrel thought, "or else she's too bad a shape for curtseying. Lucky her!"

Madame took the children into her own sitting-room. It was a charming room, but so full of photographs hung on the walls that the quite lovely blue-grey of the walls scarcely showed. Madame sat in an armchair. Hannah sat on a small upright chair behind the door, looking respectful. It was quite a little chair and she bulged over both sides.

"Now," said Madame, as if she were in for a treat, "let

us see if there is any of the Warren talent, or Margaret Shaw's charm, or your own mother's genius about you children. I don't want you to recite; I'm not fond of children reciting. Instead you will go outside the door and think out a little story, a fairy story, anything you like, and come back and act it."

In the passage outside the children leant against the wall and tried to think what they could act. Sorrel knew right away that Mark would have to be a bear, as he was in that sort of mood, and Holly would have to pretend that she was well dressed, but for the life of her she could not think at first of a story that would fit these characters. Neither Mark nor Holly were any help, for Mark kept suggesting, "Let's act the animals going into the Ark," or "Let's act the children being eaten by bears in the Bible," and Holly would only say, "I'd like to be a butterfly; no I wouldn't, I'll be a queen." Then suddenly Sorrel thought of something.

"Let's do a kind of Red Riding Hood. Let's have a little girl sent out to look for strawberries in the woods because they're hungry at home, and there's nothing to eat; and in the wood the little girl meets a bear and she's terrified and runs home, and the bear follows her and he turns out to be a prince and he marries the little girl's mother and they live happily ever after."

"Where was the little girl's father?" asked Mark.

"He died of smallpox," Sorrel invented, "and that's why they're hungry, because there's no one to work for them."

"Pretty rotten for the bear having to turn into a prince," Mark argued.

Sorrel lost her temper.

"All right then, think of a better story yourself. I've made you a bear and Holly can be as dressed up as she likes to think she is, and all I am is just an old mother cleaning the house. I think you're jolly selfish."

60

"Keep your hair on," said Mark. "We'll do your story. Only I shouldn't think you're as old as all that, otherwise why does the prince marry you? Princes don't."

Sorrel was so thankful to have got a story settled that she did not bother to argue with him.

"Come on," she said nervously. "Let's do it just once before we go in."

As soon as the door had shut on the children Madame Fidolia went to her desk and picked up a printed list and gave it to Hannah. Hannah was carrying a large brown bag with a zip fastener. She undid it and took out her spectacles. She put them on and read the list. It said across the top: "Children's Academy of Dancing and Stage Training. Rompers, two (pattern to be obtained from the Academy). Tarlatan dresses, white, two. Knickers, frilled, two. Sandal shoes, white satin. Black patent-leather ankle-strap shoes. White socks, six pairs. Face towels, rough, two. Overalls, two (to be obtained from the Academy)." And at the bottom, in large letters, "Everything must be clearly marked with the child's name." Hannah knew just what state the children's coupon books were in, so she just stared at the list, looking hopeless. Madame did not give her time to worry long.

"That's an old list, of course, from before the war. As you probably noticed at the elementary class we've just been in to, all the children's things are made of different colours, and quite a lot of them were wearing shorts. I don't like shorts myself, as they don't wash so easily as the rompers. Have the children got bathing dresses?"

"The little girls have, but Mark's are only a pair of drawers."

"Well, with their shorts and shirts and their bathing things, I expect they can manage. They must have tunics of some sort for ballet. I find that necessary even today. It's hard for a child to be graceful in a bathing dress. I may be old-fashioned. I was myself a pupil from the age of seven in the Russian Imperial Ballet School, and when I gave up dancing after the First World War, and founded my school over here, I had hoped to run it on the old Imperial Ballet School lines; but it was, of course, impossible, and so I have become the director of a school for general stage training. But dancing, classical dancing, is my life, and it is to turn out dancers that is my great ambition. Any child that shows unusual promise I teach myself; and I still insist, or try to insist, on some dress that will make the children feel in a dancing mood. White tarlatan is not on coupons, but with everybody so busy, Winifred has told me it is impossible for the mothers to keep these dresses laundered; and, instead, we have designed a short tunic with plain knickers underneath, it could be made out of anything. I think that the children's grandmother must have some old dresses put away that would alter."

Hannah was perfectly certain that she was not going to approach Grandmother. She did not mean to sound grumpy, but she did rather.

"I couldn't say, I'm sure. There wasn't nothing in the vicarage suitable, I do know."

Madame smiled.

"Never mind, I'll write to Miss Shaw."

The night before Alice had explained to Hannah that actresses were usually known by their stage names; and so, though to Hannah Grandmother was Mrs. Warren, she accepted that Madame would call her Miss Shaw.

"What about these overalls?" she asked, tapping the list. "They've got the cotton frocks they had for school."

Madame smiled.

"There we are fortunate. The overalls have always been made of black sateen from a Russian design, and have wide black leather belts. Black-out material is not rationed and these overalls are still made. The belts and the buttons we get from our old pupils. The real difficulty is shoes. The law allows that children at a recognised dancing school may have one pair of ballet shoes a month. Those have block toes, you know, but the children will not want them for a long time yet; it's the shoes for character dancing and the sandal shoes that are our trouble."

"Both the girls have sandal shoes. They had them for their school dancing. And Mark's got a pair of plimsolls, if that'll do."

Madame shook her head.

"No, they will not. But I expect we shall manage. Old pupils send us shoes second-hand; and if the girls have sandals, that's something." She looked at Hannah with a sweet smile. "You think it all a lot of nonsense, don't you?"

Hannah squeezed her bag tightly in her hands.

"It's none of what I'm used to. I give respect where respect is due, and I'm sure you mean well, Madame; but all this dancing and that isn't what was meant. The Reverend took a lot of looking after, what with being busy with his Bible animals and that, and his clothes were a perfect disgrace, with all my trying; but I could see what we were at. He was never a minute late for his services and he never missed a call from the village. Where we're living now isn't what I'm used to. No good pretending it is."

Madame nodded.

"I know, but you have to look at their grandmother's point of view. Nobody knows if the children's father will ever come back."

Hannah's hand shot up to her mouth.

"Oh, don't say that, Madame! Such a nice gentleman! And the gentlemen in the Navy only said missing, and they've never said worse."

"I certainly shall not say it to the children, and I'm full

of hope that we shall hear from him; but meanwhile there are these children to think of. They come from an immensely famous theatrical family, and blood tells. It would be a curious thing indeed if none of these children had any talent. Of course, they will probably never need to earn their living; their uncles and aunts are doing well, and their grandmother has money and . . ."

Hannah had to interrupt.

"I don't know about uncles and aunts, Madame; we haven't seen them. But the old lady hasn't any money. Alice, it's her that looks after the old lady, she hasn't known where to turn."

Madame leant forward, her voice startled.

"Really! I had no idea! Well, in that case—" she broke off and held up a finger, for at that moment the children came in.

The charade was rather fun. Holly was very pleased with herself as the child, and Mark made a really grand bear; but it was Sorrel who surpassed herself. Somehow, seeing Holly off into the wood to look for strawberries, because there was nothing to eat in the house, was so like what was really happening to them that it made her voice full of anxiety, and you could feel that she honestly minded. There was a proper mother's fussiness about the way she told Holly all the places to look for strawberries and to try very hard and not come back until her basket was full. Then, at the end, when Mark suddenly stood upright, instead of on all fours, and said in a rather disapproving voice that he was now a prince instead of a bear, that he was very rich and they would all live happily ever afterwards, Sorrel was quite overcome, it all sounded so nice, and she said, "Oh, goodness, yes, I'd simply love to marry you, *thank you so very much for asking me*," with such fervour that even Hannah smiled and Madame went so far as to clap.

When the charade was over, Madame went to a cupboard and took out a tin marked "Candies."

"These were sent me from America. From that Pauline whose picture you were looking at downstairs. I want to talk to you about those three sisters, so you each take a sweet and listen very carefully. The Fossils were brought to me because their guardian had gone away and not left enough money to look after them. Gum, they called him. It was short for Great-Uncle Matthew. He was not really their great-uncle; he was the uncle of a very nice person called Sylvia, who brought the three little Fossil girls up with the help of someone called Nana."

"Was Nana like Hannah?" Holly interrupted.

"In a lot of ways, very like her. The children did well at my school. Pauline was, and is, lovely; and while she was still quite a child she went to Hollywood and became a very great film star. One day I will take you to see her in the pictures. But to me the most exciting of the three was Posy, the youngest. You see, I am a dancer. All my life I have lived for dancing; and Posy, from a tiny child, had talent; sometimes, I thought, genius. When Posy was eleven she went to Czechoslovakia to study under the greatest living ballet teacher, Manoff. Before the Germans overran Czechoslovakia, Monsieur Manoff and most of his pupils, including Posy and Nana, who was with her, escaped to America. There, Posy and Nana joined Pauline and their guardian, Sylvia, in Hollywood. They had, of course, nothing but what they stood up in, and I'm afraid poor Monsieur Manoff went through a bad time, but finally he succeeded in starting a Ballet School of a sort in California; and, of course, Posy attends the classes when she can. Posy, under another name, is dancing in the films." Madame laughed. "She detests it, the naughty girl. I must read you her letters sometime."

Sorrel was eating the most beautiful sweet all over nuts. All the sweets in the box were marvellous. Much better than anything to be bought in England, and choosing a sweet each had distracted them a little from what Madame was saying, but they had picked up the main part of the story.

"What happened to the middle one?"

"Petrova?" Madame said the word affectionately. "Funny little girl! She is a countrywoman of my own. I am Russian. Petrova went away and lived with Great-Uncle Matthew, and learnt to fly. She is now a pilot. You know, what they call the Air Transport Auxiliary."

Sorrel moved her sweet to the side of her mouth.

"How old are they now?"

"Pauline will be twenty-two this December. Petrova is just twenty and Posy is eighteen this month. Have another sweet each." The children bent over the box and chose carefully. Mark a marshmallow thing, Sorrel a toffee in two colours, and Holly a round sticky affair made of nuts. "Now listen carefully because this is where you come in. Pauline and Posy have both felt that they ought to be back in England doing something important, like Petrova. At least, I don't suppose Posy thinks that, because Posy would dance if there were nothing but smouldering ruins left to dance on; but all the same, they would both like to help, and so they suggested something. They have sent me sums of money for two scholarships, Pauline's for someone who shows promise in acting, and Posy's for a dancer. I have not, so far, granted these scholarships; it is still the summer holidays and I was thinking of granting them next term, the money only reached me last month. I have no hesitation at all, Sorrel, in saying that I think Pauline would like her scholarship to go to you. It will pay all your fees and it will provide such clothes as we can manage, and, as well, they were both very particular about this, some pocket-money." She looked at Holly. "I'm going to start Posy's scholarship by giving it to you. I shall write and explain to her why. She asked me to find a little girl who was very clever at dancing. I can't say that about you yet; perhaps if you work hard I shall be able to later on." She leant forward and picked another sweet out of the box and put it in Mark's mouth. "As for you, my friend, we shall have to see. But I should not wonder if we found a scholarship for you too."

Mark looked up. He spoke very indistinctly because of the sweet in his mouth.

"What, from the one who flies?"

Madame got up to show them that the interview was over.

"I should not wonder. There was a very noticeable thing about the Fossil family, and that was the way they all stood together."

Chapter 7

THE FIRST DAY

The children started at the Academy the very next day. Before they got home, Madame had telephoned Grandmother. Alice told them all about it when she brought up their lunch to the nursery.

"So you're in, and scholarships too. We pretend we aren't pleased, but are we? 'Alice,' we said, 'look through my clothes and find something of soft satin that'll cut up into tunics for the little girls.' 'Half a cock linnet,' I said, my mind running through our clothes; and then, all of a sudden, it came to me: our pink that we wore in the first act of that funny little play translated from French. Just as good as new it is. You won't half look ducks in it." She put a stew in front of Hannah. "When you take them to the Academy tomorrow, you're to bring back the pattern and we're to get down to it right away."

Hannah took the lid off the stew and sniffed it with a pleased smile.

"I must say it's a treat to eat something I haven't cooked myself."

"Mostly vegetables," said Alice. "We'll do better when you've got your meat coupons. Fancy"—she gave a luxurious sigh—"a scholarship from Pauline Fossil; that really is something, that is."

"Have you seen her in the pictures?" Sorrel asked.

"Have I! I should say I have; lovely, she is. She was in

that picture all about the Civil War the Americans had. You should have seen her at the beginning in a crinoline, and a big hat. Made your heart stand still. I don't think I've ever missed her in anything yet."

Holly, who considered Posy her property, was jealous of all this talk about Pauline.

"Have you seen Posy Fossil?"

Alice looked surprised.

"What, a sister of Pauline? No, I never knew she had one."

Holly was furious.

"But she's every bit as important, more important, I should think. Madame said so."

Alice gave a tolerant smile.

"Oh, well, Madame's got a bee in her bonnet. I expect this Posy dances."

"She does," said Sorrel. "I think she's a star like Judy Garland in 'The Wizard of Oz,' only she mostly dances."

Alice laughed good-temperedly.

"No harm in thinking, but I don't mind telling you that a film star that old Alice hasn't heard about isn't shooting very far."

That night, and on the way to the Academy the next morning, the children talked a lot about the Fossil sisters. It seemed so extraordinary to think that they had once been just ordinary children like themselves, and the most comforting part of it was that it did seem that the Fossil sisters had been no more anxious to be trained for the stage than they were. They, too, had only taken it up at first because of money. Of course, the Fossils had not really been like they were. Posy must always have been able to dance, because, even if Alice had never heard of her, they trusted Madame when she said that she was a very great dancer indeed. Each of them adopted their own Fossil, as it were, and talked about them as if they were close friends.

"I bet Pauline would be sorry for me," said Sorrel, "having to go on my first day to the Academy in just shorts and a blouse. I bet she started with all the proper things."

Holly ran her fingers through her hair.

"It's funny, Posy and me both having curls. It makes us alike, somehow."

Mark was rather grand about Petrova.

"She's the only sensible one. Pretty good for a girl to be a pilot. She's the only one I'd like to know."

Hannah had implored Alice to think of some other way by which they could get to Russell Square, except on the escalator, but Alice only laughed and refused to treat Hannah's fears seriously.

"May as well learn first as last. You can't live in London and never get on a moving staircase."

"It's not Christian," Hannah said stubbornly. "We were meant to move our feet for ourselves, not have them dragged down the stairs for us."

Alice giggled.

"If my plates of meat," she winked at the children, "feet to you, had to carry the weight yours do, I'd thank my stars for anything that would move me along without my having to trouble myself." Then her face grew serious. "All the same, we can't have you going every morning with the children. Sorrel's gone eleven; she's old enough to lead the troops, and you and I will find plenty to do here. Half my morning's gone getting us up, and I'll be glad of an extra pair of hands, I don't mind telling you."

Sorrel was a little startled to hear they were going about alone in London, but there was so much that was startling going on that it did not make the big sensation that it once would have. After she and Mark had dragged Hannah on to the escalator for the second morning, she and Mark agreed that it was really a very good thing that Hannah was not going to do it every day, for after she had been on it she did look terribly like a large pale-green jelly that had forgotten to set.

The first day in any new school is confusing. Everybody else knows where to be, and what they ought to be doing, and new children feel as if they are running very fast and never being quite sure they are in the right place at the right time. At the Academy there were such a lot of things that the children could not take part in properly because they did not know any of the work that the other children did merely as a matter of routine.

Their great prop and stay was Winifred; she was an explaining sort of person and seemed very anxious that they should none of them feel worried. She told them that the term proper did not begin until next Monday, and that what was going on now were holiday classes. She told them that she herself had not been the right sort to make a success on the stage as a dancer; she had been too tall, and had not had the looks. She had done a certain amount of work as a child, including understudying Pauline Fossil when she played "Alice in Wonderland," and one afternoon she had gone on for her, and she had danced in various pantomimes. But, by the time she was fifteen, her family had decided there was not going to be a secure enough living in it for her, and so had her trained to teach. She had gone to a grammar school, and then to the London School of Economics, and then she had taken on teaching at a day school in this square.

"It was Madame's idea really; she knew we should be glad of the money at home, and so she suggested me to the headmistress because I could teach there all day and then make extra money teaching ballet here after tea."

71

THEATRE SHOES

When the war came, Winifred explained, the pupils of the school she taught in had mostly been evacuated to the country, and then when the bombing started the school had a direct hit. It happened at night and nobody had been in the building, but it had been the end of Winifred's job. She had thought then that she should join the A.T.S., but Madame had felt that teaching was valuable war work because it was important in a war that children's education should not be neglected, and so she had suggested that Winifred and two of the other teachers should set up a school in the Academy for the Academy pupils.

"In term-time you do ordinary school lessons, in school hours, just like you would anywhere else, except that sometimes you have a special dancing or acting class in the afternoon, and then you make up your lesson time after tea. There's a Madame Moulin, who's always taught French acting, and she takes you for French. There's a Miss Jones for mathematics, and there's me for everything else. We've got about seventy children here this term, so you'll be about fifteen or twenty in a class. This afternoon I'm going to set you a little examination paper to see how much you all know, but this morning you'll come to my dancing class. And then you'll go on to an acting class; then you'll do a little bit of tap work before lunch. We all have lunch together, sent in from the British Restaurant over the road."

There was never one second in that morning when Sorrel felt she was learning anything. She was in a different dancing class to Mark and Holly, and she found herself doing what they called bar work, with a lot of girls rather younger than herself. All the girls had on silk or satin tunics, split up at the sides, and she felt an awful mess in her shorts and blouse. Besides which, although she watched very carefully what her next-door neighbour was doing, it was impossible for her feet to keep pace with the feet of the rest of the class. Winifred, in her practice dress, stood in the middle of the room and rattled off instructions.

"Left hand on bar. Body erect. Don't stoop, Biddy. Right arm extended. Relax your elbow and wrist, Mildred. Don't stick your hand out like that, Poppy. All I want is a perfectly natural position. Knees bent. Now a nice arm sweep. Knees straight. Don't wriggle, Pansy. Head and eyes straight in front of you. Do you call that a first position, Agnes? Now, plié, six times. Now then, second position."

At intervals Winifred came over to Sorrel and tried by pushing to get her into the right position; but even as she pushed she was still being nice.

"Don't worry. I think you'll be in this class, but I'm going to give you special coaching to bring you up to the others; they're only beginners."

Beginners! thought Sorrel desperately. What in the world can it be like when you stop being a beginner?

The acting class was no better because it was all taken up with a performance that was going to be given for the soldiers at some hospital. It was not only acting, a lot of it was dancing, some of it was singing. The class was taken by a Miss Jay and she tried very hard to be nice to Sorrel, but Sorrel wished she would leave her alone. The children who were going to perform to the soldiers seemed so terribly efficient, she knew she could never be in the least like them, and all she wanted was to be left quietly in a corner watching; but Miss Jay would not hear of it; she came and sat down beside her.

"I think you're going to work with this class, so we must fit you into the concert if we can. What do you do?"

Sorrel fidgeted with her plaits.

"Well, I was Shylock once; and twice I've been an angel

73

at Christmas in a Nativity play, and we were children in Cranford, in a play in the village."

Miss Jay looked puzzled.

"But don't you do anything when your granny gives a party?"

Sorrel turned scared eyes up at her.

"I didn't know she ever did give a party, and I couldn't do anything if she did."

Miss Jay made a funny sniffing sound.

"Very unlike your cousin Miranda."

"My what?"

Miss Jay looked more puzzled.

"Surely you knew Miranda was a pupil here?"

"I didn't know I had a cousin Miranda."

Miss Jay broke off a moment to tidy up a hornpipe, which was being accompanied by a group of children who could whistle. Then she turned back to Sorrel.

"Miranda is the daughter of your aunt Marguerite."

"Yes?" said Sorrel politely.

"You must know that you have an aunt Marguerite?"

"No, I didn't."

Miss Jay evidently thought it was time that somebody explained her family to Sorrel.

"Your grandmother had five children: Henry Warren, the film star; Lindsey, who married Mose Cohen the co-median, their daughter Miriam is coming here next term; Marguerite, who married Sir Francis Brain, the Shake-spearean actor, and they have a remarkably clever child called Miranda; Andrew, who died, and your mother, Adeline."

Sorrel could not possibly take in all these uncles and aunts at once, so she fixed on the children.

"What's Miranda like?"

Miss Jay used a funny voice; it was as if she was being nice when she did not want to.

"Good-looking and got the Warren voice, speaks blank verse beautifully."

"And Miriam?"

Miss Jay shrugged her shoulders.

"I only saw the child for a moment or two. She's about eight, I think—a tiny, dark little thing. You'll meet them both on Monday." She got up and went over to rearrange the whistlers, but she evidently had Sorrel on her mind, for later on she suddenly clapped her hands. "I know. Lambs. Come here, Sorrel." Sorrel got up unwillingly and came to her, and glared at the floor, conscious that all the other girls were staring at her. "In that spring number we can do with an extra lamb. We'll run through that number now." She selected two girls. "You two put Sorrel between you, and she can copy what you do." She turned to Sorrel. "Clothes are always such a difficulty because of the coupons, but last time we did this we had an extra lamb who's left, and you can wear her tunic."

What followed seemed to Sorrel perfectly idiotic. First of all, one girl played on a pipe as a shepherd boy; and then another sang as a shepherdess—that part was not so bad, it was when the lambs came on that things grew unbearable. They played what seemed to her just follow-my-leader of a rather silly kind, hopping and skipping; she could not see that any of it was the least like lambs. Try as she would, she was always late and never getting in a hop at quite the same time as the others. But Miss Jay seemed pleased.

"That'll be splendid," she said in a satisfied tone. "With your hair undone, and in a black tunic, you'll look very nice indeed." And then she added, perhaps seeing rather a sullen look on Sorrel's face, "There's nothing like getting used to the feel of a stage. Never mind making a start in a humble position."

The tap-dancing class was just dull. Sorrel had not got

the right shoes and, in any case, the class were being taken through what the teacher called "a routine." The routine was part of the concert for the soldiers and it did not need the teacher's cheerful, "I think this is too much for you to pick up, Sorrel dear," for Sorrel to be certain that she could not even pretend to copy in this class. The steps went very fast, with taps from toes and heels in time to the music. There was one place, which the class practised over and over again, where the music stopped and was carried on only by the rhythm of the tapping of the girls' feet. Sorrel, sprawling on a bench, was filled with admiration but also with horror. Surely these could not just be ordinary girls like they had at Ferntree School. They must be exceptionally talented. She could not believe, however many special classes she attended, she would be able to use her feet like that.

There was no class going on that morning suitable for Mark and Holly, and so they were tacked on to a children's special holiday class. The children were all quite small and mostly came in from outside London, and were brought to their classes by very proud mothers who were sure that their children were remarkable. Most of the pupils were not dressed in practice clothes like the regular pupils of the Academy, but had proper little ballet dresses on or party frocks of muslin, and the boys wore what Mark thought very girlish-looking party suits, knickers of satin or velvet, and lots of frills about the cuffs and collars of their shirts.

The first class was with Miss Jay, and it was dancing and miming of nursery rhymes. The mothers of the pupils sat down on one side of the room as audience, and Miss Jay stood with her back to the piano and the class sat in a half-hoop on the floor in front of her. There was a small man in a warden's uniform at the piano.

"Now," said Miss Jay, "we're going to start with 'Mary,

Mary, quite Contrary.' I'm going to choose one little girl for Mary and the little boys will be silver bells and six little girls will be cockle shells, and all the rest of the little girls will be pretty maids all in a row." She looked round the class and selected a child with black curls and a very short white muslin frock. "You shall be Mistress Mary, Shirley."

Mark was not so much disgusted at finding himself supposed to take part in such a childish entertainment as refusing to believe that he was going to be so insulted. To keep his mind off Miss Jay's instructions he looked at the parents. He saw at once which was Shirley's mother, for the moment she heard that her child was to be Mistress Mary she looked round at the other mothers with an expression which clearly said, "Talent will tell." The other mothers looked resigned, as if they were just going to endure Mistress Mary while waiting for something much more important to happen. Gosh, thought Mark, fancy caring whether you were Mistress Mary or not. He came back to the class with a start to hear Miss Jay saying, "Come along, Mark, don't dream; you're the tallest, you must be the leading silver bell."

Mark flushed.

"If it makes no difference to you, I'd rather watch."

Miss Jay's eyes twinkled.

"Oddly enough, it does make a difference to me, and I'd rather you were a silver bell." She came over to him and slipped a hand through his arm. "It's all part of learning to walk to music," she explained. "You won't do it this way when the term proper starts." And then quite suddenly she added in a whisper, "Pretend it's a children's party and you're helping to amuse the little ones."

Miss Jay could not have said anything better. There had been lots of children's parties in the village at home, but the only sort where Mark himself was not one of the little ones was the parish Sunday school treat, and at that he had helped, giving assistance to the head Sunday school teacher. She was tall and grey-haired and thin and wore pince-nez, and at a Sunday school treat had tried so hard to make it a success that she never stood still for a minute but kept saying things like "Splendid! Splendid" or "Isn't it fun?" The moment Miss Jay said "helping to amuse the little ones," this woman came back into Mark's mind and in a moment he was being her and not minding the class anymore.

The pianist played a gay little polka and Shirley, holding an imaginary watering can, danced round the room. Her mother was so pleased with her that she snorted down her nose with excitement. The silver bells led by Mark then had to polka into their places in the garden and stand in a row while Shirley watered them. Mark found this easy to do, peering eagerly at Shirley through his imaginary pince-nez and whispering under his breath "Splendid! Splendid!"

Holly was a cockle shell. They had to do rather more polka-ing than the silver bells. Holly, who had never seen a cockle shell to her knowledge, had by now dressed herself in her imagination in rose pink satin, such as she knew was being cut up for their tunics, and she did not mind how much polka-ing she did.

"Mary, Mary" was followed by "Baa, Baa, Black Sheep" and "Baa, Baa, Black Sheep" by "Where are you going to?" and "Where are you going to?" by "Jack and Jill." Then they acted, "Oh, What have you got for dinner, Mrs. Bond?" and, finally, "A Frog he would a-wooing go," with Mark as the frog. In the ordinary way Mark would have enjoyed being a frog, but by the time that they got to this nursery rhyme, he was so full of being the Sunday school teacher that he could not quite get rid of her, and though he saw himself clearly in a bright-green frog suit, he also saw a grey bun of hair on the top of his head, pince-nez on his nose and he still had the anxious smile of somebody who is going to fight very hard to make a party a success. Somehow the mixture of these two characters came out, and it was funny. The parents laughed, the children laughed, and Miss Jay, who had a cheerful laugh, gave a hearty roar. When the class was over and they were going to Winifred for ballet, Miss Jay caught hold of Mark.

"What made you do the frog like that?"

Mark felt easy with Miss Jay, so he did not mind telling her. She listened quite seriously but obviously amused.

"And then," Mark explained, "though I'd stopped being her, she wouldn't go away, so I had to make her part of the frog."

Miss Jay nodded.

"I can see one of the things we shall have to teach you is not to get your parts mixed up. What are you going to do if this term you are given Puck to play in the acting class, and then Madame Moulin gives you an Archduke, or something like that, in a French play? You'll be in a terrible muddle, won't you?"

Mark thought the question over.

"I don't know. I've always been things. Sometimes for two or three days at a time. I've never had to stop being things before. Once I was William the Conqueror for three weeks; but none of it matters very much, you know, because I'm not going to be an actor, I'm going to be a sailor like my father. Really, I hope to be an admiral, so all this dancing and stuff isn't any use to me."

Miss Jay said nothing for a moment. She was nice to talk to because she obviously did not think that just because you were not grown-up you could not talk as much sense as she could. Before she spoke again she had slowed up her walk and she and Mark were quite a long way behind the rest of the class.

"I would not be so certain if I were you that none of it's going to be any good to you. Dancing is a wonderful training for muscles, you know, and balance. It teaches control, and I shouldn't think any sailor, especially one who was going to be an admiral, could do without learning control. It may be an unusual way of learning it, but it's a very good way. As for the acting and singing, all ships must need talent on them, I should think; even sailors must want concerts occasionally, and there's one part of the training which might be very useful indeed, and that's voice training. You might be a broadcaster when they want a naval officer to broadcast about things to do with the navy. Run along now, and for goodness' sake don't be a frog in poor Winifred's class. She won't like it."

Winifred, though of course she had to take an interest in all the children, was giving her especial attention to Holly. She had known about the Posy Fossil scholarship and had wondered if Madame would grant it to anybody because, in her opinion, there was nobody in the school at the moment with talent that Posy would recognise as such. It had astonished her that Madame should grant the scholarship to Holly, who obviously had scarcely learnt dancing and, therefore, showed no ability at all, let alone talent. Had Madame sensed some quality in Holly which she had missed? Winifred had suffered from the Fossil sisters. Pauline had always taken parts that she would have loved to have had. But then Pauline had not only talent but looks, and Winifred had known that she herself was plain. In a way she had envied Posy more than she did Pauline. Winifred really could dance. Had she not grown too tall she might have made a success, but just because she could dance she could recognise that something in Posy Fossil which set her apart from all

other children in the Academy. It was not Posy's looks or
Posy's success that Winifred envied, but that something
which no training can teach. The Forbes children quite
certainly had looks. Neither Sorrel nor Holly had beauty
like Pauline, her face had always been outstanding, but all
the same they were interesting and attractive. Sorrel's
shiny dark head with its two plaits and her really lovely
blue-grey eyes. Mark, with his thatch of dark hair, his big
brown eyes and high colour, gave him somehow a look of
a very expensive peach, or perhaps a nectarine. Holly,
with her short brown curls which turned up so prettily at
the back, and her eyes with a touch of green in the
brown, and her dimple. To Winifred all new pupils at the
Academy were interesting. You never knew but what you
had found something marvelous. These Forbes children,
or rather Warren, for that was how Winifred thought of
them, really were exciting. What a history! There must be
talent. There absolutely must. What fun if one of the
three proved even better than their cousin Miranda.
Winifred also thought, for she could be very human at
times, and what sucks for Miranda if they were!

Though Winifred watched with the utmost care and
gave Holly some especial chances to show what she could
do, she could not see any sign of remarkable dancing talent. Of course, she trusted Madame, but a scholarship
from Posy Fossil was something rather special. Winifred
dismissed the class feeling disappointed and low of heart.

The written examination papers in the afternoon were
easy and so were the verbal questions. The children had
been well taught in their schools and were all of them
ahead for their ages. Winifred corrected the papers and
then looked at the children with a smile.

"Very nice indeed." Then she sighed.

Mark got up and stretched himself, he was cramped
with writing.

"Why did you sigh if our papers are good?"

Winifred thought about his question.

"One of the difficulties of this sort of school is to fix the classes. It's much easier to put you in a class and leave you there for everything. You can see for yourselves that it must be. Now what am I going to do with Sorrel? She is very well on for age in lessons, but she has done no ballet at all."

Sorrel got up and pushed her chair into the table.

"Well, you haven't got to decide until Monday."

Winifred flicked over Sorrel's papers.

"As a matter of fact I've already decided about you. For everything except ballet you will work with the upper middle. The girls in that class are rather older than you, but about your level in work. It'll be interesting for you because in your class you will find your cousin Miranda."

Chapter 8

COUSINS

The children had all noticed one point about the Academy: the right thing for a proper pupil to carry was a little brown attaché case. In it you carried all your belongings to hang up in your locker; in it you carried things like your towel, shoes and spare socks for your classes, and in it you took home any of your belongings which needed to be washed. They did not want or expect the full Academy wardrobe. They were so used to coupons, or rather lack of them, that they knew they could not have clothes just because they needed them; but an attaché case was different. It was not on coupons and it was the sign of being a real pupil rather than a child who just came in for holiday classes.

They decided not to explain about the attaché cases to Hannah. Hannah could not be made to see that anything to do with the Academy really mattered. She looked upon the whole business of their going to the Academy as something that would pass, like having measles. Instead, they told Alice. Alice was the sort of person who understood how having just one of the right things could make all the difference.

Alice lived up to their expectations.

"That's quite right, that is. That's just what you do need. I'll have a word with Hannah about bees and honey, and then you can go shopping Saturday morning."

Saturday morning was wet. Hannah had a great deal to do and only terrific cajoling could get her to go out at all. Alice advised trying the King's Road, Chelsea. They could walk to it, which meant no escalators to put Hannah off. The morning was a dismal failure. They splashed along in the wet, Hannah absolutely refusing to hurry, and they went into every single shop in the King's Road, including Woolworths, that could possibly sell attaché cases. The King's Road is long, and they did not leave one suitable shop unvisited on either side, but it was not until they got to the far end where the shops finished that they faced the awful truth. Cheap attaché cases were one of the things you could no longer buy. In a few places were grand little cases of leather costing pounds and pounds, but the cheap kind could not be bought anywhere.

On Monday morning they went to the Academy each carrying a brown-paper parcel. Inside Sorrel and Holly's parcels were their black tunics, which had been given them second-hand at the Academy and brought home to be shortened, their black knickers, their black belts, their pink satin knickers and tunics, two pairs of white socks, their dancing sandals and a rough hand towel. In Mark's parcel was a bathing suit, a pair of cotton shorts, some dancing sandals and a rough towel. The nearer the children got to the Academy the worse they felt about the parcels.

"If only it was boxes!" said Sorrel. "A little box, now, would be neat, and you could carry things about in it."

Mark angrily kicked a stone off the pavement.

"Even that awful Shirley that did Mistress Mary and was only a holiday pupil had an attaché case."

Sorrel and Mark were walking fast and Holly had to run and skip to catch up.

"And so has even that smallest child who is almost a baby—she's so small that she doesn't even carry her case

84

herself, her mother does—and here's us, old enough to go to the Academy alone, and not an attaché case among us."

Sorrel slowed up because the Academy was in sight.

"I wouldn't mind if it wasn't for us being Grandmother's grandchildren. People expect us to be good at everything because of her, and because of our mother and the uncles and aunts and all the rest of it, and because of our having scholarships, and it's bad enough that we aren't good, but when as well we haven't got anything but brown-paper parcels, we really look most peculiar."

The Academy was quite a different place now that the term had started. Winifred was standing at the students' entrance with some lists in her hand, and she told the girls to hurry up and put on their black tunics with their white socks and dancing sandals, which they would wear for lessons. Sorrel and Holly had lockers side by side in one changing room, Mark's was in the boys' room down the passage. Sorrel opened her locker quickly and pushed her parcel inside and tried to unpack it in there. There did not seem to be many of the girls about that she knew, but all the same she thought she would like to get her parcel undone and everything hung up before anyone noticed. All round the room there was a flow of chatter.

"Hullo! Had a good holiday?"

"Hullo, Doris! Have you come back to live in London?"

"Have you heard Freda will not be back until half term? She's still with that concert party in Blackpool, lucky beast."

Then it happened. Somebody hurrying by tripped over Sorrel's feet and the back half of her that was sticking out of her locker and a voice said:

"Oh, bother! I nearly fell," and then added, "One of the new girls grubbing about with a paper parcel."

Holly was sitting on the floor changing her socks. She

85

did not so much care what anybody said to her, but she would not have anyone being rude to Sorrel. She raised her voice to what Ferntree School, who had not approved of such behaviour, would have called a shout.

"We would have attaché cases if we could, but we can't because there is a war on. Perhaps you didn't know that."

There was a lot of laughter, and then somebody said, "That's put you in your place, Miranda."

Miranda! Sorrel turned, her cheeks crimson. What an awful start she had made with her cousin. What an even worse start Holly had made, shouting like that. Miranda was walking up the line of lockers; she ran after her and caught hold of her arm.

"Are you Miranda? I—I mean we—are your cousins. We're Sorrel, Holly and Mark Forbes. Mark isn't here just know, he's in the boys' room changing."

Miranda turned and Sorrel gave a little gasp of surprise, Miranda was so very like what Grandmother must have been like when she was a child. The same brown hair—it hung down at the back, of course, but the top part was piled up into curls—the same dark eyes, the same effect of being a patch of colour in a dull room. Only Grandmother was like a sparkling bit of colour and Miranda was more like the last smouldering red cinder lying amongst grey ash. Miranda was evidently not a person who minded if she had been rude to her cousins or not, or rather she seemed to have forgotten it, for she put on a very grown-up gracious air.

"How do you do? I heard you were coming. We shall be quite a family gathering this term, for Uncle Mose is sending Miriam, did you know? You're a beginner, aren't you? I'm afraid that means we shan't see much of each other."

Sorrel wished most heartily that this were going to be the case, but she remembered what Winifred had said about their both being in the same class. Quite time enough, however, for Miranda to find that out if it happened. So she just smiled politely and admitted to being a beginner and went back to her changing.

Sorrel and Holly had just got into their overalls and were fastening their belts when the changing-room door was thrown open and a little girl dashed in. She had on a frock of bright orange linen, against which her thin little face looked pale and yellowish; in fact there seemed hardly any face at all, it was so surrounded by a fuzz of black hair. In one hand she carried a grand leather attaché case of the sort which cost pounds and pounds. She glanced imperiously round the room.

"Which is my cousin Holly?"

Holly was shy of being called out in front of all the big girls, and she spoke in a very small voice.

"Me."

The child dashed over to her, put her attaché case on the floor and gave her a kiss.

"We're cousins. I'm Miriam Cohen. You're just a tiny bit older than me; I won't be eight until the end of this month."

This was so insulting that Holly forgot to be shy.

"If you don't mind my saying so, I'm a great deal older than you. I shall be nine just after Christmas."

Miriam seemed to be a person who did everything quickly. She snapped her attaché case undone and threw everything in it out on to the floor.

"Never mind, let's be friends. Mum says if we're friends I can ask you to tea. I can't come to you because we're not on speaking terms with Grandmother just now. We hardly ever are, you know, except at Christmas. Of course, we always go to Grandmother's then."

Sorrel and Holly rather liked the look of Miriam, who

was, at any rate, friendly. Sorrel knelt down beside her and began collecting the things that Miriam had upset.

"I'm a cousin, too. I'm Sorrel. Do you know which your locker is?" She picked up a white satin tunic and knickers and gave them a shake. "These will get awfully dirty on the floor."

Miriam got up and began tearing her orange linen frock over her head.

"Mum's made me two tunics and two knickers. She cut up one of her best nightdresses. I think that was pretty decent of her, don't you? She said I'd have to have two, she knew I wouldn't be clean a minute if I only had one. I've got the locker next to Holly, they told me so at the door."

Sorrel hung up Miriam's tunic and knickers and her linen frock and helped her into her black knickers and tunic. Holly passed Miriam her dancing sandals.

"Are you absolutely new, like me, or have you learnt it before?"

Miriam sat on the floor to put on her sandals.

"Learnt what?"

Holly crouched down beside her.

"All these routines and things the big girls do, and that tap and that work at the bar."

Miriam tied the tapes of one of her sandals.

"I began tap when I was three, then I started acrobatic work, you know, flip flaps and all that. I learnt to sing when I was four. I did some shows with Dad for charity when I was five. I don't really ever remember a time when I wasn't learning, but mostly I went to special classes or learnt at home. That's why they've sent me here. It's to see which way I'm heading—at least, that's what Dad says. He thinks it's time I specialised. He says I'm too plain for the glamour type and I ought to do a lot of acrobatic work and become a comedienne. But I shan't, I'm going to dance.

He knows that really." She tied her second sandal tapes. "There's no doubt about it, I'm a bitter disappointment."

A bell clanged in the passage. At once there was a crash of locker doors and everyone hurried out. Winifred was standing at the foot of the stairs with a list in her hand.

"Get in line, please, children, and come past me slowly."

Sorrel leaned a little way out of the line and looked up the passage for Mark. Boys were easy to pick out amongst that mass of black tunics and white socks. Mark had changed into his sandals, otherwise he was dressed exactly as he had started out in the morning. He saw Sorrel and gave her a grin. It was a cheerful grin, but she knew that inside he was feeling very much as she was, sort of sinking and wishing they were not so new.

Winifred had stopped Miranda and told her to wait. She was standing at the foot of the stairs when Sorrel arrived at the head of the queue. Winifred laid a hand on Sorrel's arm.

"I expect you've met Miranda in the changing room." She looked at Miranda. "I want you to look after Sorrel. You two are in the same form."

Miranda gaped at Winifred.

"But she's younger than I am and she's never done a thing."

Winifred spoke nicely, but you could not help feeling she was not sorry to be able to say what she did.

"She may be younger, but from the paper I set her she's well up to the standard of work in the upper middle, and, as well, Madame has granted her the scholarship Pauline Fossil has given for dramatic work."

This last remark seemed to stun Miranda into silence. She caught Sorrel by the hand and pulled her up the stairs after her. It was only when they were outside the door of the practice room in which the upper middle worked that she suddenly stopped.

"I didn't know you could act, nobody told me."

"I don't know that I can."

"What did Madame see you do?"

Sorrel was just going to tell her and then she thought better of it. Perhaps Madame had been over-generous in granting her the scholarship. Perhaps she had not really seen very much talent, but if that was so she was certainly not going to let Miranda know about it. Like a distant light at the end of a long tunnel a thought shaped in Sorrel's head. She had not ever thought of being an actress, but she was the daughter of one and the grandchild of an actor and an actress, and the great-grandchild of a very great actor indeed, if all they said about that old Sir Joshua was right. Anyway, there was every bit as much reason why she should be an actress as why Miranda should. Why should not she see if she could be good? If she could really be worth Pauline Fossil's scholarship? She answered Miranda casually:

"Oh, just a bit of a play that she asked us to do. Is this the classroom?"

In the next few weeks the children were so busy that they had no time to think if they liked London or the Academy, or living with Grandmother or anything else. Every morning they left the house at a quarter past eight to be ready and dressed for their first class at nine. They worked at lessons until twelve. From twelve till one Mark and Holly played games with the smaller children in the garden near the Academy, but Sorrel had special ballet classes with Winifred. At one o'clock they went down to the dining-room, which was in the basement, and had lunch, which was brought in vast containers from the British Restaurant. They were then sent out when it was fine, or, if it was wet, did what they liked indoors until two-thirty; they then did lessons until four-thirty. Sometimes they had singing or dancing or an acting class in the afternoon, and then they did extra lessons after tea. Normally, tea was at four-thirty, and from five till six-thirty they had special classes; ballet one night, tap dancing the next and on each night acting in either French or English, or a mime class.

All day long, unless there was a special class, the girls worked in their black overalls, white socks and sandals; but if there was a special class, such as Sorrel's extra ballet lesson before lunch, or Holly had an extra ballet lesson in the afternoon, then down they had to rush to the changing room, get into their tunics and knickers, snatch up their towels and go up to their class. At the end of that, after a quick rub down, back they had to dash into their overalls. "It's not so bad as it used to be," the other children told them. "Now, until you get to wearing block shoes, the same sandals do for everything except tap, and the world doesn't come to an end if you just wear your tunic knickers and a shirt for tap; but when we could get the stuff there was all that changing into rompers, and we'd special satin sandals for ballet. It was change, change, all the time."

As far as the lessons were concerned the children found things easy. The Academy standard was reasonably high, but nothing like as high as it had been at their previous schools, and some subjects were dropped altogether, such as Latin, but, of course, other things took their place. There was a tremendous lot of history of dancing and of the theatre, and any amount of time given to music. They had not only to learn the theory of music, but there were special classes on rhythm and special classes on appreciation, when music was played to them on gramophone records, and they were taught how to listen to it and to understand it. Music was an afternoon class. A Doctor Felix Lente came every afternoon and taught the whole school.

The children could have kept pace with all the ordinary school things, even the music, for, as a whole, the pupils were not exceptionally musical, but it was the dancing they found so difficult. In spite of extra coaching and the fact that all three were quite intelligent, they were taking a long time to catch up. Sorrel, in fact, was obviously never going to catch up with her age, and when she was finally put to bar work with a class, it was with girls of Holly's age. Holly and Mark worked with a special little class of beginners.

As well as all the dancing they had to memorise. Each of the children had two or three acting parts. In those first weeks they frequently found themselves trying to do three things at once. Have a bath, say a part out loud, and stick out one foot, murmuring with half their minds, plié and rise, plié and rise.

Everything was much more difficult for Sorrel than for Holly and Mark. Mark took his dancing lessons very lightly. He tried to remember all he could but he felt it was a shocking waste of time for somebody who was going into the Navy. Holly had only to compete with the new girls, who knew no more than she did, and very soon she began to like dancing and became one of the best in her small class. It was not saying much, but it was something to show for the person who held the Posy Fossil scholarship. But, for Sorrel, life was pretty tough. Every girl of her age had been learning dancing for at least two years, most of them had been working on their points for quite a while. Of course the majority had been evacuated for about a year during the heavy bombing, but they had kept up fairly well by working under a local ballet teacher. Sorrel could see that however hard she worked and however many extra classes she had she was never really going to be a dancer. It was not even as though she had any especial talent. She was light on her feet and quick at remembering, but it took more than that to make a dancer. Sometimes, in the night, she thought desperately of going to Madame and asking if she could not drop all this dancing, but even before she had framed the thought she knew it would be hopeless. Madame's Academy was primarily for dancing, and to get inside those doors you had to dance.

What Sorrel did find as the weeks went by was that she looked forward to all the acting classes. Mime, where you acted scenes with no words spoken at all, she loved. Then there were her speaking parts. She had the part of the queen in a French version of "The Sleeping Beauty." She had a scene or two of Rosalind's in "As You Like It," and she had Friar Tuck in "Robin Hood." Every acting class, she liked acting more. She found things happened to her. One day, quite suddenly, she knew what her hands should be doing. Another, she discovered how she should get from one place to another across the stage. She found that she knew what it meant when Miss Jay said, "You were well in the scene, Sorrel dear." She began to know how to be acting, and yet to sound natural. Quite a lot of these things she could not possibly have explained, but they were each becoming clear thoughts, so that she knew that presently each one would be sorted out and she would be able to say, "I did that because . . ."

All the time in front of her at the acting classes there was Miranda to watch. Miranda in the school, or Miranda at a dancing class, or Miranda listening to an appreciation of music lesson was just an ordinary schoolgirl. But Miranda acting was something so special that you forgot she was Miranda. It did not matter to Miranda that she was dressed in a black overall and white socks and black sandals, and looked just like all the other girls, for when she was acting she became the person she was meant to be. As the princess as a child in "The Sleeping Beauty" you knew that she was very young and wearing stiff satin, and that she had never heard there were such things as needles in the world, and when the needle pricked her, though there was no needle there, you could see that it had gone in and had hurt her, and you could watch her going to sleep and know it was not just an ordinary sleep but would last for a hundred years. In her Rosalind scene she took the words and they sang out of her mouth in a golden stream, and yet, somehow, she made them ordinary words and Rosalind a real girl. And so it was when she played Maid Marian. Miranda always played the best parts; she never thought that she would not play them, and it seemed to be the rule that she picked out what she liked and the rest of the class shared out what was over. Both Miss Jay and Madame Moulin treated Miranda as something special when she was acting. When she was not acting they treated her as the rather conceited schoolgirl that she was. It was all very muddling. In what little time Sorrel had to think about anything except her work, she thought about Miranda. Miranda was full of talent, she had inherited all the family gifts, everybody said so. To Madame Moulin and Miss Jay it was something wonderful to be descended from the Warrens. Sorrel respected Madame Moulin and Miss Jay, and so what they thought mattered to her. She still thought of herself as Forbes, but just now and again, when she was watching Miranda act, something stirred in her, and she felt excited and then part of her mind said, "You're a Warren too. You're a Warren too."

Chapter 9

AN AUDIENCE

One morning the Academy bell clanged and all the children were summoned to the big main hall, for Madame wanted to speak to them. The big main hall ran through all three houses. At one end there was a platform with a table in the centre. The children filed in, the small ones in front and the big ones at the back. As each class arrived their teacher left them and went up on to the platform. When everybody was ready and after a little pause, Madame, in her stiff black frock and cerise shawl and ballet shoes, only this time without the stick, for the rheumatism was better, came to the middle of the stage. At once all the teachers and the girls swept big curtseys to the ground and the boys bowed; everybody said "Madame." Madame smiled.

"Sit, children." All the children sat on the floor with their legs crossed and their backs perfectly straight in the way they were taught to do in their classes. Madame waited until the last rustle of sitting down had died, then she came forward to the front of the platform. "I want to talk to you about the performances we are going to give in hospitals and for the troops. First of all I want to talk to you about transport. As, of course, every child here realises, petrol must not be wasted. Each of you will in time appear at these concerts but we shall not be able, as is our custom, to send you all in taxis. A car will be hired, or two cars if need be, to carry the costumes, and as many children as can be accommodated in the cars will travel in them. The rest of you will go in charge of your teachers by usual means of transport, whatever that may be; buses, trams, trains or the Underground railways. It is not easy for your teachers to escort a lot of children by these means and I shall expect perfect obedience from even the smallest of you. Owing to the possibility of air-raids and the distance outside London which most of you live, these concerts will take place in the afternoon, usually on a Saturday, so that you may get home well before black-out.

"Now I want to speak to you about the concerts themselves. We have in this country men of practically every nationality in the world, including the Asiatic races, who don't perhaps speak or understand our language, but every one of them has, of course, been a child himself and most of them think of children of your age whom they've left behind in their homes. We shall, of course, give of our very best to these entertainments; but each one of you will know that you're not very skillful and you've got a great deal to learn; but in spite of these defects you will perhaps get a great deal of applause from your audiences. It's about that applause I want to speak to you. I want you to remember that when you've done a little dance or song or sketch, that the applause that you get is not only because you yourself have done your best, but because each of those men is seeing in you some child at home, and because of you is able to forget for a little while the unhappiness of not being in his home, and in some cases the great tragedy of not knowing what has happened to the children in his family. I am taking you all into my confidence about this because we, as a school, are gaining a great deal by these performances. Each one of you will have an opportunity of experiencing how it is to work before an audience, and it is, therefore, of the utmost importance that none of you should get conceited. Every child in this room is a beginner, and whether you're going to be an actor or actress or a dancer, or perhaps a musical performer, you've a great deal to learn, and all your life on the stage you will go on learning, and it would be a very sad thing if a great deal of applause just now made any one of you think that you know more than you do." Madame paused and smiled. "There, I've made you all look very serious! What I want from each of you is the best that you can give and a secret knowledge in each of your hearts of how many are your faults and how much better you will do next time. That's all, children."

The children got up and curtseyed or bowed and said "Madame" and led off in neat lines back to their classes. To Sorrel, Mark and Holly, Madame's speech was rather puzzling. In the few school and village performances in which they had taken part there was, of course, applause at the end, but they had never thought that it meant anything more than that people had enjoyed themselves. What sort of applause did Madame mean that was likely to make them think that they knew a whole lot more than they did?

Sorrel was the first to find out. The upper middle concert for which they had rehearsed so long was taken down to South London to a seamen's hospital on a Saturday afternoon. Sorrel was, inside herself, scornful of the fuss that went on beforehand.

"You never saw such a fuss," she confided to Mark and Holly. "I know every skip of that horrid lamb backwards, I've known it for weeks and weeks and weeks, and yet we never seem to have finished. There's an awful thing called a lay-out. That means the order in which everything comes and giving everybody time to change. It's all written out in a prop book with music cues. What on earth would it matter if there was a little pause? I bet the seamen wouldn't mind."

When it came to the Saturday afternoon she had her first glimpse of the professional's angle of mind. Two cars took down the costumes to the hospital. Five children and Miss Jay went in one and five more and Winifred in another. Miss Sykes, the English literature mistress, who was stage managing, sat in the front of one car and Mrs. Blondin, the fat woman who played the piano, sat in the front of the other. There were seven children over, of whom Sorrel was one, and they were to be taken down by Miss Jones, the mathematics teacher.

The seven children waited in the students' entrance and it was then that Sorrel first felt nervous. Nobody could possibly be nervous about dancing a lamb with a lot of other people, but it was a catching kind of nervousness for everybody. Would everybody get there all right? Were the clothes all right? Would all the music be there? Would anybody make a mistake? Would the Academy be disgraced?

Miss Jones had a mathematical mind. She had lived and breathed figures since she was much smaller than the seven children she was escorting. Until she came to teach at the Academy she had built her life on facts. Two and two made four and so on, and that was the end of that. Since the school at which she had taught had been bombed, and become a static water tank, she had taught at the Academy, and she had found herself in a new world. First of all, the Academy being a theatrical school, ordinary lessons could not, and did not, come first. That was a big shock to Miss Jones, who up till then had thought that nothing could be more important than mathematics. Shock number two had been war conditions. Since 1939 she had seen her pupils evacuated at a moment's notice to the other end of everywhere, and found herself teaching new children for a week or two, and then they too disappeared to be evacuated. When she came to the Academy it had been another sort of life. Children travelled in from miles out for classes, and they did not come in because of mathematics or English literature, which she would have quite understood, but because of their dancing or acting classes. Now there was suddenly a full school again of children who lived in or near London, and had come back in the hope that severe bombing had ceased. She had thought then that they had come to get what she called "a proper education," but once more she discovered that it was the dancing and the acting that had drawn them back. This, in itself, would not have confused her if she had not found that children who were training for the stage, and who put their stage training first, could be every bit as intelligent when learning mathematics as a child who came to school for just ordinary lessons. Miss Jones was just as much puzzled about this performance in a seamen's hospital as was Sorrel. In Miss Jones's reckoning, if you could add and subtract and understood decimals, then you did understand them and that was that. Surely, in exactly the same way, if you learnt a dance or a song or a sketch, you could do it and that, too, ought to be that. Then what was this nervous, keyed-up feeling? The only thing she could compare it to was an examination. She knew from experience how the things that you knew perfectly well could fade from you in an examination, and she guessed that giving a performance was the same thing. So as she collected her seven children in the hall she gave them the sympathetic smile that she gave to examination pupils, and said in the same encouraging tone:

"All ready? Now, off we go."

The merchant seamen had all walked or had been pushed into one big ward of the hospital. At the far end

was a space meant to represent a stage, and at the side of
this was the piano. It made rather a good kind of stage
because there was a door each side and at the back there
was a nurses' sitting-room, which the children used as a
dressing-room. The two cars had got there before the
seven children who had come with Miss Jones arrived.
Everybody was talking in whispers and fussing about and
trying not to look excited. Winifred and Miss Jay had
rouge and some lipstick and made the children up. Mrs.
Blondin remained as detached as usual. She had not got
on her usual red blouse today, but had changed into a
crêpe de Chine one because it was a party. She stood by
the window and peered out over a lot of bomb damage to
the distant wharves, and sang under her breath "Down in
the forest something stirred." Sorrel was changing near
her and though she did not mind the song at first, she
found it a little depressing when she heard it for the
fourth time, especially as there was not a forest. Obviously, Mrs. Blondin was one of those people who got
great comfort from singing about her little grey home in
the west when she was not in her little grey home, or
about Dixie when she was in London.

The programme was to open with a speech made by
Miranda. For it she wore her school black overall. The
clock struck three and Winifred looked round and beckoned to Miranda. She tried to beckon to Mrs. Blondin,
but she was engrossed in singing "It was only the note of
a bird," so she did not notice things like beckonings, and
Winifred had to tap her on the shoulder. Miss Jay looked
round the room.

"Absolute silence, children."

As Miss Jay said those words and the doors shut behind
Mrs. Blondin and Miranda, Sorrel felt not herself, but
part of everybody left behind in the dressing-room. She
felt her breath coming in little short gasps, she felt she

100

could hear her heart beating and she felt her fingers grow sticky. Miranda's voice, in a muffled way, came through the closed door. She was speaking beautifully, telling the seamen how proud they were to be allowed the chance to amuse them, how they would please remember that they were only children and how they were going to do their best, and how immensely grateful they were to them because they knew, but for the men who were the audience and men like them, they would have starved. And then, in quite a different voice, she began to recite Kipling's "Big Steamers."

As Miranda finished, the heads of all the children turned towards the doors and Miss Jay and Winifred exchanged glances. Everybody was waiting, and then it came—the applause. Sorrel, because it was her first performance with the Academy, did not understand why that clapping with its roaring, pleased sound meant anything to her. Of course, Miranda was her cousin, but why should she care so much how Miranda was doing? Why did she feel that what Miranda did was part of what she did? Winifred was shepherding through one of the doors children who were dancing in a little ballet which was to come next. They were being sent on through the same door as Miranda had gone in by, and as they went on Miranda came back through the door on the other side. Miss Jay gave Miranda a pleased nod and Miranda ran to the corner where she was changing and pulled off her overall. Winifred closed the door behind the last of the ballet and came across to Sorrel. She picked up a brush and began brushing Sorrel's hair.

"They're warming up nicely."

Sorrel liked Winifred and ventured a question.

"Does it make a great difference if a thing starts well? I mean, if Miranda had forgotten her words, which of course she wouldn't, it couldn't have spoiled the ballet, could it?"

There was a very little bit of curl at the bottom of Sorrel's hair. Winifred made the best of this, twisting it round her fingers.

"It always matters. This sort of show has to be built up. If anything goes badly and the men don't like it, then you've lost something, the interest and so on of the seamen, and you've got to start again to get it back."

Winifred went away after that and Sorrel, who was in her black crêpe de Chine lamb's tunic and had nothing further to do for the moment, leant against the wall and thought. If in a performance like this to seamen just done by children at an Academy everything mattered so much, what on earth could it be like when you were a real actress like her mother had been? If you were bad in your part for even a moment, if you became yourself and slipped out of the play for a second or, most awful of all, if you forgot your words, how fearful it must be, everybody else who acted with you having to work doubly hard to get the audience back to the mood of believing in you, which they had been in before.

The lambs' turn came in the last half of the performance. Sorrel was the third lamb from the end, and she stood in a queue by the door, fiddling with her tunic and seeing that her shoes, which she had just taken off, were where she could find them again, and looking at Winifred with an anxious eye. Then the shepherdesses' song was over, the door was opened and Mrs. Blondin started to play one of Schubert's "Moments Musicaux." Sorrel held out her arms and raised her right leg.

It was impossible while Sorrel was being a lamb for her to think about the audience. Even simple work such as the lambs did took all of her mind. Toes had to be pointed just right, hops had to happen exactly on a beat, and she had to make her exit on exactly the right bar. But at the end when she ran on to curtsey with the rest she had a chance to look round. In the front of the ward were the beds, behind them the sitting chairs and behind that were the walking cases. It was then that Sorrel saw what Madame had meant about all nationalities. There were black faces and yellow faces and white faces. There were bandaged heads, limbs in plaster of Paris, there were some men so covered with bandages that you could hardly see them at all. A whole lot of the seamen, especially three Chinese, she was certain could not understand anything that was said in English, and yet everybody was smiling and looking pleased. Because of Madame's speech she could see why, and what she had meant about conceit. Of course, it was not anything much that they had just done. They had spent a lot of time on it and there was no muddle or anything like that. Probably any children anywhere could have done it. But these broad smiles that were greeting them were because of some other children somewhere else. Just as, if she were away, she might think some boy or girl somewhere like Mark or Holly. When she ran back the second time to curtsey with the rest of the lambs she gave an especial smile to one of the three Chinese. He had one arm in plaster of Paris and, as far as she could see, the rest of him was in plaster of Paris too. Anyway, he was lying very stiff and flat in his bed, and in spite of it all he was managing to smile.

It was hard for Sorrel, having got her lamb off her chest, not to burst into excited talk with the others, but Miss Jay and Winifred were strong on discipline and at the first sound of a raised voice they flew to the culprit with an angry face. Those of the lambs who were not taking part in any other act huddled together by the window.

"Seemed to go all right, didn't it?"

103

"I nearly tripped as I came on; there was an awful rough bit on the floor just there. Did you see?"

"Nancy's got her shepherdess dress on wrong. Those panniers ought to stick out."

"She sang all right, though."

"Did you feel nervous, Sorrel? Didn't make any mistakes, did you?"

The entertainment finished with another short speech from Miranda and then all the children came on in the dresses in which they had last appeared and sang "There'll always be an England" and "God Save the King."

It was while they were changing to go home that the exciting thing happened. The Matron of the hospital came in and spoke to Winifred and Miss Jay. Winifred and Miss Jay had a puzzled conversation and then Winifred called out, "Will all the lambs come here a minute?" Surprised, the lambs stopped dressing and came over to her. Matron looked at them all and then laid her hand on Sorrel's arm.

"I think this is the little girl."

Winifred finished fastening Sorrel's frock and tidied her hair.

"We'll send her out and see." She turned to Sorrel. "There's a sick Chinaman who wants to speak to one of you."

Matron took Sorrel by the hand and led her over to the bed of the Chinaman in plaster of Paris. There was no doubt that it was Sorrel he wished to see, for he nodded. He was too weak to say much, but he smiled and whispered.

"Makee plesent." He then fumbled under his pillow and brought out a queer little china fish on the end of a string.

"It's a present for you, dear," said Matron. "Speak slowly if you want to thank him."

Sorrel went round to the left-hand side of the bed because that hand was free from the plaster of Paris. She laid her hand in his.

"Thank you so very much," she said, speaking every word slowly. "I will keep it always."

The man smiled.

"Makee mluch luck."

Back in the nurses' sitting-room, the other children crowded round Sorrel.

"What was it? Who wanted you?"

Sorrel told them. Then she held out the little fish.

"He gave me that."

"Why you? What on earth for?" asked Miranda.

Sorrel was so frightfully pleased at having been given the little fish that she hardly noticed the rude way in which Miranda spoke.

"Just for luck."

Miranda opened her mouth as if to say something, and then she shut it again. It was as if words were tumbling into her head and she was swallowing them. Then finally she blurted out, not in the lovely voice in which she spoke on the stage, but in the voice of a jealous schoolgirl.

"Well, I hope it does you good. If you're going to be an actress I should think it would take a row of fishes to make you a success."

Chapter 10

NEWS

It was lucky in a way that the children had to work so hard, for really it was very peculiar living with Grandmother. Fortunately, it did not seem as peculiar to them as it would to most children, because they had got acclimatised in the holidays at the vicarage to a rather odd way of living. There had been Grandfather, much more interested in Bible animals than he was in them, so their holiday life had centered round Hannah. At Number 14 Ponsonby Square there was Grandmother living a quite separate life from the children. Quite a lot went on in Grandmother's drawing-room—people came to call, the telephone rang—but none of it concerned the children. Their world was upstairs with Hannah, and with Alice when she could make time.

Next to Hannah and Alice the nicest thing about Ponsonby Square was the garden. Before the war, when there were railings round it, it had been a garden beautifully kept up at the expense of the people who lived in the Square. Even in wartime you could see somebody was trying about it. The grass was cut, there were Michaelmas daisies of all colours in the beds, crab-apple trees with crab-apples hanging all over them, and endless shrubs with gay leaves and berries. At one end of the garden vegetables were being grown, but right down the centre of the vegetable beds were some incredibly old mulberry trees, fairly dripping with mulberries. Two aged gardeners looked after the garden, and they became great friends with the children. The head gardener told them that before the war dozens of children had belonged to the garden and played there regularly, but they were all evacuated now. He said that he missed them very much and hoped that now that this there 'itler had stopped making a nuisance of himself they would come back.

"A garden ain't rightly a garden," he would say, shaking his head, "without children in it."

The whole of one half of the garden was divided into allotments, most of which belonged to wardens. Every Sunday after church the children would walk round the allotments to see how everything was getting on, deciding which allotment they would give a prize to. Their choice always fell on the same allotments because the wardens who owned them had not only grown cabbages and things like that, but had put in a few flowers as well.

In the middle of the garden was the lawn and all over this, on Saturday afternoons and Sundays, which were, of course, the only days when the children saw the garden, people lay in deck-chairs asleep. Most of the people were very nice to the children and talked to them; but somehow, just being three in a garden full of grown-up people, they never felt they could be really noisy. Sometimes, of course, they made a mistake and shouted; usually when they did, an old lady woke up with a jump and dropped her knitting, or an old gentleman's eyebrows shot up, and then they went back to playing quietly again. Fortunately, the lawn was not the only place. There was a shrubbery path all round the garden, which was very good for hide-and-seek, and when they felt energetic there was a low overhanging branch which made a bar for practising their dancing exercises.

In the house, Alice and Hannah had done everything that could be done to make their rooms look nice. They had bought some gay green paint and painted up both

Mark's room and the nursery. Alice had found some old curtains and she and Hannah washed them and cut them up and hung them in Mark's room; and she had found a red table-cloth, and that made curtains for the nursery. Sorrel had been given a latchkey, which was hung on a piece of string round her neck so that they could always let themselves in, and save, as Alice said, "Somebody's understandings on the old apples and pears." But, in spite of a latchkey, either Hannah or Alice always managed to be about, looking pleased to see them when they came in.

Hannah, after a lot of searching, had found a church that she approved of in the neighbourhood, and the moment she found it, and had got used to the times of the services, she began to feel at home. She considered the children ought to go to a children's service in the afternoon on Sundays, but, as there were so few children in London, there did not seem to be any children's services to go to. Instead, she took them to a morning service and managed to keep for each of them what she called "Sunday clothes."

"You may laugh, Alice," she said when Alice was amused at these efforts, "but I know what's right and proper for Mr. Bill's children, and I'm going to see it carried out."

From the moment that Hannah found her church and got the children's church-going settled, she became much more herself. All day long the sound of hymn-singing was heard on the top floor:

> "The rich man in his castle,
> The poor man at his gate.
> What have I done with my thimble?
> And ordered their estate."

And when Harvest Festival time arrived:

> "We plough the fields and scatter

108

The good seed on the land.
What an awful hole Mark's made
In thi-is sock."

Every day or two, one or all of the children were sent
for to visit Grandmother. It was a queer kind of visiting
of Grandmother, the children thought, because it was like
going out to pay a call. A message would come to say that
they were being received, and then a lot of tidying and
brushing-up went on by Hannah before they were passed
over to Alice, who escorted them downstairs just as if they
did not know their way, and announced them like proper
visitors.

"Here's Sorrel, Miss Shaw dear," or

"Here's the children to see you, Miss Shaw dear."

Thanks to Miriam, the children were beginning to
learn about their family. Miriam's mother, the children's
aunt Lindsey, was the eldest of Grandmother's daughters
and she had not married very young, and before she
married, Grandmother had come to depend on her being
about the house to see to things and to talk to. Then one
day she had brought home Mose Cohen, the comedian,
and said she was going to marry him. Grandmother had
not been able properly to disapprove of Mose Cohen, because he was a very great star on the music halls; but she
was rather jealous of him because he had taken away her
Lindsey, and so, because she was not always very polite,
the Cohens got out of the way of calling on Grandmother, and only came when they had a proper invita-
tion. Sometimes, Miriam said, Grandmother forgot she
was angry with her father and then they were round
seeing her every day or so; but just at present they were
not on very good terms.

"It's like that with Aunt Marguerite, too," Miriam explained, "only it's worse for Aunt Marguerite because she
thinks Uncle Francis the most marvellous actor in the

109

world and Grandmother doesn't think he can act at all and always says so. You wait till Grandmother imitates Uncle Francis, and then you'll see. As a matter of fact, I expect Grandmother will see more of them soon because of Miranda. Everybody, even Uncle Henry Warren in Hollywood, is pretty excited about Miranda. Somebody to carry on the tradition, you know."

Mark had puzzled about this.

"But when Miranda goes on the stage she'll be Miranda Brain, so I shouldn't think anyone would know or care about that old tradition."

Miriam was amazed at his stupidity.

"Of course everybody knows. Who married who and what happened to everybody. When Sorrel's old enough for a licence, you'll see. It doesn't matter that she's called Sorrel Forbes; all the critics and most of the public will know she is Aunt Addie's daughter. Just like me, when I'm old enough they'll know, of course, that I'm Mose Cohen's daughter; but they'll know at the same time that my mother was a Warren."

Everybody had to talk to Miriam as though she was a great deal older than she was. She was an only child and had been brought up mostly with grown-up people, and everything to do with the theatre was in her blood. Masses of theatrical people came to her parents' flat and they talked theatrical business in front of her, so that on that particular subject she was much older than her age. When it was anything to do with the theatre, Sorrel always asked Miriam's advice, as though she were a grown-up person.

"If," she said anxiously, "everyone knows we're great-grandchildren of Sir Joshua, doesn't it mean that people will expect us to be fairly good?"

Miriam nodded soberly.

"You bet it does. As a matter of fact, we won't be allowed to go on with it if we aren't. My mother didn't do much; she started off with a bang when she was about eighteen and then she got some bad notices and then she got smaller parts, and then she gave it up. Mum says it was simply awful; she knew she couldn't do it. There were just two that were any good in the family, Uncle Henry, of course, and your mother. It's the most awful blow to Grandmother that Uncle Henry's gone on the pictures and lives always in Hollywood. He was pretty terrific on the stage, Mum says. I was too little, I never saw him. He came over just before the war, but I never spoke to him much; there was always a howling mob round his hotel wanting his autograph."

"What about Aunt Marguerite?" Sorrel asked. "Didn't she act?"

Miriam lowered her voice.

"Well, that is one of those things that makes Grandmother angry. Grandmother never thought she could act, and nor did Grandfather when he was alive, but she went on the stage and she didn't do so badly; and then she married Uncle Francis. Well, he made her his leading lady, mostly in Shakespeare. Sometimes Grandmother goes to see them act; and then on Christmas Day, and times like that, she shows Aunt Marguerite how she looked when she was being Lady Macbeth, or whatever it is." She giggled. "It's awfully funny. Dad adores it and leads Grandmother on to do it, though Mum always tells him not to. But then Dad's in a special position. Grandmother can't imitate Dad, and though she'd die rather than say it, she thinks he's awfully funny. I've sat in boxes with her and I've seen her laugh so much that all the paint comes off her eyelashes."

Ever since she had been living with Grandmother, Sorrel puzzled why, with one son who was a film star and a son-in-law who was a very successful comedian and another son-in-law who was Sir Francis Brain, the well-known Shakespearean actor, Grandmother should be so poor. It was again Miriam who explained.

"Grandmother simply doesn't understand money; she never has, Mum says. Of course, it's better now because there aren't so many things she can buy; but even now she spends all the money that she has, mostly on things she doesn't want. I don't exactly know, but I think that now Mum and Aunt Marguerite give money for Grandmother to Alice, but Uncle Henry still sends it to her. Mum says he's just like her and spends every penny he has himself, so he never has much to give away, however much he earns. But I think it's Aunt Marguerite and Mum that see that Grandmother's all right."

Sorrel, Mark and Holly heard this in silence. It was clear from the way that Miriam was dressed and all the things she had, like a good leather attaché case, there was lots of money in her home; and it was equally clear that Miranda was so used to money that she took it for granted that she could, as far as the war allowed, have everything she wanted. So it seemed a bit odd that if Aunt Lindsey and Aunt Marguerite were really giving Alice money for Grandmother, that they gave her so little. Alice had been quite right when she said bees and honey were words they would often hear her say. It was clear there was very little bees and honey in the house; but, of course, they did not say this to Miriam, they hardly could suggest her own mother was mean.

Grandmother's favourite of the three children was Mark. She saw him at least twice to Sorrel's and Holly's once.

"Give me boys," she said. "I always preferred them. I blamed Fate for giving me only two sons, and one of those died when he was a baby." She would talk to Mark about his uncle Henry. "I should like you to meet your uncle. There's a man! Can say more with his little finger than that ham actor, your uncle Francis, can say with all the breath in his body. We must turn you into an actor like your uncle Henry."

Mark was not at all afraid of Grandmother.

"I've told you hundreds of times I'm not going to be an actor. I'm going to be a sailor. In fact, I'm going to be an admiral."

Grandmother swept him on one side, leapt off her chaise-longue scattering her shawl and cushions all over the floor, and putting on a deep voice like a boatswain, quoted from "The Tempest":

"Down with the topmast! Yare! Lower, lower. Bring her to try with main course. A plague upon this howling! They are louder than the weather or our office."

Mark hated Shakespeare—and, particularly, he hated him when Grandmother recited him.

"They don't say things like that in the Navy now, whatever they did in that old Tempest." He picked up the cushions and said hopefully, "Can I tuck you up again, Grandmother?"

Grandmother saw why Mark was being so polite, and it made her laugh.

"Getting your own way? Come on, then. You shall amuse me. Tell me how Miriam's getting on. I don't care for Jewish humour myself, but he's a clever fellow, her father. Needs to be, for your aunt Lindsey was always a stick. 'Never give that girl a part that wants any warmth,' your grandfather used to say. Still, the child might have talent. Pity she's so plain."

Mark lay on his face on the floor and dug little holes in the carpet with his finger.

"Miriam can dance. Winifred thinks that Madame's going to teach her next term."

"Doesn't she teach all of you?" said Grandmother, surprised. "I thought that was what she started the school for, because she wanted to teach dancing."

Mark had been a pupil at the Academy sufficiently long enough to be appalled at such ignorance.

"Of course she doesn't. Hardly anyone. You've got to

113

be absolutely outstanding for her to teach you by yourself. Of course, she comes to classes and looks at all of us, but she doesn't teach."

"Stupid waste of time, too much dancing; but good for deportment. I always said to Fidolia that she'd end by having a school for the theatre, that it's all-round training that we want; and I was right. Hope she doesn't waste too much of Miriam's time. Dancing's all very well in its proper place, but I've hopes for Miriam. We don't want anyone making a dancer of her."

Mark scooped amongst the wool of the carpet with his fingernail. He knew that Miriam considered that she was going to be a dancer, but it was never actually mentioned because her family wanted her to be an actress. But he was beginning to have ideas about Grandmother. It seemed to him that everybody treated Grandmother all wrong, and it was because they treated her wrongly that she was so stupid about things like money, and not seeing that her grandchildren had proper furniture in their rooms. He was not absolutely decided, but he was beginning to think that perhaps he ought to be the person to start making Grandmother sensible. He made a first effort in this direction.

"If Miriam can dance and can't act, wouldn't it be a good thing if she was a dancer?"

Grandmother sat up. She had on that day a dress of grey with blue on the falling sleeves. She took a deep breath and threw out an arm, and said in a very grand voice:

"A Warren and not act! Never!"

Mark hurriedly got up off the floor and tucked Grandmother in again in case, having started to get up, she would get right up and recite some more Shakespeare. Having tucked her in, he was not going to relinquish his point.

"But just supposing, I said. After all, just because your

114

grandfather and your great-grandfather and all the rest of it were actors, you needn't be one. Somebody must start somewhere being something else."

Grandmother smiled.

"Are you arguing with me?"

Mark was annoyed and scowled at her.

"If an interesting discussion has to be called an argument, just because I'm a child and you're grown-up, then I am."

Grandmother leant down and pulled his face up to look into hers.

"Warrens act, my dear grandson. They live to act. Get that into your head. They act, not dance, nor do they become sailors."

Mark shrugged his shoulders.

"I've heard what you've said, but you can't stop me thinking what I do think, and what I think is that it's silly to talk like that, and I shall go on thinking it whatever anybody says."

Grandmother looked as though she was going to shake him. Then all of a sudden she laughed.

"Run away, my dear grandson. I'm glad that you are not a manager whom I have to see about a salary, for I feel you'd be a very hard nut to crack. Be off, now."

Sorrel's visits to Grandmother were usually spent in Grandmother asking questions about Miranda. Grandmother would lie back against her jade cushion, pull her Spanish shawl up round her and throw out gentle little questions to Sorrel, and when Sorrel answered she would find Grandmother's sparkling dark eyes glued on her face.

"How did my eldest granddaughter do today?"

Sorrel was nothing like as unafraid of Grandmother as Mark was. Grandmother's polish and finish made her feel all elbows and hands, and she was shy of Grandmother's quick, vivid way of talking. She always had a feeling that

Grandmother was wondering how on earth, in a brilliant family like the Warrens, they had managed to produce a person as dull as herself.

"We did 'As You Like It' after tea. Miranda was Rosalind to-day; she was lovely. I was just being a forester."

Grandmother was looking at her hands.

"How do you mean, lovely? Like a girl who had fallen in love, or like a schoolgirl reciting?"

Sorrel glanced up to catch Grandmother's twinkling eyes fixed on her.

"Well, I've not been in love much myself; and, of course, Orlando's only one of the girls, but I think she's like Rosalind. She certainly isn't a bit like anybody reciting."

Grandmother chuckled.

"And a very good thing, too. You've not met your uncle Francis. Now, there's a real actor!" She giggled as she said this. "All wind and roar. One of the few sensible things they ever did was to send that child to Fidolia. She won't be allowed any of those tricks in her school."

Sorrel felt for words.

"I don't think Miranda wants to do any tricks. Miss Jay never teaches her much and she generally does things right all by herself."

Grandmother gave her shawl an angry shake.

"It maddens me to think that when that girl appears her father will say she has inherited his talent. His talent indeed! He doesn't know the meaning of the word. If he had even a grain of understanding, he would never allow your poor aunt to play the parts that she does. You've not met your aunt Marguerite; she never had much talent, but the poor girl deserved a better fate than to be Lady Brain. Your uncle Francis was a young man when we first met him, playing in our company. It was a costume piece and he was very good-looking, though just as much of a ham actor as he is today. Your aunt Marguerite had a

116

little part and the poor girl could hardly get through it for goggling at Francis. She thought him a genius, and still does if it comes to that. There they go, round and round the provinces with occasional trips to South Africa or Australia. There's scarcely a corner of the British Empire that has not had to endure your aunt Marguerite in such parts as Lady Macbeth, for which she's totally unfitted. How upset your poor grandfather would be if he could see her."

"What happens to Miranda when they're away?"

Grandmother waved a hand as if these domestic problems were of no importance.

"A governess, a good soul; and her doting parents come home practically every weekend."

"But they couldn't from Africa or Australia, could they?"

"Naturally, with the war on, they remain in England. When they went overseas they took the child with them. They dote on her." Grandmother stroked the shawl and pleated it over her fingers. "Let them. That child is pure Warren. The Warren voice. The moment she sets a foot upon the stage, the critics will all say so. I would give a fortune to see your uncle Francis's face when he reads that sort of notice." She suddenly remembered that Sorrel, too, was training. "And how are you doing, child?"

Sorrel was so afraid of being asked to recite that she purposely made very little of her parts."

"Well, of course, it's my first term. I'll have bigger parts later on."

"I must see Fidolia and enquire after you all. Mark, now, I'm sure there's talent there."

This pulled Sorrel out of her shyness.

"Oh, no, I'm sure there isn't. There wouldn't be likely to be, you see, he's going to be a sailor."

Grandmother would allow Mark to argue, but not Sorrel. Her eyes flashed.

"Mark will do what he's told. I've only one grandson and I pin great hopes on him. Great. Run along, child. Run along."

Holly looked forward to coming to see Grandmother because of the things there were to play with in the drawing-room. The green-jade horse was still her favourite; but there were other things as well, ivory fans, and a silver cart, and a case full of bangles. It was an understood thing that if she put everything back, she could play with what she liked while she was in the drawing-room. Holly amused Grandmother.

"Well," she would say, watching Holly pull a row of native bangles on to her arm, "who are you now? Tell me all about it."

Holly would start describing how she was a princess, or a fairy, or a child at a party, and then Grandmother would add to the story until Holly was the centre of an imaginary room full of people.

"Look over there, Holly. A hundred and seventy-two fairies in cloth of gold have come to bring you birthday presents. And look, isn't that a frog, all in white satin, coming in at the door? And here's Cinderella and her fairy godmother."

Holly would get excited.

"And look, there's Cinderella's mice, before they became ponies."

Sometimes, Grandmother would join the party herself and sweep round the room with her shawl trailing behind her, curtseying to everybody and speaking to Holly about their guests. They would be so carried away that they never noticed the time until Alice opened the door.

"Time young Holly was in bed. Come on, Holly. Hannah wants your head on your weeping willow, pillow to you."

Because visiting Grandmother was an event, and because they lived so much more in the world of the Acad-

118

emy than the world of home, the children never felt that
there was excitement in the house. They knew Grandmother was out a lot, but they never thought of asking
why. Then, one night when Hannah was giving them
their supper, Alice came in looking important.

"I'll bet you a lord of the manor none of you three'll
guess my bit of news." Mark was trying very hard to think
what a lord of the manor might be. Alice ruffled his hair.
"A tanner. A sixpence." The children were all looking at
her and she could not keep her secret any longer. "We're
working again; we've got a new part and a very good
part. We start rehearsing the week after next, and our
play opens in January."

Although, of course, they knew Grandmother was an
actress, they had somehow never thought of her as going
to act any more.

"Do you mean Grandmother's got a part?" Mark asked,
obviously amazed. "She must be acting somebody very
old, mustn't she?"

Alice laughed.

"'Tisn't only young nippers like you that people see in
plays. All ages, all types, they are." She lowered her voice.
"If you'll all swear not to repeat it, I'll tell you something
else. Come on, touch your loaves of bread." All the children put their hands on their heads. Alice took a deep
breath. "There's a little girl in the play and your grandmother wants young Miranda to play her."

"What, in a real play?" said Sorrel. "She told me she
wasn't going on the stage until she was eighteen."

"That's what she thinks; but we think differently, and
we're seeing Sir Francis about it, and we generally get our
own way. So you can take it from me that, in the next few
days, you'll see young Miranda setting off to apply for a
licence."

Chapter 11

MOSTLY ABOUT MARK

Grandmother got her way. Miranda was to act in the play with her. Miriam told the children bits of the excitement that had gone on about it.

"Aunt Marguerite telephoned to Mum about every twenty minutes all last night and all the night before. Dad says he thinks they never went to sleep, but rang each other up instead. Uncle Francis thinks it would be better if Miranda waited to make her first appearance under his management. When Mum heard that, she just threw her telephone down and left it hanging from the wall without even putting it back on its rest. I heard it growling and sighing, and went and put it back for her. Mum said to Dad, 'That's all this awful jealousy; he thinks nobody in the world can teach anybody to act but himself.' Anyway, in the end, Grandmother got her way. I couldn't think what Mum and Aunt Marguerite were fussing about, because I knew she would, she always does."

Mark scowled.

"I know one thing she is not going to get her way about, and that's me. She won't put me on the stage and make an actor of me, whatever she does."

Miriam had been doing some foot exercises when she was speaking. She did eight battements in the fourth position front before she answered him. Then she gave a little flourish with her foot to show that she thought he was talking stupidly.

"You wait and see, my boy. You've not really come up against our grandmother yet, and when you do you'll know."

Miranda's engagement caused a certain amount of stir in the Academy. It would have caused more, only it was the autumn term and quite a lot of the other girls who were old enough for a licence had got engagements, too. Most of the other children's engagements were for pantomime though; two of them were going into "Peter Pan"; and, of course, Miranda's acting part was something rather grand and special. But an engagement was an engagement, and just because Miranda's was for acting and most of the others were for dancing, that was no reason for her to think she was of more importance than anyone else.

Every pupil at the Academy, as they were nearing their twelfth birthday, prepared what they called "m'audition," which was their way of saying "my audition." This meant that they had learnt a speech or a recitation that suited them, and that they had a song ready which had a dance to a repeat of the chorus, or special music to which they could do a little dance. Of course, this was the full audition. If a child was going about a singing part or a dancing part, or an acting part only, naturally they only sang or danced or acted; but for a pantomime they usually did all three. Nearly forty of the children were over twelve and every day one or two were standing in the hall in the best frock or suit they had, waiting to be inspected by Miss Jay or Winifred before they went to their audition. The rest of the school, passing them, would call out "Good luck, John," or "Good luck, Mary." Sorrel had studied the twelve-year-olds waiting in the hall pretty carefully. Next April she would be twelve and perhaps sent for an audition, and she wanted to get a good idea of what ought to be worn, and the right sort of face to put

121

on. It was not at all a good thing to look cocky, because, if you did and then came back without the engagement you had gone after, you looked a fool. On the other hand, it was not a good thing to look nervous and miserable because then the school said, "Gosh, I shouldn't think anyone would ever give her a job; she looked as if it had been raining for a week."

Miranda's rehearsals were not starting for ten days and she was to continue with her ordinary training until they did; and, as far as possible, while rehearsals were in progress. Until the Christmas holidays began, she had to get in five hours' lessons a day by law, and in the meantime the management were trying not to call her to rehearsals until the late afternoons and on Saturday mornings. Miranda resented having to come to the Academy at all. To Sorrel's great surprise, she chose her to confide in.

"It's a long and difficult part. I ought to be at home studying it. It's ridiculous to waste my time bringing me here."

"Couldn't you arrange with Madame only to do dancing, singing and lessons, and drop the acting classes? I shouldn't think anyone would mind if you did."

Miranda looked at Sorrel as if she were a worm.

"So that's what you think, do you? I suppose it has never struck you to wonder what would happen to these troop concerts if they hadn't got me to keep them together."

Sorrel had no wish to quarrel with Miranda, but she did wonder how anybody could be as conceited as she was, and she could not help her voice showing a bit what she was thinking.

"I suppose somebody else could do your part. I mean, they'd have to if you weren't there, wouldn't they?"

"I'd like to know who," said Miranda, and stalked away.

As it happened, a concert for the troops was at that very moment being discussed by Madame and her staff.

"They want us to give a matinée for the Forces in the Princess Theatre, or rather, they want us to take over one half of it. The rest will be music-hall turns. It's to take place just before Christmas. I had said 'yes,' intending to use Miranda; but now I don't know what we are going to do if we can't have her. I don't think we've any other child competent to act as compère. However, I've written to her management to ask if they will release her from rehearsal for that one afternoon, and we must wait to see what they say. For the rest we'll use the best of the items in the various other programmes that we have given this term. And I think, as it's a Christmas entertainment, we should put in a Christmas ballet and perhaps a carol, or something like that. Has anyone any ideas?"

The result of that conference began to filter through the Academy. Winifred started some strenuous rehearsals on the new ballet. The best of the school dancers were not able to take part in it as they would be rehearsing for their pantomimes, so the second-best team had to work very hard indeed to be sufficiently good for Winifred to pass them. Miriam was, of course, too young to be allowed to work on her points; but she was so very much the most promising dancer in the school that the ballet was to centre round her in the part of the child. Miriam, to the children's surprise, was not at all pleased at what the rest of the Academy thought her good fortune. She tried to explain to them why.

"It's very important at my age that I shouldn't be brought forward in any way. I should now be getting my technique firm, so that in a year's time, when I begin to work on my points, I can take my training seriously."

Sorrel had to laugh.

"You can't say you don't take it seriously now, Miriam. You never think about anything else."

"That's perfectly true. But it isn't only making me do too advanced work that I'm worried about, I know neither Winifred nor Madame would allow that; but if I dance in public, there's almost sure to be notice taken of me and then Dad'll hear, and then probably there'll be a row. Not, mind you, that a row is going to make any difference at all, I'm going to be a dancer whatever anybody says; but it could be tiresome, and I don't want it to be."

Sorrel, in her free moments, thought a lot about these conversations with Miranda and Miriam. How confident they were! And how different about it. Miranda was conceited somehow and spoilt, but Miriam was like a person following a path through a wood. There might be a lot of other interesting paths branching off at the side, but Miriam only saw the path that her feet were on, and nothing could distract her from it.

Miriam was not the only person who came into prominence over the Forces matinée. The juniors were dancing and miming some of their nursery rhymes. Most of these were accompanied by Mrs. Blondin on the piano and an orchestra, but for four of the songs the rhymes were to be sung as a solo. "I Had a Little Nut Tree," "I Saw Three Ships Come Sailing By," "Baa, Baa, Black Sheep" and "Little Boy Blue." Dr. Lente was asked to pick a child for these solos. To everybody's surprise, because he had never said anything about him before, he at once mentioned Mark. Dr. Lente did not speak English very well.

"The little Mark, when he is trying, which is by no means always, has the voice of much charm, true and clear."

At the next nursery-rhyme rehearsal, Mark was placed beside the piano and Mrs. Blondin, and told to sing "I Had a Little Nut Tree." Miss Jay had got used to Mark by

124

now and knew he liked to find something that he personally thought interesting about what he was asked to do, or
else it was very difficult for him to attend properly. Dr.
Lente having said that Mark could sing like a bird, Miss
Jay built on that idea.

"I want you to think of yourself as rather an important
kind of bird singing on a bough. All the rest of the class
are hopping about on the ground, but you are by yourself with nothing but sky over your head and the sun
shining."

Mark considered this.

"What sort of a bird?"

Ornithology was not Miss Jay's subject. She could only
think of larks and nightingales as having singing voices,
and off-hand she could not remember how either bird
looked, and she knew that Mark would want to picture
himself in feathers.

"A special bird. A foreign bird. I think his feathers are
blue and green and he has a scarlet crest."

Mark visualised such a bird and before he knew where
he was he was thinking of himself as being the bird with
feathers such as Miss Jay had described, singing against a
blue sky. Then his eye fell on Mrs. Blondin. She was in
her red blouse. She had on that morning a small green
felt hat with a little feather in it. She was gazing into
space humming "I know where I'm going." Mark lowered
his voice. Not that he worried really whether Mrs. Blondin was listening, because everybody in the Academy
knew she only heard the words "Begin" and "Stop"; but
he felt the subject called for a confidential tone.

"What's she doing in the wood with me? Is she a bird
too?"

Miss Jay also believed Mrs. Blondin to be deaf to ordinary conversation, but she was certainly not going to risk
offending a good accompanist, so she moved away, saying

125

with that sort of dismissing smile grown-ups use when they do not want a child to go on with a conversation:

"Of course, dear, a lovely bird."

Mark, mentally swaying on his bough, his feathers gay in the sun, was still being a boy with part of him, and that part of him was trying to imagine some sort of bird which could possibly be identified not only with Mrs. Blondin but with a piano.

Miss Jay had got the grouping for "I Had a Little Nut Tree" ready, she was holding the Queen of Spain's daughter by the hand. She turned her head towards the piano and barked in the only tone that was known to penetrate Mrs. Blondin's dreams:

"Begin!"

Mrs. Blondin played the opening bars and Mark, proudly swaying on his branch, began to sing:

"I had a little nut tree and nothing would it bear," then he stopped. He turned a pleased face to Miss Jay. "Not a bird at all; one of those monkeys that's got no fur behind but blue and pink instead, and its fingers are moving all the time because it's looking for fleas."

The children laughed, though nobody except Miss Jay knew what Mark was talking about. Mrs. Blondin certainly had not heard because she was still playing, for Miss Jay had not said "Stop!" Miss Jay looked severe.

"I'm not interested in anyone in this particular forest except a bird that I'm waiting to hear sing." Then she changed her voice to a bark. "Stop!" Mrs. Blondin's fingers shot off the piano and fell in her lap. Miss Jay went over to her and tapped her shoulder. "We're doing that all over again." She returned to the class and put a restraining hand on the Queen of Spain's daughter. "Begin!"

Mark's singing really was a lovely noise. He had an absolutely true voice, and now that he had placed Mrs. Blondin as a mandrill, he was able to dismiss her from his

126

mind and sing with the unforced ease of a bird, which was no wonder, as, by the time he was half-way through the verse, he was certain he was one.

Though, of course, the Academy was primarily a dancing school, credit brought to it in any artistic direction was a pleasure to all the staff and, particularly, to Madame Fidolia. There were a lot of hopes built on Mark. It did seem likely that he might be the big hit of the afternoon. Then came discussion about what he should wear. All sorts of ideas were put forward, most of them impracticable, because, of course, everything had to be either in the wardrobe or cut out of old things, or made of unrationed goods, for, naturally, there were no coupons to spare for one matinée. Then an old student of the Academy, who was visiting and had been brought to see the beginners' class rehearse, made an offer. Her little boy had been a page at a wedding at the beginning of the war. He was at the time younger than Mark, but he was big for his age, and Mark, like all the Forbes children, was small for his. Her son had worn a Kate Greenaway suit with a very frilly white shirt, blue satin trousers, white silk socks and blue satin shoes. Everybody was enchanted, and from Madame Fidolia down they said so in their own way.

Madame said, "That would be perfect; he will look a picture."

Winifred: "Won't he look a duck!"

Madame Moulin: *"Tout à fait ravissant!"*

Dr. Felix Lente: "I know not this Kate Greenaway, but if he is made to look as pretty as 'is voice, then I satisfied am."

Miss Jay, because she had produced the nursery rhymes, was more pleased then anybody.

"I shall have him on all the way through the scene with his hands in his pockets, leaning against the proscenium

127

arch. When it's his cue to sing, he can stroll to the centre of the stage; he moves very naturally; the effect ought to be simply enchanting."

They had all reckoned without Mark. The box with his clothes arrived one morning and Mark was sent for to try them on. Out of the box came a heavily-frilled shirt, and was held up against him, then, with squeaks of pleasure, Winifred and Miss Jay unpacked the blue shoes and blue trousers. Finally, Winifred discovered, rolled up in the corner, a pair of white silk socks. She turned to Miss Jay beaming.

"Well, isn't that thoughtful! Fancy lending us the socks too!"

Mark, who had been gazing at the clothes in an almost trance-like way, pulled himself together.

"Who is going to wear this?"

Winifred opened her mouth to say "you" when Miss Jay gave her a little nudge. She had caught a look in Mark's eye she did not like.

"Kate Greenaway designed clothes very suitable for singing nursery rhymes," she said briskly. "When she was alive, boys of all ages were dressed like this."

Mark looked at the socks and shoes and dismissed what Miss Jay was saying as sheer foolishness; and, indeed, the exact argument about that set of clothes was not worrying him, for he had no intention of wearing them, but he was furious with Miss Jay. He considered her a friend and thought she had let him down.

"You promised me I was dressed in blue and green feathers with a scarlet crest."

Miss Jay wished with all her heart she had never invented his bird. It had never crossed her mind that Mark thought he was going to be dressed in feathers. She was a scrupulously fair woman and would never pretend that something was going to happen that was not in order to

128

bribe a child to work well. She decided that she must have time to think of the right approach to Mark before she forced the clothes on him. She put the lid on the box and put her arm round him.

"Sorry, I had never planned you should be dressed as a bird. I had only imagined you singing like one; but we'll see what can be done."

It was no surprise to Miss Jay at the next nursery-rhyme rehearsal that Mark sang very badly. She was sorry, but she would have been sorrier still if she could have known how violently angry and hurt he was. He confided just how he felt to Sorrel.

"It isn't only they thought they could dress me like a girl in blue satin. I'm used to all that sort of thing. After all, when you're made to put on white socks for every dancing class, you can get used to anything; but it was her absolute promise that I was to be a bird that I mind. I just hate the way grown-up people make promises and then break them. She says she didn't, but she absolutely did. I was being a bird on a branch, and the only person near me was that Mrs. Blondin, and she was a mandrill looking for fleas."

Sorrel had known, from Mark, that he was going to be dressed as a bird and that he was pleased about it; but this was the first time she had known to what lengths his imagination had carried him.

"But, Mark, Mrs. Blondin's going to be sitting at the piano in the orchestra, where all the audience can see her. You couldn't really have thought she was going to be dressed as a mandrill." She thought a little more on the subject and then added: "A mandrill more than anything, seeing how they are behind."

Mark's imagination, when in full flood, was quite incapable of being checked by material difficulties. He could only repeat, in a voice suffocated with anger:

129

"It's what she said and what she promised. Anyway, there was being a branch built for me up above everybody else. I shouldn't have been looking at mandrills or anything. I was just looking at the sky and the sun. That's what she said, and it was an absolute promise."

Miss Jay went to see Madame and told her the whole story. All her life Madame had worked with imaginative people; and though, of course, now she was able to keep her imagination from running away with her, she had known what it was, when she was Mark's age, to build a completely imaginary world from fragments of conversation overheard, or things invented by herself. She remembered her first interview with Mark and how he had said "Madame" in a low, deep growl, and when she had asked him how he was dressed when he bowed to her, she had got him to confess that he had thought he was a bear in the Antarctic who had travelled miles to call on the Queen.

"Send Winifred along here, will you?" When Winifred in her practice dress came dashing in, Madame pointed to a chair for her to sit on. "Miss Jay and I are in a dilemma. It seems that Mark Forbes understood Miss Jay to promise that he was going to be dressed as a bird, and as a bird he was singing like a bird. Now he feels unjustly treated and is singing very badly. Miss Jay thinks that it isn't naughtiness, but that he really feels so hurt and angry that he can't use his voice properly. Now I think, since we can't dress him as a bird, that we'll have to suggest a compromise. Could we put a Polar bear into the winter ballet? We've got that white cat's skin in the wardrobe we could alter, and I expect we can hire or contrive a white bear's head, and we must make a stumpy tail. Anyway, it would be near enough."

Winifred got up and hummed the ballet music. Now

and again doing half a step demi-point. She turned to Madame.

"Why shouldn't the child, when she wakes up in the land of winter, find herself lying with her head on a Polar bear? As a matter of fact, I wanted to think of something that would add to the fairy-tale atmosphere of that scene. It's very difficult to get the effect before the ice fairies and snow fairies come on. Mark can't dance much, of course, but he can manage a few simple steps and he'll certainly add to the charm of the scene."

Winifred was sent to fetch Mark. He came in to Madame's sitting-room, bowed nicely, and said "Madame," but his eyes were not the friendly eyes that Madame usually saw, but hard and angry. She smiled at him.

"Well, my son, I hear we've disappointed you."

Mark was fair enough not to blame Madame for what had happened.

"It was an absolute promise, blue and green feathers and a red crest."

Madame spoke quietly.

"No, Mark. It was not an absolute promise. You thought it was a promise, but it was a misunderstanding. Miss Jay wanted you to sing like a bird. She had never pictured you dressed as one." Mark moved forward to speak. Madame lifted her hand and checked him. "And what is more, my child, you cannot be dressed as a bird because we have not got anything at all in the way of a costume for a bird; and, as you know, we cannot waste coupons on materials for these things. Before we go any further with this discussion, I want you to apologise to Miss Jay. You should have known her too well to think that she would make you a promise and not keep it."

"But she did promise. And Mrs. Blondin was a mandrill."

131

This was too much for Madame. She laughed.

"Nonsense, Mark! I do not care how vivid your imagination may be; but you cannot seriously, even at your age, think that Miss Jay was going to dress Mrs. Blondin as a mandrill." She changed her tone. "But I do think you thought there was a promise and, because you thought that, when you have apologised to Miss Jay I shall tell you what we propose to do to make it up to you. I don't expect you to apologise for anything except allowing your imagination to run away with you to such an extent that you could think Miss Jay would break a promise."

Mark wrestled with himself. He was so convinced that he had been promised, that it was very hard to be fair about it, but at last he managed to say to Miss Jay:

"Well, I'm sorry if I said you broke a promise when you didn't."

Miss Jay accepted this.

"Thank you, Mark."

Madame beckoned him to her and held out a hand.

"Now hear what we have planned for you instead. How would you like to be a bear?"

Mark's world reeled. He flew off his branch, cast aside his feathers and dressed himself in fur.

"What sort of bear?"

"Polar," said Madame.

Mark turned to Miss Jay.

"All the songs will have to be set very low to be sung in a growl."

Miss Jay had a horrifying vision of what Mark, as a bear, might do to her nursery rhymes. She spoke slowly and rather severely, so that there might be no mistake this time.

"The nursery rhymes come first, and for those you wear the Kate Greenaway suit that you saw in the box.

You will sing the nursery rhymes just the same as you did when you were a bird, but you will be dressed as a boy."

Madame took up the conversation.

"You know all about the ballet in the second half. We want a Polar bear in that. If you sing the nursery rhymes well you shall be that bear, but one of the other children will understudy you, and if you don't sing well then you won't be the bear."

Mark took most of the day to get his ideas sorted out, but after tea there was a rehearsal of the winter ballet, and he was given two or three steps to learn, including some pas de chats, which, in his opinion, were just right for the movements of a bear. Coming home on the Underground he was in the wildest spirits and told Sorrel and Holly all about it.

"He's not one of those slow, heavy bears. He's a very gay, light-footed bear. The best dancer in the Antarctic."

Sorrel spoke cautiously.

"What's happening about the clothes for the nursery rhymes?"

"Oh, that! I wear the most awful suit, all frills and blue satin, but the boy who's wearing it doesn't feel a fool in it because he knows he's under a spell, and when the witch that made the spell is dead, he'll be a bear again."

"I see," said Sorrel. "Well, for goodness' sake don't let the witch break the spell in the middle of the songs."

Mark was clear about that, too.

"She won't. If she breaks the spell one minute too soon, then that boy will never be a bear again, never, never, never."

Holly was looking forward to the matinée. She was small and pretty and what the staff called "dressable." All the clothes came out of the wardrobe, of course, there was nothing new; but she was given three little parts, and for each she had something pretty to wear. She was the buttercup in Miss Mary's garden. She had a crinoline and bonnet in a singing number, and a flame-coloured tunic in a little dance.

Sorrel was the only one of the family to stay in the background. She still had nothing to do but dance as a black lamb. She tried to pretend she did not mind. She told herself she never had wanted to be an actress anyway, so what did she care; but actually she did mind very much indeed. She had been getting on well in her acting classes, both Madame Moulin and Miss Jay said so, and as soon as she had heard of the matinée she had a secret hope that she would be given a little part in a sketch, not a big or showy part, just something quite small. There were some small parts going. It had been a blow and made her feel discouraged when the parts were handed out and she had nothing. To make things worse, because she had so little to do she was made to take Miranda's parts while Miranda was at her play rehearsals. Miranda, of course, got to hear about this.

"You'll have to stand-in for me again today, Sorrel. They need me at the theatre."

Sorrel tried not to be rude, but it was difficult.

"I'm not standing-in. If it's anything, it's understudying."

"Call it what you like. You ought to be pleased, it's admirable experience for you."

When a notice was put on the board to say there would be a dress rehearsal at the Princess Theatre on the morning of the day before the matinée, Sorrel was delighted.

"They can't get that awful old matinée over quick enough for me," she confided to a fellow lamb. "I'm so bored with it, it makes my mouth yawn every time it's mentioned."

A SWOLLEN HEAD

Alice took the children to their dress rehearsal. Hannah did not exactly refuse to go but she said, looking very stubborn, "she couldn't seem to fancy it." Alice was glad of the opportunity to get inside any theatre.

"We've gone to our rehearsal," she said, "and we can manage by ourselves for one morning, and I know my way about behind the scenes, and there's nothing like understanding how things ought to be done, so you can trust old Alice to see the children through."

Sorrel found, as she had when she went to the performance for the seamen, that she felt wormy inside; at least, that was how she described her feelings to herself. When she woke up she felt as if a big worm was turning round and round in her middle. It was not, of course, anything to do with her. She was not really worried about being a lamb; she had danced all right at the seamen's hospital and there had been plenty of rehearsals since. It was a mixture of things. Worrying whether Mark would sing all right, wondering if all Holly's dresses were there, if the girls would turn up in time, and how it would feel to be on a real stage in a real theatre.

The dress rehearsal was supposed to start at half-past ten; but, like most dress rehearsals, it did not start punctually. The stage was hung with curtains of a pale-grey shade, coloured lighting was to be used to give different effects to different scenes. Miss Jay and Winifred had written out what lighting they wanted for the different items; but that did not seem to satisfy the electrician, and for quite a while there was a great deal of "Put in your ambers, Bill," "Might try a frost on that," "Would you like it all frost, miss? You get a colder look that way." Miranda, in her black overall, and the children who were taking part in the small ballet which followed the prologue, stood on the edge of the stage watching and whispering and trying to keep quiet, but not succeeding very well because they were all rather excited and it is difficult to behave quietly when you feel like that. Miranda was very quiet, but that was because she was very annoyed. She considered herself a star now, and was furious at being kept waiting.

"It's disgraceful, keeping me hanging about like this. If I had known I'd have come much later. My management didn't let me off my rehearsal for this sort of thing."

The other children got bored with Miranda for making such a fuss. One of them said so.

"Why don't you go and tell Miss Jay about it? Tell her that, with a person as important as you in the cast, we've simply got to begin."

The girl was, of course, trying to be funny. To everybody's surprise, Miranda took her quite seriously. She tossed her head and said, "I think I will," and marched down to Miss Jay, standing by the footlights. The other girls, their eyes round with horror, watched her, holding their breaths for the explosion which was bound to follow. Miranda spoke to Miss Jay quite quietly. Miss Jay, busy talking to the electrician, did not hear what she said.

"Thank you very much," she called to the electrician. "That's exactly the effect I want." She turned to Miranda. "What is it, dear? You can see I'm busy." Miranda lost her temper.

136

"I was asking if we could begin. It's really ludicrous to bring me here at this hour of the morning to hang about."

Miss Jay, a very steely glint in her eye, was turning to answer when a voice came from the dress circle. Nobody had seen Madame arrive, for she had come in quietly and sat down, and there was very little light in the theatre. The group of dancers, quite cold with fright for Miranda, hurriedly curtseyed and said "Madame," but Madame was not attending to them.

"Miranda, would you please repeat clearly the words you have just used to Miss Jay."

Miranda had the grace to look a little frightened. She dropped a beautiful curtsey and said "Madame" before she answered.

"I was just asking if we couldn't begin."

"And why, pray, did you take it upon yourself to dictate to Miss Jay when the curtain should go up?"

"Well, I've got a morning off from my rehearsal to come here and it seems a most awful waste of time. I mean, it isn't as though it was a real performance or anything like that. I mean . . ."

"I see quite clearly what you mean; but I see no point in your argument. I have here a letter from your management saying that you may have the morning off and that they would not have needed you this morning in any case, as they are not taking your scenes. I'm most distressed, Miranda, that a pupil of mine should behave as you've just behaved. Because you have been engaged for a part in a production, that is no reason for you to behave in a spoilt and vulgar manner."

Miranda felt the girls behind her were enjoying the row, and that the electricians were looking on, and that Miss Jay was delighted that Madame was telling her off, and she lost her head.

137

"I do think it's inconsiderate. It's an important part and, naturally, I'm nervous. I think it was a bit too much to expect me to do this matinée as well."

There was an awful pause. Then Madame's voice, at its coldest, rang across the theatre:

"Miss Jay, Sorrel Forbes knows Miranda's lines, I think."

Miss Jay was in a quandary. Sorrel did know the lines, but she had only just rattled them through; and in any case, she could hardly hope that Sorrel could be as good as Miranda, but she knew Madame. It was no good saying things like that. Madame would far rather have a part less well played than have one of her pupils get away with bad behaviour such as Miranda had just shown, so she nodded.

"Yes, she knows the lines. There was no thought of her playing, as you know, so I've not rehearsed her in them."

"Then please send someone to tell Sorrel that she will be taking over Miranda's parts and, as soon as she's changed and you're ready, the rehearsal can begin."

Miranda was like a pricked balloon. All the arrogance had blown out of her.

"But Madame, I didn't mean it, truthfully I didn't. I'm awfully sorry. I want to take my parts in the matinée."

"You should have thought of that before," Madame retorted. "If you will change, I will see that some arrangement is made for sending you home."

Sorrel was talking to Alice in the passage outside the dressing-rooms.

"The call boy comes along when they're ready to start," Alice was saying, "and raps on each door and says, 'Overture and beginners, please.'"

"What does he say when they aren't beginners? I mean, when they are proper actors and actresses?"

Alice was quite shocked at such ignorance.

"It's nothing to do with how long you've been working. It means the overture is going to start and everybody who

138

is concerned in the beginning of the act goes down on the stage. When it's a proper play, like the one your grandmother is rehearsing now, he calls people by their names. He'll rap and he'll say, 'Overture and beginners, Miss Shaw, please,' and then he comes to the room where Miranda's dressing and then he'll say, 'Overture and beginners, Miss Brain, please.' When the play's been on a bit of time I'll take you round one matinée. You won't be allowed to come in our dressing-room, anybody about gets us in a fidget, but I'll see if I can get the stage manager to let you stand down in the prompt corner."

One of the children had been selected by Miss Jay to find Sorrel. She came tearing up the passage. Her words tumbled out in a jumble.

"Sorrel, there's been the most fearful row. Miranda's sauced Madame, and Madame told her off good and proper, and she isn't to take part in the matinée, and Miss Jay says you're to take all her parts, and will you go to number three dressing-room where the clothes are? If you can't find a black overall for your first entrance, it doesn't matter; you can wear your shoes and socks and your lamb's tunic."

Alice was the one who grasped all this. An understudy thrown on in a hurry was the breath of life to her. She snorted like a hunter who hears hounds.

"Come on, ducks, here's your chance. Fancy, the very first time too! The numbers of understudies I've known who have waited from one end of the run to the other for something like this to happen. Even got so far as to grease the old apples and pears, hoping for a sprained ankle or something. And here, you're going on the very first time!"

Sorrel clutched at Alice, as if Alice was the only piece of wood and she was a drowning mariner.

"Alice, I can't. I don't know it. I mean I've never acted them properly, or anything."

Alice took her firmly by the arm.

"Nonsense! Come on now, you show young Miranda she's not the only member of the family who's inherited the Warren talent." She pulled Sorrel into dressing-room number three. "Sit down, ducks, while I comb out your hair and give you a bit of make-up." She turned to the girl who had come to fetch Sorrel. "Nip along to the room we were in, number nine it is, and get Sorrel's socks and sandals."

Sorrel thought that morning the most awful she had ever lived through. Miranda, besides compèring the whole show, took part in two little sketches; and, of course, being Miranda, they were both leading parts. Miranda was bigger than Sorrel, and none of the clothes fitted properly. Because she was nervous, Sorrel stammered over some of her words. In the little sketch in which she wore a crinoline, she tripped over her frock. She felt in such a rush and tear; there was never time to be sure what she was doing with anything. Now and again, she cast anxious glances at Miss Jay and she saw that Miss Jay looked harassed, and she did not blame her. Poor Miss Jay! How sickening for her to have the show ruined like this!

At the end of the performance, Miss Jay asked to have the curtain raised. She called the children on to the stage to receive notes from Madame. Madame came down to the front of the stalls. She had a page of notes in her hand. First of all, because it was the subject she liked best, she spoke to the dancers. She had been, she said, exceedingly pleased with the winter ballet. The fairies had kept their line very well, but she would like this afternoon to take them herself, the glissades were not clean cut, and the line was untidy during the pirouettes. Then she turned to Miriam. She spoke in a warm voice, which all the Academy pupils knew meant she was pleased.

"You seemed to be having a very happy time." She nodded to Mark. "And as for Mark, you were really a most energetic and sprightly bear. A most realistic study, I thought."

When she had finished with the dancers, Madame turned to the singing numbers.

"I was pleased with the nursery rhymes, but, Holly, I thought you were a very restless buttercup. What was happening to you?"

Holly came down to the footlights.

"I thought there was a little wind blowing through the garden and it was blowing me from side to side, so that all the other flowers could see if the gold of me showed under their chins." Then she remembered that perhaps Madame was not so well informed as she was. "If you hold a buttercup under your chin, and you can see yellow, it means you like butter."

Madame laughed.

"Well, it's no good any of the flowers liking butter in wartime, so I don't think we'll have any wind blowing, Holly. I want a very grand, proud buttercup who stands still and shows off her petals."

She turned back to Mark.

"That was very nice indeed, Mark, though there was one moment when I was a little nervous whether I was going to be able to see you as a bear later on."

Mark was still in his bearskin, but he had the bear's mask under his arm. He raced down to the footlights, his words falling over each other.

"It wasn't anything to do with bears, it was a hiccup!"

"I see. Well, I suppose hiccups happen to even the best singers; but I very much hope nothing like that will happen tomorrow. It would be most disappointing if I were unable to see you as a bear a second time. Now all the dancers and singers can go. I only want those concerned with the sketches to remain."

Sorrel wriggled her way to the back of the waiting children. "Oh, gosh!" she thought. "Now it's coming. She's going to tell me I was terrible, and I know it's perfectly true."

Madame waited until the last of the dancers and singers had gone through the pass door.

"The sketches which concern Sorrel were, naturally, a little ragged. You're used to playing with Miranda, so that is only natural; but on the whole, I am very pleased with you all. When we get back to the Academy, Miss Jay will, of course, take you through them again and give Sorrel a chance to feel easy in her parts. Now where is Sorrel? Come here, my child. I'm really delighted with you. It's your first term, your clothes don't fit; they will, of course, be altered today. You have in no sense been the official understudy, so really it was a splendid effort. Now, don't feel anxious or worried. I'm sure we are all going to be very proud of you tomorrow."

Sorrel went back to her dressing-room, hardly knowing that she was walking. She had been so certain that Madame was going to say that she was going to send for Miranda after all, that she had hardly taken in what had been said to her. As she changed, she told Alice all about it.

"I'm going to do it tomorrow, all of it. The two long speeches at the beginning and the end, and the three little ones—the one explaining about the nursery rhymes and the one explaining about the winter ballet, and the one telling about the songs. I don't mind them so much; it's the sketches, particularly that awful one where I am a picture come to life. Of course, the thing I step out of

142

may look like a picture on an easel from the audience: but I feel that I'm twitching all over and that everyone knows from the beginning that I'm not a painting. Then, in the scene where I'm a schoolgirl who dreams that she's in a Victorian schoolroom, I feel all legs. I suppose it's because the others have got long skirts and pantalettes. I'm not a bit good at all that lacrosse and tennis talk. I don't know how Miranda managed to sound as though she was; but she did, somehow. The awful part is, I'm meant to be funny. Of course, I know there was only Madame in the theatre this morning; so, of course, nobody could laugh. But won't it be awful if nobody laughs tomorrow! The seamen laughed and laughed when Miranda did the part."

Alice plaited Sorrel's hair.

"Now don't go working yourself up into a state. All you have to do is to go on and do your best, and nobody can't ask for more. If I hadn't had young Holly to keep a hold on, I'd have nipped round in front to have a look at you; but I'll manage to have a squint tomorrow."

The next afternoon Sorrel stood beside Miss Jay. They peered at the audience through a little hole in the curtain. It was a special performance for Forces on leave, and the house was full of battledress and the khaki of the girls' coats and skirts and the navy blue of the sailors and of the W.R.N.S. and the light blue of the Air Force and the W.A.A.F. Because everybody was on leave, and, therefore, in good spirits, there was an absolute roar of conversation and laughter, and the theatre was grey with cigarette smoke. Sorrel looked up at Miss Jay.

"They don't look as if they needed amusing very much, which is a good thing, isn't it?"

Miss Jay laughed.

"We shall soon know if we don't amuse them; they won't mean to, but they'll shuffle their feet and cough.

143

Even the nicest audience can be turned very easily into a nasty one." She was holding Sorrel's hand, and she gave it a squeeze. "Not that I'm worrying about you. I'm sure you're going to be a great success."

"If only something didn't seem to be turning round and round in my front."

"Everybody's got to be nervous," said Miss Jay. "But there's some things you can do to help it; try taking very deep breaths."

Sorrel tried. But somehow the breath got stopped half way.

"I can't. It's coming out in little pants, like a dog in the summer."

"Try again," Miss Jay encouraged, "and I'll try too."

Miss Jay breathed and Sorrel breathed, and all of a sudden Sorrel found it was quite true, the deeper her breaths the less disturbed her front felt.

Winifred came over to them.

"I've got a message for you from Madame. What do you think is waiting for you at the Academy when we go back after the matinée?" She saw that Sorrel was not going to guess and was bursting to tell her the news. "It's a letter from Pauline Fossil, and there's one for Holly from Posy."

Miss Jay looked at Winifred.

"This theatre must bring Pauline back to you."

Winifred nodded.

"I can see us as if it were yesterday, sitting side by side at the audition, me looking a perfect fright in brown, and Pauline looking simply lovely in black chiffon velvet. I knew it was hopeless for me from the beginning and that she'd get the part of Alice.

"Curious," said Miss Jay, "how history repeats itself. That little scene yesterday morning must have reminded you of when Pauline put on airs and graces, and you were sent on to play for her, do you remember?"

"Of course. Will I forget? But Pauline was never a bit like . . ."

Miss Jay laid a hand on Winifred's arm and stopped her.

"Well, it must be about time we were ringing up. Come along, Sorrel dear."

Sorrel followed Miss Jay back to the prompt corner. She knew they were not going to ring up, but that Winifred had been going to say that Pauline was never a bit like Miranda. Obviously she could not have been, because everybody in the Academy had been fond of her. Though everybody in the Academy admired Miranda's work, nobody was really fond of her. It seemed so queer to think that Winifred had been a pupil of Miss Jay's. Somehow, when a person was grown up and teaching you, you thought of them just as grown-ups and teachers, and forgot that there were all sorts of ages in grown-ups. Winifred had not stopped being a child very long. It was all queer, very queer. It made Sorrel feel confused. Then suddenly, the orchestra stopped playing popular songs and began Roger Quilter's "Children's Overture." It was their own music. She clutched at her front.

"Oh, goodness, that means we are going to begin, doesn't it?"

Miss Jay kissed her.

"It does. As you are down already and won't be called, I shall say to you, 'Overture and beginners, Sorrel, please.'"

The curtain was up. Sorrel had to come through the front cloth to speak the prologue. The front cloth was of a light lemon colour, and Sorrel, who was not very tall for her age, looked small against it, standing there all by herself. Then her dark hair and black tunic stood out clearly, and the effect was nice. For one or other of these reasons, or perhaps just because the Forces were on leave and in a very good temper, before she could speak at all they began to clap. Sorrel had never thought of clapping to start with. Why indeed, should there be when you had not done anything? She tried to speak through it. The audience saw her mouth moving and, whilst some of it was still clapping, the other half were saying "shush." Then from the prompt corner in just as ordinary a voice as she used in the classroom, Miss Jay said:

"Make a nice curtsey, Sorrel, and begin all over again."

It seemed queer to Sorrel to hear her voice in that great big place and the first few words left her mouth in a very wobbly condition. Then all of a sudden the audience's friendliness came to her like a hug, and she spoke directly to it as if it were an old friend. Her prologue was one of welcome, it explained what they were going to try to do to amuse, and finished by announcing the ballet that was to follow. Then she curtsied. There was a roar of applause. She slipped back through the curtain and joined Miss Jay on the side of the stage. Her first entrance was over.

The ballet was not Miss Jay's business. It was Winifred's. Winifred watched it from the wings muttering, "Look at Angela's posture! That's a queer sort of jeté. Oh, what a shocking pirouette!"

Miss Jay drew Sorrel against the wall.

"Very nice, dear."

"I'm sorry about the muddle at the beginning, but I never expected them to clap."

They were, of course, speaking in whispers. Miss Jay leant down.

"Never mind, you've learnt a very valuable lesson about speaking through applause."

Sorrel's next entrance was to announce the nursery

146

rhymes and then she had to change for her first sketch. Mark came through the pass door and strolled down to her. He looked absolutely unconcerned, and he also, though Sorrel would not have dreamt of telling him so, looked awfully nice in his Kate Greenaway suit.

"Alice has gone in front. Hannah won't sit in the dressing-room. She said when Holly's face was painted that Holly was like Jezebel, you know, the one the dogs ate."

"How do you feel?" asked Sorrel anxiously.

Mark looked surprised.

"I wasn't feeling ill."

Sorrel did not want to put it in his head that he might be nervous, but it did seem queer that anyone should be so calm.

"I meant about singing."

Mark put on a lordly expression.

"Everybody keeps fuss, fuss, fuss, except me; and I just don't see anything to fuss about."

"Except," Sorrel reminded him, "that if you don't sing well, you can't be the bear in the ballet."

"And who said I wasn't going to sing well? I just know that I am, so why should I worry?"

Mark was perfectly right. He sang quite beautifully. What was less certain, he strolled to the centre of the stage to sing in just the right way. He was so enchanted at the volume of applause that greeted his songs that, without being told, he gave the same beautiful bow that he gave when greeting Madame, and that made the audience clap louder than ever. Miss Jay, standing on the side of the stage with Winifred, looked at him with amused admiration.

"In any other child this performance would need checking; one would have to be careful that the child didn't get its head turned and didn't get hold of stagy tricks; but I take a bet with you that Mark has no conception at this moment that he's Mark. Whatever else he's been this afternoon, it's not Mark Forbes."

Nothing could be encored on the programme because there was only an hour and a half allowed for the Academy, and they had a programme lasting exactly that long; but if it had been possible to encore, then Mark's singing would have been. As he came off, Miss Jay beckoned to him.

"Well done, Mark! That was very nice indeed. Now run quietly off to your dressing-room and put on your bearskin."

Mark looked at her disapprovingly.

"We have been," he said, "receiving our subjects. We shall not be giving any further audiences today."

Miss Jay was a quick thinker.

"I see, sir. And I take it that it is your royal wish that your understudy should appear as the bear."

Her words broke the dream world in which Mark had been living; he might be royal at that particular moment, but he was not so far away in his imagination that he could not shoot back to cling on to his bearskin. He grinned at Miss Jay.

"From this minute I'm a bear, a very quiet bear, skating very softly, so softly you won't hear me go."

The other big success of the matinée was Miriam. Her dancing absolutely charmed the audience, who shouted for her when the ballet finished. Winifred watched her and there were tears in her eyes.

"What extraordinary fortune! You would think that a school that had produced Posy Fossil would not get the same luck twice."

Winifred had spoken her thoughts out loud. Sorrel thought she was speaking to her.

"But they had you, too."

"Me, Sorrel! You're only a beginner, but can't you see

that something about Miriam's work that makes it quite different from what people like myself do, quite different, in fact, from what one dancer in every million does. Of course, it's too early to be sure yet, but I think she's got that something that'll set her quite apart."

It was most disheartening how ordinary everything became the second the matinée was over. The dressing-rooms were inspected to see they were perfectly tidy for the real actors who would use them that night, and then Sorrel and Mark and Holly were walking to the Underground with Hannah and Alice. Three ordinary children whom nobody could see had been a leading lady, a big singing success and a Polar bear, or worn such elegance as a buttercup dress only a short while before. Sorrel said:

"Nobody would think, looking at us, what an exciting afternoon we've had."

Hannah had been rather proud really, but she was not going to say so.

"I should hope not. You look like three children who might be going to tea at a vicarage, and very proper, too."

"But the afternoon's not over yet, Sorrel," Alice said. "You and me are going round by the Academy to fetch some letters."

In a minute the world stopped looking grey, flat and dull, and was as gay as a chalk butterfly. Sorrel skipped with excitement.

"My letter from Pauline Fossil! Isn't it super it turned up just this afternoon!"

Sorrel could not wait to get home to read her letter. She and Alice read it in the Underground.

DEAR SORREL,
    This is difficult to write because it's odd writing to somebody you've never seen. I shall find it

much easier when I've had an answer from you. I am very glad that Madame has given you my scholarship, and I hope it will be useful to you. My two sisters and I had a great deal of help from all sorts of people when we were your ages, and that's why Posy and I thought it would be most awfully nice if we could give some help back. We have felt rather out of things here, everybody in England has been working so hard, and had such a bad time with the bombing that my guardian (Garnie we call her) and I have often wished we could come back ourselves and do something strenuous, but we can't. Luckily, my sister in England, Petrova, is doing so very well that perhaps it makes up a little for what Posy and I aren't doing. It seems so idiotic just to make films when Petrova is flying planes, but even if I came home I wouldn't be able to fly a plane, I never was mechanically minded. Garnie says I am more useful doing what I do best, and entertainment is badly needed.

Madame has told me about Mark, and I have written by this mail to Petrova and told her about him, as I think she would like to give him a scholarship in the way that Posy and I have to you and Holly. I expect Mark will be hearing from her. Tell him not to mind if she doesn't say much, she's very busy, and anyway, she never was a person who expressed herself much. She lives in a cottage near where she flies, with Gum (our great-uncle Matthew). Gum used to collect fossils but he can't now and, instead, he collects babies; we were the first three. Now he runs a whole wartime nursery of them, and loves it.

When you answer this, will you tell me exactly
how Madame looks and how the school is run
now. I hear you do lessons there as well as stage
training. We never did in my day and I can't
imagine it somehow. Do you still wear black
overalls and white practice dresses for ballet? I
hope they've changed the design of rompers for
tap, we always hated those. I am sending over
some money for you to buy yourself a Christmas
present. I know you are not allowed to write to
America to ask for anything you want or I would
have tried to find out and send to you from
here, which would have been much easier, but
Posy and I think it'll be nicer for you to have the
money and buy things for yourselves. We were
always wanting things so dreadfully when we
were your ages, and we never had the money to
buy them, and I daresay you're the same.

Please give Winifred the most enormous hug
and tell her not to go and see my newest film
called "Look Up and Laugh." It's all about entertaining soldiers, and I was made to do a song
and a dance, and it so reminded me of the first
audition I ever went to, and how she said to me,
"You were out of tune in the song, and your ankle shook awfully in the arabesque." Please remember me affectionately (and respectfully) to
Miss Jay and Madame Moulin. I have written to
Madame by this post. Please write soon.

Yours affectionately,
PAULINE.

Posy's letter was in such a sprawling, difficult handwriting that Alice read it to Holly:

151

THEATRE SHOES

MY DEAR HOLLY,

I've heard from Madame that she's given you my scholarship. She says she is not sure whether you are going to dance in the way I meant, so I have written to her and said to give you a scholarship anyway, and find another dancer for me, as that is what I really want. I am not liking it here. Ballet is most unsatisfactory on the screen. It is all right during the shooting and much of the choreography is lovely, especially as in my last picture, which Manoff directed; but when you see it, it goes too fast, the space is too small, and much of the footwork gets blurred. Garnie and Pauline say it's a very good thing I have a contract because it will mean I can have some money for afterwards when Manoff starts his ballet. I am to be one of his prima ballerinas. We've planned to do some beautiful things, and he will collect many of his old company. I think it's bound to be a success; but Pauline, Garnie and Nana say they think it will be that kind of success when it will be a very good thing to have money behind you.

Have you been to see the Sadler's Wells ballet? If not, please do, and write to me all about it. If my contract was finished I would have liked to have come over and danced with them, but it would be difficult to get a passage, and Nana (our nurse who was with me in Czechoslovakia) says she won't cross the ocean again in this war and nobody will let me go alone, so it's no good my writing to Ninette de Valois, which I should like to have done just in case. Madame tells me that Margot Fonteyn's work gets more beautiful each season. She's very lucky to have the oppor-

tunities that she has and I'm very jealous of her.
I'm sick of being in pictures, it's a stupid life.
There's just one comfort, they wouldn't let me
use my name; they call me Posina, which is
pretty frightful; but it's a secret, so don't tell anybody. They thought it was better to leave Pauline
the only one with the name Fossil. I am very
glad about this because, when the war's over, I
mean the name Posy Fossil to be known by
everybody who loves dancing, and that certainly
won't happen now with the sort of pictures I
dance in. I have sent over two pounds for you to
have a Christmas present. Nana says you'd better
spend it on woollies because she always thought
the Academy cold; but, of course, you won't. I'm
only telling you because she asked me to. Please
give all my love to everybody in the Academy
that I know, and tell Madame that every day, no
matter what happens, I do her six special exercises, and I have worked out a message which
my feet say to her every day.

With love,
POSY
x x x x x

Chapter 13

CHRISTMAS DAY

Christmas Day in every family is built up on little bits of custom. Something happens one year and it is amusing and gay and Christmassy, and so it becomes part of all future Christmases. Christmas Day in Guernsey had been full of things like that. The children's father had come into their nursery for the opening of their stockings and there were always band instruments in each stocking, and when the stocking opening was finished they played "Good King Wenceslas" with their father singing the solo part of the King and Mark singing the page, and a lot of repeat verses for the band only. There had been visits to friends after morning church and a lovely party with a Christmas tree in somebody else's house in the afternoon.

When the children came to live with Grandfather, Hannah did the best she could with Christmas. She managed the band instruments in the stockings and she tried to sing "Good King Wenceslas." This was lucky, because that first Christmas of the war with their father away had felt a bit queer and miserable, but Hannah singing the King's part in "Good King Wenceslas" was so funny that they all laughed until they felt sick. As Hannah could not sing "Good King Wenceslas," they made her sing "The First Noel" as a solo, with the children helping in the Noel bits; and this, having happened for three Christmases, was now an established custom. There were other

154

things that had happened in the vicarage on Christmas Day that had become customs. There was a party in the afternoon in the house of a big family where there was a Christmas tree, and charades were played, and Christmas Day had finished with a special supper of scrambled eggs made by themselves, eaten in the kitchen with Hannah.

This year Christmas was obviously going to be quite different from anything the children had known before. They were keeping, of course, a few of their own customs, but mostly they were going to be part of Grandmother's. Christmas Day was the day when she received her family. She had them all to dinner in the evening. It made the day exciting in a way to be going to meet Aunt Lindsey and Uncle Mose and Uncle Francis and Aunt Marguerite, and to be going to see Miranda and Miriam away from the Academy.

"Proper set-up it is," said Alice. "I'm worn to a shred by the time I've laid the Cain and Abel, and when it comes to dishing up I never know how to drag my plates of meat up the apples and pears. This year it won't half be a set-up. We're receiving in style. We've got a part. We're on top of the world. We shan't half see that we're number one at our own party."

Because of the Fossil scholarships, Sorrel and Holly had a shilling pocket-money every week. This, divided into three, made eightpence each. They spent some of their eightpences on their month's sweet ration, and they each gave a penny a week to the Red Cross; and there was, of course, a penny for the collection on Sundays, but what was over they had saved for Christmas presents. They could not buy much because there was nothing much that was cheap to buy; but they managed parcels all round. Sorrel had bought a party hair bow on a slide for Holly, and some pencils for Mark. For Alice there was a calendar with a picture of people about a hundred years

ago drinking round an inn on a very snowy day; for
Hannah there was also a calendar, but hers had a little
wreath of holly and a verse that might have been part of
a carol. Mark gave Sorrel and Holly some drawing-pins,
which seemed a funny present, but was one of the few
things he could afford to buy that was useful. For Hannah there was a little wooden ruler, and for Alice some
tin-tacks. Holly had never been able to grasp how coupons worked. Up till almost Christmas Day she hoped to
buy soap for everybody, because she liked the smell.
When at last she realised that it made no difference what
shop you went into they would all want soap coupons, it
was Christmas Eve and the shops were nearly empty, so
in desperation she bought buns, not even nice buns, but
the sort you would expect to get when you queue up for
them on Christmas Eve. For Grandmother the children
had put their money together. They bought a white
heath in a little pot. It was really a tiny plant and it cost a
fearful lot, but it was the best they could manage; so that
was that.

Christmas Day started in a proper way. There were the
stockings and there was Hannah.

"Happy Christmas, dear," she said to Sorrel. "Don't
you touch your stocking now, I'm just popping along to
fetch Mark and Holly."

Holly sat in bed beside Sorrel, and Mark sat at the
other end, and Hannah sat on the side of the bed. Of
course, the stockings had not got in them the good things
they used to have because things like that were not in the
shops anymore. But the fun of Christmas and stockings
and presents is obviously not in what the presents are
made of, for though the trumpets were cardboard instead of tin, and the drum was only paper and the triangle was very small, and the mouth organ only had four

notes, it was all the funnier trying to be an orchestra with them.

Alice came as audience.

"Happy Christmas, everybody. I thought I better hear old Hannah sing her carol. I was afraid if I wasn't here to shout to the neighbours, we might have the police in."

It was a very nice carol singing, and when Hannah got to the bit:

"They looked up and saw a star
Shining in the East beyond them far.
And to the earth it gave great light,
And so it continued by day and by night,"

it was as much Christmas Day as ever it had been. Alice wiped her eyes.

"Christmas carols always make me cry, and that's a fact." She laid four little parcels on the bed. "You pay your money and you take your choice."

How Alice had managed to save the sugar and get the treacle off the points, nobody knew and nobody asked; but there were four packets of toffee, homemade, brown and stiff. There were no sweets in the stockings this year and Christmas Day cannot be said properly to have begun without that sickish feeling that comes from eating sweets before breakfast; so the hat was, as it were, put on the day when they all had a piece of Alice's toffee in their mouths.

Hannah's church was very nicely decorated. There was not much holly, but the decorators had done very well with evergreens and red berries from other plants wired on to look like holly berries. In an alcove there was a beautiful crib, with stars shining through the back of the stable and the Virgin Mary sitting by the manger with the

157

Baby on her knee, and two sheep and a donkey and four cows kneeling in the straw, looking reverent. The hymns met with everybody's approval. They began with "Hark, the herald angels," and they sang "While shepherds watched" during the collection, and "God rest you merry, gentlemen," as they went out.

"Just what we might have had at home," said Hannah. "I can't praise higher."

In the afternoon it was not a bad day, so the children went over to the Square garden; and there, on the grass, were two boys and a girl kicking about a football. Evidently, what the head gardener had said was true. Now that the chance of bombing was less, the children were beginning to come back. Holly and the smaller boy, whose name was Robert, went off to ride on his tricycle that he had been given that morning, and Sorrel and Mark played football with the other two children. They got very hot and the time passed extraordinarily quickly, and they were amazed when the nurse belonging to the other children came along and said it was nearly time for tea.

Sorrel did wish she had got something nice to wear. She had her school velvet, but it had been outgrown before Grandfather died, and she had been meant to have another as soon as the coupons would run to it. Although she did not seem to have grown very much, the frock seemed to fit her a great deal worse since she last wore it. She seemed to have got broader. It was difficult to get it to fasten at the back, and when it was fastened it made her feel short of breath. It had luckily got short sleeves, but they seemed disobliging and cut into her arms. It was not so terribly wrong in length; she had thin legs and a short frock did not matter. As well as fitting badly, it was shabby looking. It had thin places where there hardly seemed to be velvet any more, but only the stuff that velvet is made on, and it had lost its colour in places. It was meant to be green, but Sorrel noticed as she put it on that in quite a lot of spots it was much nearer grey. "If only this wasn't the first time that the uncles and aunts are seeing me!" Sorrel thought. "They're bound to expect rather a lot from Mother's child, and really, I do look pretty drab. I do hope Holly and Mark will make a better impression. It wouldn't be so bad if only I could put my bad clothes down to the war; but Miranda and Miriam live in the war too, and I bet they look quite nice."

Mark was looking ordinary except that he was unusually well brushed and clean. He wore his grey shorts, a white shirt and his school tie. Alice had said that she thought he should wear white socks and that Grandmother would expect it. Luckily, Mark had not heard this suggestion and Hannah treated it with scorn.

"I know what's right for Mr. Bill's children, and that's how things are going to be."

Holly looked rather nice. She was at the right age for party clothes, and with her curls she was the party-frock sort. She had, of course, got all the clothes Sorrel used to have and had now outgrown. She was wearing a white crêpe de Chine frock, and the little cherry-coloured bow that was Sorrel's present in her hair. Hannah would not have said so for the world, but she was very proud of Holly when she had finished with her. Sorrel hoped when she came along for Alice to inspect her that perhaps she did not look as bad as she thought she did, but what Alice said was:

"Well, there's a war on and you're at least covered, and I suppose we mustn't expect more."

Which, the more you thought about it, the less encouraging it was.

To save heating and trouble, dinner was being served in one end of Grandmother's drawing-room. The children thought when they were dressed they would go down, but Alice had given her instructions.

"Nobody takes a step till I fetches them. We are more fussy about Christmas Day than anybody would believe. All kinds of goings on we have. You'll see."

When the children were called down, Alice did not do what she usually did and announce them, but she led them into the drawing-room, which they found entirely empty. By the fire was an armchair with Grandmother's green cushion in it. The sliding doors were closed. Alice, who was rushed because of cooking the dinner, gave Sorrel her instructions.

"You stand round your Grandmother's chair until your uncles and aunts arrive, and then you'll do what the rest of the family do, you can't go wrong if you keep your eyes open."

They longed to ask "wrong about what?" but Alice had dashed out shouting to Hannah to come and lend her a hand.

Sorrel looked at Mark and Mark looked at Holly; and all of a sudden it seemed so silly standing solemnly in a row round an empty armchair that they began to giggle. Mark giggled so much that he had to lie down on the floor. Then they heard the front door bell. Sorrel pulled him to his feet.

"Oh, goodness! There's the uncles and aunts! Do get up, it's most terribly important that we shouldn't be a disgrace. We don't want them to despise the Forbes."

A perfectly strange man dressed as a butler threw open the drawing-room door and roared out, "Mr. Moses Cohen, Mrs. Cohen, Miss Cohen."

The first person to come in was Miriam. She stood just inside the door, and in a very affected way that was not a bit like her, said:

"This is my daddy, and this is my mummy." As the

children knew quite well that she called her parents Mum and Dad, and as Miriam was never affected, they stared at her in amazement. Miriam saw their faces and added, in a hoarse whisper, "We always work up everybody's entrance on Christmas Day."

Aunt Lindsey came in. She was dark and rather severe looking, and very smart. She stood in the doorway with both hands outstretched, and said in an acting sort of voice:

"Little Addie's children!"

She then stood to one side. There was a moment's pause and there was Uncle Mose with a tiny cardboard hat on the side of his head, rubbing his hands in front of him.

"Vell! Vell! Vell!"

Evidently saying "Vell! Vell! Vell!" like that was something for which he was famous, because as soon as he had finished saying it, Aunt Lindsey and Miriam laughed.

Once the laugh was over and the Cohen family safely in the room, everybody began to behave in an ordinary way. Miriam raced across and hugged her three cousins and said "Happy Christmas," and told them what she had been given for presents. Aunt Lindsey kissed them and was very nice, and Uncle Mose told them to feel in his pockets, and out came three envelopes marked Sorrel, Mark and Holly, and in each one was a ten-shilling note! He kissed Sorrel and Holly and rubbed Mark's hair the wrong way, and told them what he would like them to do would be to buy a book each, but that the money was their own and they could spend it how they liked. They took a great fancy to Uncle Mose.

The Cohens had no sooner got safely into the drawing-room than the Brains arrived. The strange man dressed as a butler said, "Sir Francis and Lady Brain. Miss Mi-

161

randa Brain." This time Miranda came in first. She stood
in the doorway, and said in her lovely voice:

"A merry Christmas, everybody." Then she turned and
held out both hands, and added in a surprised voice, as if
she had not known she was there, "Mummy!"

Aunt Marguerite was shorter than Aunt Lindsey, and
thinner. She had an anxious, strained expression. She put
one arm round Miranda.

"A happy Christmas." And then, holding out her free
hand into the passage, "Look who's here! Come to say
merry Christmas to everybody."

Uncle Francis was a large man with a big, booming
deep voice, which sounded as though he kept it mellow
by giving it caramels. He looked round the drawing-room
as if he were surprised to find himself there. He stood
between Aunt Marguerite and Miranda, an arm round
each.

"My dear wife, my little daughter, this is an occasion."
And then, with a big smile round the room, "A merry
Christmas to you all from the Brain family."

The moment this introduction was over, Aunt Marguerite ran across the drawing-room to hug Aunt Lindsey, but her eyes were on the children.

"Oh, isn't this fun! I have so wanted to meet you, but
we've been touring." She kissed each of the children in
turn. "I didn't know what to bring you, dears; it's so hard
these days to find anything nice." She turned to Miranda.
"Run and get the parcels out of the hall."

Miranda and Miriam were both looking as well dressed
as Sorrel was afraid they would. Miranda had on a party
dress of green taffeta, and Miriam was in white with an
orange ribbon round the waist. Sorrel felt at her worst, as
if she were sticking out in all the wrong places.

Miranda, who had gone into the passage to fetch the
parcels, came back with her arms full. Aunt Marguerite

162

selected three of the parcels and handed them to the children.

"Don't undo them until Grandmother comes. We keep the presents until then."

Grandmother's arrival was announced. The butler threw open the drawing-room door:

"Miss Margaret Shaw."

Grandmother stood in the open doorway. She was wearing a dress of black trailing chiffon, and fox furs, and her hair was held up on the top of her head with a diamond comb. There was not very much light in the hall and as she stood there she did not look like an old lady, but like somebody out of a fairy story. She stretched out both arms.

"My children! Now this is really Christmas."

The children that she referred to were, of course, Aunt Lindsey and Aunt Marguerite, and they hurried forward and kissed their mother.

"Darling Mother."

"Mother dearest."

Then Uncle Francis came across the room and kissed Grandmother's hand.

"Wonderful, wonderful woman!"

Uncle Mose followed Uncle Francis. He kissed Grandmother's hand, too. All this time Sorrel, Mark and Holly had been waiting to do something, and now they had their cue. Miranda and Miriam danced across the room.

"Granny, Granny!"

Uncle Mose gave a wink and a jerk of his head to Sorrel. She caught hold of Mark and Holly and they hurried forward. After kissing Grandmother, the right thing to do seemed to be to lead her to her chair. She sat down, shook out her skirts, rested her back comfortably against her cushion and twinkled up at Aunt Lindsey.

"Well, what is it this year?"

163

Aunt Lindsey looked positively nervous as she produced her parcel.

"I do hope it's something you'll like, darling; but you know how difficult things are."

Aunt Lindsey, being obviously so nervous, seemed to affect everybody else, and they all leaned forward while Grandmother opened the box. Inside was a beautiful handbag.

Of course, Sorrel thought, one shouldn't criticise one's grandmother, but she did seem to take presents in a funny way. She turned the bag upside down, she smelt the leather, and she looked at the lining; and it was this that took most of her attention, for when she had examined it carefully she said to Aunt Lindsey in a shocked way:

"Artificial."

"I know, dear," Aunt Lindsey agreed, "but there is so little real silk about these days."

Uncle Mose gave Grandmother an affectionate tap on the shoulder.

"You've fooled her as usual, Mother. I know you're not looking at the lining; you're hoping to find the price ticket."

Grandmother twinkled up at him.

"Quite right. I love knowing what things cost."

Aunt Marguerite laid her present on Grandmother's knee. This time it was a thin parcel. Inside was an umbrella.

"I know, dear," Aunt Marguerite said, "that you never have used an umbrella, and that you never walk anywhere; but now that you're going into this show, I do think you ought to be prepared in case you have to, there are so very few taxis."

Grandmother turned over the umbrella as if it were some curiosity from a foreign country.

164

"Interesting. I remember I carried one just like this in the first act of 'Aunt Celia.' You remember, that was the play when I had to try and look dowdy."

Uncle Francis cleared his throat.

"Good umbrellas are scarce today, Mother."

Grandmother answered him in a very good imitation of his own voice.

"Then it was very kind of the Brains to give it to me." All of a sudden, her manner changed and she swung round in her chair and looked at the children. "Now, what about the children's parcels? Where are they? Bring them out."

Aunt Marguerite's parcels were opened. In Sorrel's and Holly's were very pretty strings of beads, and in Mark's a penknife. As well, there was a parcel each from Aunt Lindsey. A book by Ransome for Sorrel, a torch for Mark and a game for Holly. They took a very good view of their aunts' ideas of presents.

The children had made Grandmother's heath look better by putting round the pot a bow that Alice had found. They had given it to Alice to put on the table. Now Sorrel began rather to wish they had not. Evidently this was the right time to give presents, and anyway it looked pretty shabby of them not to have got presents for at any rate Miranda and Miriam; but even with the presents they had given they were cleaned out.

They need not have worried; their present was a great success. Grandmother said she should put it on her dressing-table at the theatre to bring her luck.

Dinner was tremendous fun. Grandmother and Uncle Mose were both terribly funny and always funny about things to do with the children. First, it was about Miranda, and then Sorrel perhaps, and then Mark. It seemed to be that kind of party when nobody minds how excited you get or how noisy you are. There was turkey

165

to eat. Uncle Mose had managed to get it from a friend and he told a long, silly story about how he had led it on a gold ribbon right up from the city. Of course, they all knew it was not true, but they enjoyed it just the same. There was plum pudding of a sort to follow and some mince pies. The children all chose the plum pudding because, as Alice laid it down, she said:

"There's a thimble, a china baby, a horseshoe and a sixpence in there, and I want everything except the sixpence back for next year, so mind you don't swallow them."

The thimble and the china baby were found by Holly, the horseshoe by Miranda, and Uncle Mose got the sixpence. Uncle Francis had brought with him a bottle of port wine, which he said he had got from his club, and when dinner was over, everybody, including the children, were given some to drink. It was for toasts. There seemed to be a custom about this. First of all, Grandmother's health was drunk, and Uncle Francis made a speech about it. Then Aunt Lindsey fetched an enormous photograph of Uncle Henry and put it down by Grandmother's side, and Grandmother made a speech about "my eldest boy," and everybody drank to Uncle Henry. Then Grandmother made a speech about the Cohens and another about the Brains. The children, who had not had very much port to begin with, began to wonder how many more healths were going to be drunk, because even though they took only teeny little sips they had not much left, when Grandmother suddenly held up her hand for silence.

"There's someone we specially want to drink to tonight. These children's father. May he be home with them by next Christmas."

It was quite awful; but somehow, thinking of its being Christmas and even imagining him home by next Christmas was so absolutely gorgeous, it made Sorrel want to cry. She looked at Mark and saw he was going to cry too, and then she looked at Holly and saw that she was, too. Fortunately, Sorrel was not the only one who knew what was going to happen. Uncle Mose was quicker than she was. Before more than two tears had flopped down Sorrel's cheeks and Mark had only got to the making-faces stage and Holly was just puckering up, he had got off his chair and was walking round the table on his hands.

None of the children had ever seen a person do that before, and they were so interested watching him that the crying moment passed, and they were back feeling Christmassy again.

After dinner they played charades, and the man dressed as a butler, Alice and Hannah came in as audience.

The charades started like ordinary party charades, only of rather a grand kind. Uncle Mose, Grandmother, Miranda, Holly and Aunt Lindsey made a side. They acted "manifold" but the word did not seem to have much to do with it. It was just thinking of amusing things to give everybody, especially the children, to do. The second charade was acted by the rest of the family. This was more serious because Uncle Francis seemed only to play serious parts, and so that charade was not very funny. It was when they were playing the third charade that Grandmother and Uncle Mose got together.

"You must do Jaques in 'As You Like It,' Uncle Mose urged, "only, instead of the apple, I've got a prop for you."

The children had never seen Uncle Francis act. So it was not half as funny to them as it seemed to be to the others.

Grandmother, with an overcoat on to show she was being a man, stood with an enormous carving knife in one hand and peeled a pumpkin. And while the skin fell on the floor she rolled out very slowly the Seven Ages of Man speech. There were immense pauses when she looked up and did things with her eyes, and this simply convulsed Aunt Lindsey, Uncle Mose and Alice. Alice laughed so much that she had to hold her inside, and she kept murmuring to the butler:

"She'll be the death of me."

Hannah, sitting beside her, never laughed at all. Alice had told her that this was Shakespeare—and Shakespeare, according to what Hannah had heard, was not a thing to laugh at. After that, Uncle Mose, pretending to be Aunt Marguerite, and Grandmother, pretending to be Uncle Francis, did a scene from "Macbeth." Sorrel, who had learnt "Macbeth," knew that neither of them was using the real words, but making it up. Some of the things that Uncle Mose did were really funny, but otherwise the people who enjoyed themselves most were Grandmother and Uncle Mose. Uncle Francis was not amused at all.

Then the charades were over. Grandmother went back to her chair and Aunt Lindsey looked at her watch.

"I think it's time we started the carols."

They sang "The First Noel" and "Good King Wenceslas." And then Grandmother held out a hand to Mark.

"Come here, grandson. I hear from Madame Fidolia that you can sing. What carol will you sing for us?"

Mark did not want to sing at all. It was that sort of party which, as nobody was stern with anybody, had got to the point when knocking other people about, especially grown-ups, was fun. Mark felt more in the mood to stand on his head than to sing a carol, but Grandmother was holding him firmly and she obviously meant to have her way.

"If I sing one you won't say 'sing another,' will you?"

Grandmother looked round at her daughters.

"See how he bullies me; you'd never have dared to do that. Very well, Mark, just one carol and I won't ask for another."

They had learnt at the Academy, "I Saw Three Ships." It was easy to sing without a piano, and Mark liked it. He leant against Grandmother and sang it all through.

There was complete silence when he had finished. Sorrel did not wonder, for, really, Mark's singing was a very nice noise. She looked at him with pride. It was a good thing that one of them could shine in this clever family. Uncle Francis was the first to speak, and he used his most caramel voice:

"Beautiful, beautiful."

Aunt Lindsey kissed her mother.

"I think that's the right ending to a lovely evening. We've hired a car, you know, and it ought to be here any minute."

Grandmother was kissing everybody.

"Good-night, dears. Good-night, Francis. Good-night, Marguerite. God bless you all."

Chapter 14

FIRST NIGHT

Holly woke very early one morning and thought about the two pounds Posy had sent her. Holly was not exactly vain, but she liked nice things, and all through the term she had to look at Miriam, who was given the best of everything by Aunt Marguerite, but the best thing of all in Holly's opinion was her attaché case. Not having an attaché case mattered much more to Holly than it did to Sorrel or to Mark. Holly was forgetful and could easily drop a thing and not notice it, and she was not very good at tying up a parcel. Almost every day she dropped a sandal or a tap shoe, or a sock somewhere in the Academy, and though at first people had been kind and helpful about it, now everybody groaned, "Oh, Holly!" When Holly woke in the mornings she made the most splendid resolutions. "When I go up to my class today I won't drop anything. I'll come with all the right things folded neatly inside my towel like Winifred showed me, and then everybody will say, 'Well done, Holly!'" Unfortunately, these splendid resolutions never went beyond Holly's bed. She generally left something behind in the bathroom as a start to the day, and then Hannah said:

"Your head will never save your feet."

It was still dark and it was very cold; but Holly, as soon as she had thought of the attaché case, was so thrilled about it, she simply had to tell Sorrel. She got out of bed very quietly, for the iron beds that she and Hannah slept on creaked horribly if anyone moved quickly. She managed to find her dressing-gown, which was lying over the end of the bed. She could not find her slippers, so, though it was not allowed, she ran up the passage without them.

Sorrel was asleep. Miles and miles down in sleep, dreaming one of those nice dreams where you keep meeting people all together who in actual life could never meet at all. Her father was having a talk with. Madame and she pulled forward a little girl and said, "This is my best pupil," and one moment the little girl was Sorrel and the next it was her mother at the same age. And then Hannah came running in with a huge tray of ice-cream, singing, "Pease porridge, hot!" Sorrel had just taken an enormous strawberry ice-cream with real strawberries in it and whipped cream on the top, the sort of thing even in peacetime would have been something to remember, when Holly woke her. She tried very hard to be nice; but really, what with missing the ice-cream and just waking up, she did not feel nice. Holly sat on the edge of the bed.

"I simply had to come. Do you think I could buy a real leather attaché case, the grand sort like Miriam has, with the ten shillings Uncle Mose gave me, as well as Posy's two pounds?"

Sorrel thought about it. She remembered the shops they had been to and the attaché cases they had seen.

"I am awfully afraid we couldn't. Those nice ones we saw were five pounds, I think."

Holly was wriggling her toes to keep them warm.

"Could I get into bed with you? My toes are awfully cold. Well, that's what I thought, so I wondered if we could buy just one and take turns with it, you one week, me one week, and Mark one week. That would be fair to

171

Mark because he hasn't got anything except his ten shillings."

Sorrel shuddered as Holly's feet touched her.

"Oh, goodness, Holly, your feet are cold! Whatever will Hannah say!" She made room for Holly and pulled the eiderdown round her. "It's a very good idea about the attaché case, but I don't know whether having one just for one week out of every three wouldn't be worse than never having one at all. And then there's who's going to look after it? I mean, it's bound to get scratched and marked—they do—and who's going to be to blame?"

Holly looked up at the felt doll which was on her side of the bed head.

"I wouldn't mind something like that if I can't have an attaché case. Do you think you can buy them now? Or I'd like a white cat to put my pyjamas in just like yours. When we first came here and you let me have that white cat to sleep with me, the nursery was quite different. I've wanted a cat like that ever since."

Sorrel always laid the white cat on a chair for the night. She leant out of bed and pulled it to her by its tail. It was a nice-looking beast and she had grown fond of it.

"Do you think I'm awfully mean not to give it to you?"

Holly had no idea what she was talking about.

"Why should you give it to me? I wouldn't give it to you if it was mine."

Sorrel looked round at her blue chintz curtains and her pretty dressing-table with the silver dressing-table fittings, at her white furniture, and her carpet with pink flowers, her bedside lamp and the green frog, the picture of the cornfield and her books.

"It doesn't seem quite fair, it never has since we've been here, that I should have everything and you and Mark nothing."

Holly, without knowing it, had been harbouring a

172

grievance; and now you could feel it was a grievance, from the way she spoke.

"I don't see how you can say Mark hasn't anything when you've given him your fourteen bears."

Sorrel wrestled with herself. It was not for herself that she wanted the things in her room, though she did want them, but it was because of the way they somehow made a picture of her mother. In the months they had been in the house she had felt that she knew her mother better every day, and not only as the girl she had been when she had this room, but as she had been when she had been her mother. She had felt that her mother had told her on the night before the matinée not to be a fool; that, of course, she could do it. She had thought that her mother had told her to worry and fuss less about the ordinary things that went on every day. If she had a bad day at the Academy and got into trouble, or was rude and cross to Hannah, or snapped at Mark or Holly, she had begun to feel that when she got into her bedroom and shut the door, somebody laughed and said, "Who's got a black dog on her shoulder?" And then she felt quite different, and stopped wanting to be angry. Because of all these things that she would not tell anybody, she dreaded seeing anything leave the bedroom. These things were her mother's; these things her mother chose, and if anything left she might stop being so real a person. On the other hand, it did seem pretty sickening for Holly. The one thing she really wanted was an attaché case, and she could not have that, and her next choice was to have things like there were in her mother's room. It really was frightfully unfair if you looked at it that way, that she should have everything and Holly nothing. She gave the cat an affectionate stroke.

"You needn't buy a cat, you can have this one."

173

Holly gazed at her speechless for a moment, and then she flung her arms round Sorrel's neck.

"Darling Sorrel! I think this is the most beautiful thing that has happened to me ever." She examined the cat with her head on one side. "What shall I call him?" Sorrel did not answer. So Holly answered herself. "When he's got one's pyjamas in him he's fat, and when they're out he's thin. He really wants a sort of in-and-out name. I know, I shall call him Hannah-Alice. Hannah for the fat all-day part, and Alice for the thin all-night."

Sorrel was not really attending, but she managed to sound as though she was.

"That'll be very nice." She pleated the eiderdown. "As a matter of fact, I've got ideas about my money. I want to buy a frock. You know what mine looked like on Christmas Day."

Holly stroked Hannah-Alice.

"Pretty awful. It doesn't look as though it could possibly button; it's a surprise it does. And where it buttons it kind of pleats, and that makes your vest show, and the velvet looks as if it had been left outside all night, and it had rained; otherwise, it's all right."

"What I'm afraid of is this first night of Grandmother's. Did you notice when we were down last night seeing her, that she said something about our coming to the first night?"

Holly bounced with pleasure.

"Oh, goodness, I hope she meant it!"

"It's all very well for you, Holly, you've got all my party frocks passed down to you; and it's all right for Mark if they don't try and dress him up, and they can't because they haven't anything to dress him up in; but it's absolutely awful for me. I know what's going to happen. Grandmother will go pushing us about and saying we're

174

her grandchildren and there'll be me looking a disgrace
to any family, especially the Warrens."

"If you can't get a frock for your money, you can have
mine; and I expect Mark would give you most of his ten
shillings if we had the coupons."

"If we had the coupons I don't think I should need any
extra money. I could buy a utility frock. That dress that
Mary had for her audition was utility, and I thought it
looked awfully nice."

Holly recalled Mary standing in the hall in something
green and tailored.

"It did. Much nicer than I thought Mary ever could
look. How much was it?"

"Less than two pounds."

Holly was giving her whole attention to Sorrel's clothes.

"I don't think you wear things like that for first nights.
When Alice told me about them she said all the ladies
wore satin and velvet and diamonds and foxes, and all
the gentlemen had top-hats and black tails. What do you
think men wear tails for at a first night?"

"Not the sort of tail you mean. It's some black bits hung
down at the back of their coats. Men wore them at parties
before the war. Daddy had them, I remember quite well.
What you said about satins and velvets is what's worrying
me. I don't believe we've got many coupons left, and I
don't think Hannah will let me spend them on a real
party frock."

"Couldn't you get another velvet?" Holly suggested.
"Only one that fits."

"I thought of that, and I could if they're cheap enough;
but I think Hannah will think it ought to be in a service-
able colour—a dark red or navy blue, or something like
that. And what I think I need is a party frock; something
really party that rustles and sticks out."

175

The door opened and Hannah's face, with her nose red with cold, appeared.

"I'll rustle and stick out you, Holly. What are you doing along here without your slippers?"

Sorrel held out a hand to her.

"Hannah, darling, come and sit here a minute. Holly and I will do without my eiderdown, so it can all go over you and keep you warm. I wanted to ask you something."

Hannah sat down on the bed. It was a well-made, well-sprung bed, but sagged under Hannah. She could not really have been any heavier when she had not got her stays on; but in her red dressing-gown, with no stays, she looked twice as big as usual, but rather less like a loaf because there was nothing to tie her in.

"Well, what is it?"

Sorrel explained about her money and the first night.

"You see, Hannah, I'd have to have a new dress anyway, wouldn't I? I mean—that velvet's finished, even if it would let out, which it wouldn't."

Hannah nodded.

"Shocking it is. If we could get you something new, I'll put it on one side; or maybe cut it up for a pair of knickers or something, later on. You haven't enough coupons in your book, but you can have a few from young Holly and a few from mine; but you'll have to buy something big with room for turnings, nice, solid, dark stuff that'll last."

Sorrel leant against Hannah and looked up feelingly in her face.

"Oh, Hannah, I knew you were going to say that; but it's a party dress I want. That's what I was saying when you came in, something that would rustle and stick out. Don't you think we could possibly spare the coupons for that? After all, it wouldn't be wasted, I could wear it to church on Sundays in the summer."

"There's enough funny goings-on in this house," said Hannah, "without my taking a dressed-up monkey that ought to be on a stick along to church of a Sunday." But she did not say it with any conviction. She was obviously worried, and after a moment she added: "Something pretty in white you ought to have, with a sash; like the one's you've passed on to Holly."

"I'd have liked something a little more grown-up," Sorrel pleaded. "Just think, Hannah! Suppose it could be yellow. Crêpe de Chine or silk net over taffeta."

Hannah got up. Her voice was cross in the way it was when she had to hurt and disappoint one of the children.

"It's no good talking like that, Sorrel dear; and well you know it. What with things you've got to have, like shoes and socks and warm clothes, and you all growing, I don't know which way to turn for coupons as it is. Yellow silk indeed! You know we couldn't manage it, so what's the good of talking. Come on, Holly."

Sorrel did not give up the party frock easily. And Hannah, who was really very sorry about it, patiently went with her from one big store to another. There must have been hundreds of dresses, but not one that met even halfway between Hannah's idea of sensibleness and usefulness and Sorrel's of what she should wear at a party.

A fortnight before Grandmother's first night the children were officially told they were all going and that they were to sit in the stalls. Alice had told Sorrel that she thought they would sit in a box, and "If you do, dear," she said, "there's no one behind to see if your frock's too tight." There was no comfort like that about sitting in the stalls, and it was the very day Sorrel heard it was to be stalls that she gave up the search for the frock.

"Don't let's try any more, Hannah. I'll wear the old velvet. It's silly to spend the coupons or the money on something dark and sensible, because I don't want that kind of

177

frock for anything. I'll keep the money and buy something with it later on."

She said this so nicely that neither Hannah nor Alice grasped how despairing she was inside, though they watched her carefully to see.

"I do hate to disappoint the child," Hannah said. "But even if we had the coupons, which we haven't, what could she do with a frock made of silk and that? I wouldn't have minded if she'd wanted something white. We could have bought it far too big, taken it in and turned it up, and then when this first night was over, folded it away for her confirmation; but she wouldn't hear of white. They wore white for best at that Ferntree School, that's why Holly's got two white frocks."

Alice was having such a time with Grandmother, she had not a great deal of time to spend worrying about other people.

"I wish I could help, dear, I do, indeed; but we're very nearly demented, if you ask me. To see us get up in the morning is a proper pantomime. Acting bits of scenes as we pull on our clothes, and when I'm doing our hair the brush is snatched away and the script shoved under my nose. It's 'Hear my lines, Alice. Start at the top of page so-and-so.' Then we get a line wrong and I correct us and we say, 'Don't interrupt, don't interrupt. How can I ever learn this part, you fool of a woman, when you jabber all the time?'"

Hannah was clearing away the supper things during this conversation. She paused in the doorway with the tray.

"Ever since I've been in this house, I've wondered how you stood it, Alice; and the more I hear the more I wonder. What you want to do is to take a place in a vicarage where there's nice Christian goings-on and never anything more out of the way than a parish social."

FIRST NIGHT

The week before the first night the three children were asked to spend the day with Miriam. Uncle Mose was going on tour for E.N.S.A., and he had a week's rest; and the moment he knew his holiday was fixed, he told Aunt Lindsey to settle a day and get Sorrel, Mark and Holly along. They chose to go on Holly's birthday.

It was a lovely day with a nip of frost in the air, and the sun caught the silver of the defence balloons and turned them into gigantic pink and gold fish. Most of the things the children thought they would do in London and had been hoping were going to happen happened that day. They went to the Zoo, and they went to Madame Tussaud's. Uncle Mose said that he would have taken them to the Tower of London only you could not see it in wartime, and then he laughed and said that much though he would have liked to have shown them the Tower, in his opinion the Zoo and Madame Tussaud's were enough for one day, and it was an ill war that did nobody any good.

After tea, at which there was a cake with nine candles, they sat round the fire and roasted chestnuts. The Cohens had a lovely flat, all white paint and very shiny. The children had liked Uncle Mose from the beginning and they had always been fond of Miriam; but now they discovered how nice Aunt Lindsey could be. She had not gone with them to the Zoo in the morning because she had to cook the lunch, nor to Madame Tussaud's in the afternoon because she had to get the tea; but now that there were no more meals to see to, she settled down in an armchair and talked in a friendly way as if she had known them always. She asked a little about Guernsey and a great deal about the vicarage. She and Uncle Mose laughed and laughed when they heard about Grandfather and the Bible animals, and then she began asking about living with Grandmother. Were they comfortable? Mark was busy with the chestnuts.

"Sorrel is; she's got our mother's room."

"And you?" Aunt Lindsey asked.

Sorrel managed to kick Mark to remind him that Grandmother was Aunt Lindsey's mother. Mark looked over his shoulder and made a face at her to show that he had not forgotten.

"Quite, thank you," he said politely.

Aunt Lindsey looked down at Holly.

"Which room have you got?"

Holly wriggled up to her aunt and leant against her knees.

"I think it was your nursery. Mark's in the room next to me."

Aunt Lindsey turned to Uncle Mose.

"He must be in the little room that the kitchen-maid had. I suppose Mother's put them on that floor because that's where Addie's room was. Henry and Marguerite and I slept on the floor below."

"I daresay you did," said Mark. "Those rooms haven't any furniture in them now."

Aunt Lindsey laughed.

"You can't have lived in that house for quite a number of months, Mark, and think that; as you know, there's hardly room to turn round for all the furniture Mother's collected."

Sorrel was so afraid that Holly's face, gazing up into Aunt Lindsey's, would give her away that she pulled her arm.

"I think your chestnut's burning."

Miriam, by accident, led the conversation away from Grandmother's house.

"Do you know that Mum's written to ask whether, as Dad will be away for Grandmother's first night, you could all sit in the box with Mum and me? What are you going to wear, Holly? I've got a blue silk frock. Mum's let it out and altered it, and it looks very nice now."

"I've only got white," Holly explained. "But I've got the coral beads Aunt Marguerite gave me, and I'm wearing a coral bow."

"And what's Sorrel wearing?" Aunt Lindsey asked kindly.

There was an awful pause while Mark and Holly looked at Sorrel to see what she would say.

Uncle Mose had his eye on Sorrel. He caught hold of her arm and pulled her to him, and made her sit on the arm of his chair.

"Come on, what are they dressing you in? Something you don't like?"

The most awful thing happened to Sorrel. Because she really was so worried about the frock and the shame of wearing it, and because Uncle Mose was so nice, she suddenly found herself crying. Uncle Mose did not seem in the least upset by this. He pulled her off the arm of his chair and on to his knee, and found his pocket-handkerchief and mopped her face and said he would like to hear all about it.

Sorrel had reached the cry and hiccup stage; but somehow she managed to tell the entire story, reminding him what the velvet frock was like, and about the shopping expeditions she and Hannah had been on, and what Hannah wanted and what she wanted, and the dreadful story of the coupons.

When she had finished, Uncle Mose looked at Aunt Lindsey.

Aunt Lindsey got up.

"You come with me, Sorrel. If there was one thing I was extravagant about before the war, it was evening

181

dresses, and I'm a very good dressmaker. Let's see what we can find."

They did not find yellow, but there was a white evening dress made of stiff rustling silk, with bunches of yellow flowers embroidered all over it. Aunt Lindsey had piles of picture papers lying on the table in her bedroom. She kept turning these over until at last she came to a picture on the cover of one. It was coloured and showed a girl of about Sorrel's age in a party frock with puffed sleeves. Underneath it was written, "It may be wartime, but Miss Adolescent wants her fun!"

"There!" said Aunt Lindsey. "How would you like that frock?"

Sorrel could not believe it was true. She kept fingering the stuff.

"Do you mean honestly made of this?"

Aunt Lindsey had whipped up a yard measure from somewhere and was measuring Sorrel. She stopped measuring for a moment and held Sorrel's chin between her fingers and looked into her eyes.

"Of course I mean it, goose; it'll be fun. You'll look a darling in it, but never let me hear of you crying and worrying about anything like this again. You come straight along to us; that's what uncles and aunts are for. There's no dressing-up at first nights these days, so I shall make you the smartest person in the theatre. You'll see."

The children had heard about first nights from Alice and from Miriam. Fortunately, Miriam's theatre-going had been mostly during the war. If they had relied on Alice's story of what happened, they would have been bitterly disappointed at the real thing.

Alice, through long years of dressing Grandmother, had seen the splendid sort of first nights that there were in peacetime; when the whole road was blocked with cars driving to the front of the house; when the foyer was full of lovely clothes, and all the smart people who had come to the first night stood packed together talking to each other while the more important of them were photographed.

A first night in wartime was not a bit like that. Nobody, of course, came in a car; but a few lucky ones, including the children, came in taxis. In the days of first nights that Alice talked about, plays had begun quite late in the evening, eight or half-past; but now, because of the black-out and getting home, no play began later than half-past six. Grandmother's was to begin at six-fifteen. The children had a high tea; that is to say, they had a piece of cold spam with their ordinary tea. It was not the sort of day when any special cooking went on. Grandmother, and Alice too, if it came to that, were in such a flutter and excitement that the only thing for other people in the house to do was to keep out of the way, not to argue about anything, and to want as few things as possible. Alice had offered Hannah a seat in the upper circle, which she said she could get her. But Hannah said no, she would rather wait and go later on to a matinée, if that was convenient, she could not seem to fancy being out in the black-out. Actually, when it came to the day, the children could see she was rather sorry that she had said that. With everybody else going to a first night, it seemed a bit flat to be at home by herself. And it was clear by about tea-time that she felt this, because even when she was in the kitchen getting tea she did not sing.

"Not even one line of hymn," said Holly. "Poor Hannah! I bet she's wishing she was us."

For fear of getting messed up, the children did not change until after tea. Hannah had laid Sorrel's frock out on her bed. It looked, Sorrel thought, quite lovely against the blue eiderdown; and she stroked it a long time before she began to undress. Aunt Lindsey had made it beau-

183

tifully, and she had not only made the frock but she had
sent some yellow ribbon which matched the flowers for
Sorrel to tie on her hair. Hannah, coming in to see how
Sorrel was getting on, found her just standing there
stroking, and she had to hurry her up.

"Come along, now, I've had Holly dressed this last ten
minutes."

Sorrel looked at her with shining eyes.

"I shouldn't think there was ever a prettier dress in this
room, would you? I mean, even when my mother lived
here."

Hannah privately thought the dress rather too grand,
but not for worlds would she have told Sorrel. Sorrel had
got as far as her knickers and socks and shoes, so Hannah
lifted the frock off the bed and put it over her head. Sorrel really did look very nice. Hannah felt a swelling inside, she was so proud of her. She did not, of course, say
anything, as she thought flattery was a sin; but when Sorrel passed her her comb and asked her to plait her hair,
Hannah suddenly put the comb down.

"How about you not having plaits? Supposing you use
these bits of ribbon to tie bows on the sides." Hannah's
great belief in neatness and plainness was such a feature
of her that Sorrel gaped. Hannah was embarrassed with
herself, but she stuck to her point. "No need to stare at
me as if I had said something queer. There's a right and
a wrong about everything; and plaits, which are right and
proper at most times, wouldn't seem to me to fit in with
your aunt's frock. Give me your brush. I'll just twist these
ends round my fingers."

Mark and Holly were immensely impressed by Sorrel's
appearance. Holly said that she looked as if she came out
of a fairy story.

"It isn't a taxi that is going to take us to the theatre; it's a beautiful coach, sent by Sorrel's fairy godmother, and I'm a lady-in-waiting and Mark's a lord-in-waiting."

Mark had been staring at Sorrel in silence, for he found it very hard to believe that something odd had not happened to her. He had, of course, seen her in party frocks before, but not for a long time and never in a frock as grand as this. Now Holly's suggestion that she was a princess made everything fit into place. Sorrel was an ordinary girl who for one night had become a princess. They were going into a magic world and he was to be a lord-in-waiting. He glowed.

"Every time Sorrel wants anything, you and I, Holly, will have to run and fetch it; and I shall bow and you will curtsey."

Sorrel saw in a second what was going to happen to this evening, unless she was careful. She spoke to Mark very severely.

"I'm not going to have you make a fool of me. I'm not a princess, I'm Sorrel Forbes, going to my Grandmother's first night in a frock made out of an old evening dress of Aunt Lindsey's." She tried to think of something that would pull Mark to his senses. "And I'll tell you one thing which will show how ordinary I am: if you make even one little bow, or behave like anybody but Mark Forbes, the moment we get back here tonight I'll take away those fourteen bears I lent you. I always told you they were only a lend."

Mark felt the excitement die out of him. He was back in London. It was a dark cold night in January; they were three ordinary children going to the theatre in a taxi. It was a pity. It would have been so easy to have made this night all magic; but when Sorrel spoke like that she meant what she said and he had no intention of losing his fourteen bears.

There was only a little cloakroom at the theatre, and with the three of them and Hannah in it, there was not room for anybody else, and Sorrel could see that the attendant was as glad as they were when Hannah said, "There, you'll do. Now come outside and find your aunt."

They stood by the fireplace in the foyer. There was very dim lighting for fear of it showing in the street, and they were terribly afraid of missing Aunt Lindsey. They need not have worried, because Miriam had eyes like a cat. She was no sooner inside the door than she shrieked "There they are!" and came burrowing her way through the people and flung herself at Sorrel, who was the first of the Forbes children that she found.

Miriam could never look pretty. She had not got that sort of face, but she could and did look very smart. She had on a white ermine coat and a blue crêpe de Chine frock and white socks and silver shoes. Holly and Mark began stroking her the moment they saw her.

"White fur," said Holly. "Oh, Miriam, how lovely to be dressed all in white fur!"

Aunt Lindsey, who had forced her way to the children, stooped and kissed Holly.

"It looks all right in this dim light, Holly; but it's not so good in the daylight. She's outgrown it, the fur is getting very yellow looking; but it's got to last for the war, we've no coupons for another."

"She's exactly like I was as a Polar bear," said Mark, "only, of course, I was fur all over, including my legs."

Aunt Lindsey had her arm round Sorrel.

"Well, let's come into the box and examine each other. I can't wait to see how Sorrel looks in my frock."

Aunt Lindsey was a very thoughtful person. She had guessed that Hannah would leave the children's coats in the cloakroom and she knew how badly heated theatres were in wartime; but she knew, too, that however badly

186

heated they were, neither Sorrel nor Holly would want to wear school coats over their best frocks, so under her arm she had brought a white angora rabbit jersey of Miriam's for Holly to wear, and for Sorrel there was a white jersey of her own. Holly, of course, could not be quick enough to put on the angora rabbit; it looked simply lovely, but Sorrel thought nothing of the plain white cardigan that she was offered. Aunt Lindsey quite understood that.

"You won't wear it in the intervals, of course, darling; but you can put it on when the curtain's up, and I expect you'll be rather glad of it."

The theatre was, of course, a blaze of light, and Aunt Lindsey seemed to know dozens of people. First one waved and then another, and she was always waving back and getting Miriam to wave too.

"Look, darling, there's old Sir Richard smiling at us." "Look, darling, there's Aunt Meg and Uncle Sam." Everybody seemed to be an uncle or an aunt to Miriam.

Mark and Holly found all this waving entrancing. They leant on the edge of the box and peered at the people, and every time anyone waved they drew their aunt's attention to it.

"There's two ladies waving." "Look over there, three ladies and a man."

Sorrel felt shy. It was as if everybody in the theatre was looking at them, and she wished they would not. Her cheeks burned, and she wished the curtain would go up and the lights would go down. The audience was exactly as Miriam had said it would be, and not a bit as Alice had described it. The women were in uniform or dark overcoats, and most of them had big boots with fur linings. The men were in uniform, or exactly as they had come on from work. Nobody was dressed up. Aunt Lindsey was looking very nice in a black frock and fur coat, but only nice in the way that anybody might look in an afternoon,

187

and not a bit as if they had come to an evening theatre; but one thing that Alice had promised was there, and evidently had nothing to do with clothes. The excitement. From far up in the gallery, down to the upper circle, down through the dress circle, through the pit, up to the front row of the stalls, everybody was keyed up, just chattering to fill in the time until the moment when the curtain would rise. She turned to Aunt Lindsey.

"I wonder how they're all feeling behind."

Aunt Lindsey laughed.

"I can easily tell you that. Sick as dogs." And then she said, "S-ssh" and leant forward, and Sorrel could see she was clutching the front of the box so hard that her knuckles shone white. The lights dimmed, the orchestra's music faded away. The curtain rose.

The play was in costume. It was about people in the reign of Queen Victoria. The children had only heard of the play from Alice, Grandmother and Miranda, and from all three they had got the impression that Grandmother never came off the stage at all, and most of the time she was talking to Miranda; so it was a great surprise to them all when the curtain rose and neither Grandmother nor Miranda appeared. The play was about a family of girls and what seemed to be their unkind father, whom they called papa, and their very kind mother, whom they called mama. It seemed to be funny because the audience laughed a great deal, but most of the time the children could not see anything to laugh at. They liked the play very much indeed, but it seemed to them the people were real. It was a proper family, and nothing to laugh at. The eldest girl wanted to marry a nice man, but for some reason all the family knew that papa would never allow it.

It was about half-way through the act that Miranda appeared. She had been out with her governess, and she came in wearing a funny little hat and holding a muff, and in the play she seemed to be quite a different person from the Miranda they knew every day. She was the youngest and everybody's pet, including papa's; her name was Sylvia. Perhaps because she was the youngest, or because she was born that way, she was the family rebel. She could not believe that her sister Letty was going to be weak and stupid, and not marry the man she was fond of just to oblige papa; and, as well, she thought it was very foolish and wrong of Letty because if only she would marry him it would mean that she, Sylvia, and the rest of her sisters could be bridesmaids and wear lovely dresses. Both Sorrel and Holly sympathised with Sylvia entirely about this.

All through the act it was known that papa's mother, grandmama, was expected. It seemed that grandmama had never been to stay before, but she had brought papa up and almost every time papa opened his mouth he said something about "My dear mother," so the whole family knew what to expect, and the thought of grandmama's coming caused a cloud, especially it depressed poor Letty, who felt that with grandmama backing papa there would be no chance of persuading papa to let her marry Albert. At the end of the act the sound of horses' hoofs was heard outside, and all the family held their breath; then the door was flung open and there was grandmama. The grandmama of the play was, of course, Grandmother, and she was just as big a surprise to the family on the stage as Grandmother in real life had been to the children. She was a mass of feathers and bows and colours, and had a manner about her and a twinkle in her eye which made the family on the stage gasp and the audience clap and clap and rock with laughter. She said something that none of the children understood, but the audience found very amusing, and the curtain came down in a storm of applause.

In the interval all kinds of people came to the box. Some of them were critics and some of them were actors, but to them all Aunt Lindsey said:

"These are Addie's children."

Everybody in turn looked puzzled and as if they were searching in their memories, and then Aunt Lindsey added:

"She married a man in the Navy called Forbes."

And then each of the people nodded as if they were remembering. The children thought that most of them were thinking of the wedding that their mother ought to have been married at when, instead, she had run away with their father. Several people commented on the children's looks. Some said they had Warren noses, some said they had Warren eyes, and everyone said they had the Warren hair. Mark, in each case, stood up for the Forbes side of him.

"Our father has dark hair, too. It isn't only Warrens that are dark."

In the next act grandmama was ruling the household. There were all sorts of changes, but the biggest change of all was in papa, who had ceased to be unkind and had become almost humble, so much so that the children felt sorry for him. But not only the children felt sorry, because, oddly enough, now that papa was down, all the family except Sylvia rose up to protect him. This led to all sorts of muddles, and the worst muddle of all was that Letty did not seem to be going to marry Albert. Grandmama did not approve of him, but not for the reason that papa did not, but simply because she said he was dull. This gave Miranda her big scene, for either because she was a born meddler, or just for fun, she stirred Albert and Letty up and planned an elopement for them. It was

190

this elopement which finished the act, for just as it was taking place grandmama discovered it.

This act did not get quite so much applause as the first act, which made Aunt Lindsey worried and restless, and she said she was going out into the foyer to have a cigarette. There they met one of the critics who had come to the box in the first act. He talked about Miranda.

"Quite a part for your little niece," he said. "It's very difficult at that age to distinguish precocity from talent."

Aunt Lindsey got a cigarette out of her case.

"It was Mother's doing. Francis was against it."

The critic lit her cigarette.

"Of course, there's plenty of precedent for it. Ellen Terry was a very small child when she started, but the theatre was a different place in those days. I don't fancy that much spoiling went on."

Aunt Lindsey laughed.

"You don't know Miranda. She's a very mature young lady. I don't fancy that anything that any of you say will affect her opinion of herself; and don't think by that I mean conceit. I think she's just got it in her and she's got confidence."

He was moving off to speak to somebody else, but he changed his mind.

"You tell Marguerite from me, if she must stick the child's press cuttings into a book, not to let her know that she does it. How old is she?"

"Thirteen."

He turned to Sorrel.

"What about you? Are we going to see you soon?"

Sorrel nodded.

"Yes, if I can get a part. I'll be old enough for a licence in April."

The critic was looking at Mark.

191

"What about you? Are you going to follow in your uncle Henry's steps?"

Sorrel answered for Mark.

"No, Mark isn't going to be an actor. He's going to be a sailor. He goes to the Academy with us now, but he isn't going when he's eleven; his birthday's in September."

Ever since Holly's birthday party, Mark had felt dimly aggrieved about his birthday. It had come in the early days of term, and except for a special supper when they got home and some presents, it had not, in his opinion, been properly spent at all.

"I shall be glad to go to a different school. At the one I was at before, people paid attention to birthdays, which they don't at the Academy."

Aunt Lindsey was looking amused. She shook her head at the critic.

"I don't know what all this sailor talk's about. He's following in the usual family footsteps as far as I know."

The critic moved away, and as he went Sorrel suddenly stopped enjoying the evening and felt worried and depressed. Alice had promised that Mark should be properly educated in the autumn, but could Alice? Could anybody? What happened if your uncles and your aunts and your grandmother were all against you? How was she, all by herself, going to get things done? It was not even as though she could absolutely rely on Mark. In theory Mark wanted to be an admiral, but quite little things could change his mind. It was quite certain that if he was given a part which meant dressing up as a dragon, or something like that, he would forget all about the Navy.

Aunt Lindsey was leading the way back to the box. She drew Sorrel's hand through her arm.

"Tired, darling?"

"No. I was thinking about what you were saying about Mark."

Aunt Lindsey was not quite herself that evening. Her mind was wrapped up in the play, she so badly wanted her mother to have a success. If she had not been thinking so much about the play she would probably have probed further into what Sorrel was saying. Instead, she just squeezed her hand.

"I don't think we need worry about Mark yet, darling. He's only a little boy; plenty of time to worry when the time comes."

The last act the children thought lovely. Things began to come right just like a fairy story. The act opened where the last one had ended, and there was grandmama searching through the family unable to believe that Letty had the spunk to plan an elopement, and sure enough she presently found that Sylvia was the culprit. Sylvia came down in her dressing-gown escorted by her governess, and that was the first time papa and grandmama were completely in agreement.

"That child," said grandmama, "must be whipped."

Mark, who was hanging over the edge of the box, bounced on his seat.

"Goody, goody, goody. I bet she hates that!"

Aunt Lindsey told him to be quiet, but Mark gave Sorrel a nudge to show that, although he was going to be quiet, he still thought that being beaten was a very good idea.

The curtain was dropped for a moment in the middle of the act to show the passing of time, and presently grandmama's boxes were being carried downstairs, and grandmama, all feathers and twinkles, was going to drive away again. Then, even before the last of the horses' hoofs had clopped out of earshot, you could see papa swelling and going back to his ordinary self, and he was ordering his family about just as he had before grandmama had arrived. Of course, things were not quite the

193

same, because Letty was being married, and there was something to do with debts and money that was not going to happen, and Sylvia had been beaten. Unbelievable though it might seem, papa even forgot that his family now knew what his mother was like, for just as the curtain fell, he said:

"As my dear mama . . ."

Grandmama held Miranda's hand when they took the final curtain. All the ladies curtseyed to the ground and the men bowed and the audience clapped and clapped, and the author, who was dressed as an officer in the Air Force, came on and bowed and made a speech, and then the play was over. Aunt Lindsey took the children through the pass door across the stage to see Grand-mother. Seeing Grandmother in the theatre was very like seeing her in the drawing-room. Aunt Lindsey knocked on the door and Alice looked out and then went back into the dressing-room.

"Mrs. Cohen and the children to see you, dear."

Aunt Lindsey, when she got inside, behaved, not like herself, but like Aunt Lindsey on Christmas Day. She held one of Grandmother's hands in both of hers and said, "Wonderful, Mother! Wonderful!"

Grandmother had taken off her stage dress and was in a dressing-gown. She pretended to be seeing to the frills on it, but really you could see she was attending entirely to Aunt Lindsey.

"How do you think it went? Was I really all right? They seemed to like it, didn't they?"

"Ate it," said Alice. "I told you from the beginning it was just the sort of sentimental stuff they would eat."

Grandmother turned to the children.

"And how did you like it?"

"It was super," said Sorrel.

Miriam leant against her grandmother's chair.

"I thought it was a lovely play."

Grandmother looked at Mark.

"What about you, grandson?"

"I liked every single moment of it, but best of all I liked the bit where Miranda was whipped. But I thought it a pity that happened upstairs."

"I thought you had such lovely dresses," Holly broke in. "I would like to have a little hat and muff like Miranda wore."

Grandmother was looking severely at Mark.

"You're a bad boy." She turned to Aunt Lindsey. "Miranda's done very well. The children might go up and see her. She's on the next floor."

A lot of people came in to see Grandmother, and Alice was busy showing them in, so the children went alone to find Miranda. They would have been shy about finding their way if Miriam had not been there, but Miriam was quite used to the back of theatres. She led the way along the passage and up some grey stone steps, and pushed her way through the people who were standing in the passage, and read the names on the different doors until they came to a door marked number nine, which had a card on it, "Miss Miranda Brain." Miriam thumped on the door.

"It's us, Miranda. Can we come in?"

Aunt Marguerite and Uncle Francis were on tour, so Miranda's governess had brought her to the theatre. The children had not met her before, and she looked, they thought, rather nice. She had pretty grey hair and a smiling face. Miranda was sitting at her dressing-table taking off her make-up.

"Hullo! Did you like it?"

Miriam was prowling round examining Miranda's clothes, which were hanging on pegs on the walls.

"You were awfully good. Everybody thought so."

Miranda seemed much easier to talk to than usual. She swung round in her chair.

"I was dreadfully nervous at the beginning. Did it show? Do you like my clothes? Grandmother said she was pleased. Did she say anything about me to you? Did . . ."

Miranda's governess gently patted her shoulder.

"Come along, dear, get your make-up off. The car will be here and I want to get you home for your supper." She turned to the children. "Her father has hired a car for tonight as it's her first night, and I don't want her to be late because we've got two shows tomorrow."

Sorrel awfully wanted to have a real look at Miranda's clothes, and to read all the telegrams she had got pinned up on the wall, but she could see the governess did not really want them in the room.

"Well, we just came to tell you how good you were, Miranda, and, anyway, I think we ought to be going, we left our coats in the cloakroom when we came in." She hesitated by Miranda. It seemed rude just to walk out, and yet she was not the sort of person you kissed.

Miranda surprised them all. She jumped up and kissed each of them.

"Good-night. I'm glad you came round. Hold your thumbs for me; I am so terribly fussed what the papers will say tomorrow. It's sickening Daddy and Mummy can't be here. It's so flat just going home."

Grandmother was being taken out to supper, so Alice took the children home. It took ages to get a taxi, and when they had got into it safely, what with the excitement and one thing and another, they were all half-asleep. Alice put Holly on her knee and Mark leant on her one side, and Sorrel on the other.

"That's right," said Alice. "You make yourselves at home. That's what shoulders are for. Make very comfortable weeping willows."

Chapter 15

HOLLY

Miranda had made an immense success. The notices said such things as "the evening really belonged to little Miss Brain." "This latest shoot from the Warren tree seems to hold promise of bearing a crop of talent unusual even from a branch from this parent stem." The other type of paper, which did not write in that grand way, said such things as "Miranda romps home" and "Child star born in a night." One paper was tactless enough to say that Miranda acted everybody, including her grandmother, off the stage. The children did not see these notices themselves, but they heard Alice telling Hannah about them at meals.

"We've taken it very well; I must say that. No one can say that we grudge the child her success, but we're afraid of early success, and quite right, too. A child star born in a night, indeed! One cloud no bigger than an acorn and that star will be out. We know; we've seen it."

"But if Miranda takes her part so nicely," said Hannah, "that's not to say she couldn't do another, is it?"

Alice spoke with the weight of one who knew.

"It isn't that they mean any harm, these critics, nor the public don't either, but they rocket somebody into the sky and there they sit sparkling and twinkling with no more to keep them there than one of these tracer bullets. Then everybody's surprised when they drop. You see, the next part may be more difficult or wrong for their personality or that, and they haven't the technique to put it over, then what happens? Screams from the papers: 'Mr. or Miss So-and-so doesn't fulfil early promise.' 'I was disappointed in the performance of Miss So-and-so.' No, there's just one way for sure success and that's building up your knowledge and your reputation together, and when you do that you can't topple off, it's like having a concrete house under you."

Sorrel broke into the conversation.

"Don't you think that perhaps Miranda's different, that she just has to be good?"

Alice nodded.

"Shouldn't wonder at all; clever as a cartload of monkeys. But that won't stop her having her ups and downs like the rest; the higher she climbs the harder the bump when she falls. There isn't such a thing, from what I've seen, as an easy road to success."

Oddly enough, success did not seem to have done Miranda any harm, but neither had it done her any good. She went on being very much herself. Because of her theatre work she no longer came to the Academy for lessons, but did them at home with her governess. She came to the Academy only for special dancing. Two ballet classes a week and two tap and all in the mornings. Sorrel met her at only one of these classes. The work was really too advanced for her, but it so happened that there was no other dancing class on that particular day which could fit in with her school work, and so she attended the dancing class with her lesson form. As the work was too advanced for Sorrel, she sat down and watched a lot of it, and this brought her in contact with Miranda's governess, Miss Smith. Miss Smith had, in a long career of governessing, been used to houses in which, at suitable intervals, cousins came to stay, and it worried her that the Forbes children never came to the house, or Miriam either, if it came to that.

"You see, all the autumn your uncle and aunt were rehearsing as well as working," she apologised, "and now they're away on tour and, of course, Miranda and I live very simply. You've no idea how hard it is now term has begun to fit in her lessons as well as eight performances a week, and her dancing classes. She gets very tired, poor child."

Sorrel looked at Miss Smith's nice face and thought that it looked tired, and she was not surprised, for she could imagine that Miranda tired would make anybody who had to look after her very tired indeed.

"One day," said Sorrel, "Alice is going to take me behind for a Saturday matinée. She's going to get Grandmother to ask the stage manager if I could stand on the side of the stage. Perhaps that day I could come up and see Miranda."

Miss Smith looked pleased.

"Of course. You'll come and have tea in the dressing-room. I'll ask Alice to let me know in plenty of time that you're coming, and I'll run out in the morning and see if I can get something nice. There's a shop near us where, if you're early enough, you can get a sandwich with a kind of cream spread. Of course, it isn't cream spread really, but I think you'll like it."

Sorrel, though she knew that she would like the cream spread, felt Miss Smith had too much to do to go trotting about buying cakes for her.

"Please don't bother to get anything extra. We hardly ever do have cake, so I wouldn't miss it."

Miss Smith looked at her with fondness.

"That's nice of you." She lowered her voice. "But as a matter of fact, it will be nice for Mary. She's the understudy, such a dear little girl. She sits in our room because, as of course you know, somebody has to be with her, and I can save her poor mother. There are four other children at home and her father's in the Army, so I'm glad to help. It isn't much fun understudying, I'm afraid, and one way and another she has a hard time."

Sorrel thought about Mary. That must be a very nasty job understudying Miranda. She could just imagine how it would be. Miranda very much owning the dressing-room and expecting you to sit in the corner and be humble.

Miss Smith was looking at Sorrel's shoes.

"How worn your dancing sandals are getting."

Sorrel sighed.

"Everything about me is getting worn. I'm still wearing my school uniform because it lets down, but it's getting pretty shabby and there's something about wearing the uniform of a school that you don't any more belong to that is humiliating. The only thing I've got that's really good is that simply lovely frock Aunt Lindsey made for the first night, but I shouldn't think I'd ever put that on again, because we never go to any parties, and Hannah says it's too smart for church. I've got enough coupons for a dress if I absolutely had to have one, but, as a matter of fact, I don't absolutely have to have one, so I expect they'll go on shoes and underclothes."

Miss Smith laughed.

"What a dreary picture! But I can tell you one occasion when you'll be able to wear a frock. Your uncle and aunt are going to do 'The Tempest' for a season in London, in about May or June, and you can wear the frock for the first night then, and if the worst comes to the worst we must give a party for Miranda's fourteenth birthday. It couldn't be a very big party, of course, because of the food, but we could mark the invitations 'party frocks will be worn.'" She looked again at Sorrel's shoes. "Miranda had to have some new shoes lately; she's still wearing her old sandals and tap shoes, but I was thinking the other day she ought not, they're pinching her toes, and she's got a lot of pairs of socks that have shrunk in the wash. You're so much smaller than she is, so they will either fit you right away or you can grow into them. I'll bring the things to her class tomorrow and put them in her locker, and you can fetch them from there. We've got an old attaché case I'll put them in; it'll make it easy for you to carry them home."

The next evening Mark and Holly saw the attaché case in Sorrel's hand. They asked so many questions about it that they fell out on top of each other.

"Whose is it?"

"How did you get it?"

"Is it your very own?"

"Could I, oh, could I carry it?"

Sorrel explained the sad truth that it was Miranda's, but she was very fair about it. She agreed that each of them in turn should carry it. Holly as far as Russell Square station, Mark on the Tube, and she from Knightsbridge home, and the next morning the system would be reversed. Holly would carry it from home to Knightsbridge, and she would carry it on the Tube, and Mark from Russell Square to the Academy. Holly was so shocked at this arrangement that she stood still, as if her legs were refusing to walk anymore.

"But, Sorrel, Mark's doing the one bit that matters. He's carrying it where all the Academy can see him; couldn't, oh, couldn't I have that bit?"

As a matter of fact the moment Sorrel had divided up the carrying arrangements for the attaché case she had realised that she had given Mark the one bit that mattered, but even as she had made the arrangement she had seen his face, and it would be impossible for anyone

201

to look more pleased, so she gave Holly a little push to hurry her along.

"No, I've said that's what's going to happen, so that's what is going to happen, and it's no good arguing." Then she turned to Mark, "But at the bottom of the Academy steps you'll hand it to me, for I've got to put it back in Miranda's locker." She passed the attaché case to Holly.

"There you are. Make the best of it, you've only got it as far as Russell Square."

They walked along in silence for a bit, eyeing the case, and then Mark said what was in all their minds.

"To think there could be a person in the world with an attaché case like that that was only their second best."

For Mark, Miranda's attaché case was eclipsed the next day by a letter from Petrova.

DEAR MARK,

I've heard from Pauline about you and I have written to Madame to say that I will give you the same as Pauline gives Sorrel and Posy gives Holly. This will, of course, include a shilling pocket-money. I have also sent two pounds for your Christmas present. I would have written before, but I have been posted to a different place for a week or two, and Gum (my Great-Uncle Matthew) never can remember to forward letters.

I hope you like the Academy. I simply hated it myself, but then I had no talent.

Yours,
PETROVA.
P.S. Let me know if you want anything special—a spanner or anything like that.

Madame sent for Mark and told him she had got his

two pounds and he could have it whenever he liked, and that she would give him his shilling every week as she did Sorrel and Holly. She said that she was going to make a formal announcement about the scholarships and she had only been waiting for this letter from Petrova to do it, and would he find Holly and send her to her.

Holly was devoted to Madame. She came skipping along the corridor and only collected herself at the door of the study. However devoted you were to Madame she was not the sort of person that even the most careless child would burst in on. She pulled her black tunic straight, pulled up her socks, felt her hair ribbon to be sure it was holding back her curls properly, and tapped on the door. In answer to Madame's "Come in," she opened the door and made a really beautiful curtsey before saying "Madame."

Madame was sitting at her desk. She held out her hand. "Come here, my child." When Holly came to her she put an arm round her. Holly wanted to play with the fringe of Madame's cerise shawl, but Madame took hold of her hands and held them. "I want to talk to you about Posy's scholarship. As you've heard from Posy, she's making another scholarship especially for you. What she means by that is that she would like to pay for the training of somebody at the Academy, but that her scholarship and all her interest and her letters are to go to a dancer if I can find one. Posy was always like that. She eats and sleeps and lives dancing. I was afraid that I wouldn't find her the sort of dancer she wanted, as we haven't had one since she was here, but now I think I can say I've found a dancer, and you know who that is, don't you?"

Holly nodded. All the children in the Academy knew that.

"Miriam."

Madame held her tight.

203

"Yes, Miriam. Would you mind very much if you only just had the money? You'll get your pocket-money every week and birthday and Christmas presents, but it is only fair to tell you that when it comes to writing letters, at which Posy was always very bad, I think they'll go to Miriam."

Holly was finding it difficult to concentrate on what Madame was saying, because, leaning against her, she found how silky and rustly was the black silk of her dress, and she was imagining herself dressed like that and living, because it seemed the proper place for black silk, in a palace. But she was just sufficiently attending to catch Madame's question, and she knew what every pupil of the Academy knew, that when Madame asked a question it had to be answered. She could not, at the moment, see why Madame should suppose she would mind. It was nice to get a letter, of course, because everybody at the Academy wanted to see it and read it, but it was the presents and pocket-money that were really important. She looked up at Madame.

"No, I wouldn't mind."

Madame gave her a pleased squeeze.

"I'm very glad, Holly. You have worked very hard and I shouldn't like your feelings to be hurt, and your dancing's coming on very well indeed, but we can't pretend you're the same sort of dancer as Miriam, can we?" She gave Holly a kiss. "Run along now, back to your class."

That afternoon the school was summoned to the big hall. After they had greeted Madame the pupils were seated in the usual rows across the floor. Madame addressed them from the platform. She told them about the scholarships.

"All you children know, I think, that last term I was given scholarships from Pauline and Posy Fossil in Hollywood. I expect you children are tired of hearing about

204

the Fossil girls, but we're all so proud of them. Last term I granted the scholarships temporarily to Sorrel and Holly Forbes. Pauline's scholarship has to be given to a child with marked acting talent whose career would be helped by financial assistance. After Sorrel's performance at the matinée at the end of last term I made up my mind that she was exactly the right person for that scholarship and, therefore, she will hold the Pauline Fossil scholarship for the rest of her time here." She searched the rows of children. "Congratulations, Sorrel." Everybody clapped. Madame waited for them to finish clapping and then she went on: "Posy's scholarship was for a dancer, and I granted it to Holly because I knew that last term I had no one in my mind entirely suitable for it, and when she came to an audition here she certainly was promising. Well, since then somebody else has come along who is the sort of dancer Posy wants to help. Miriam." Everybody clapped again.

"In your case, Miriam, you will keep the scholarship just as long as you go on showing the sort of talent, together with hard work and application, that Posy meant. Now we come to a third scholarship, which is not for any particular talent, but is presented by the third Fossil pupil, Petrova. Petrova, as you all know, is on our honours list of Academy pupils who are serving. We are, I think, more proud of Petrova than almost any of our girls because she is a ferry pilot. Petrova is giving her scholarship because the Fossil sisters always stuck together and did the same things, and so, because I know that's what she would like, I'm giving it to Mark." Everybody clapped again. "The money will be useful to him in his career, and I'm sure he'll work very hard to deserve it. Posy has made a little arrangement to make up for Holly's disappointment, and so we have a family of brother and sisters with scholarships from a family of sisters, and that, as everybody who worked here when the Fossils were here will know, is exactly what they would like. Their family feeling ran very high indeed. Thank you, children."

It was when Holly was back with her class in the classroom that she realised she had lost something very important. Everybody thumped Miriam on the back and most people said, "Bad luck, Holly."

Miss Jones, who was taking the class for arithmetic, said to Holly in what was meant to be a kind way:

"Well, dancing isn't everything, is it, Holly?"

Holly, sitting at her desk and trying to look as though she were attending to the arithmetic lessons, felt as if all of a sudden she had grown older. All her nine years she seemed to have been drifting along with people making plans for her and she was just a little girl and, of course, nobody would be deliberately unkind to a little girl. Nobody was being deliberately unkind now. They had made her see herself as she was, and that hurt. She suddenly saw how inferior she was to the other children. To begin with, everybody else had a mother and, because of these mothers, they were always a bit better dressed than she was. Hannah and Alice did their best, but they did not take you suddenly to a hair-dresser to see if something more amusing could not be done with your hair, which was what had happened to two of the girls in her class last term. They did not embroider your name inside the hem of your tunic so that it would be easy to pick out from all the others. They did not worry quite so much if your dancing tunic was a little bit too long. Hannah was fond of saying "It'll do." Mothers did not seem to do that. Then, of course, there was bees and honey. With the scholarships they were not badly off, but the house still looked awful. It was not a lovely flat like Miriam's, where you would be proud to ask anyone to tea. Then there were the attaché cases. This term she was the only child in the class who was carrying her things about in a brown-paper parcel. The more she thought about things the worse she felt, and suddenly she knew that she was going to cry. She could not cry, she simply could not, everybody would think she was crying because she was jealous of Miriam. She asked to be excused, and ran downstairs to the cloak-room, and sat behind her locker where nobody would see her, and cried and cried.

Of course, the awful thing about crying is that even when it is over it leaves you swollen up and looking like it. Holly, after one horrified glance at the looking-glass, knew she simply could not go back to her class looking like that, so she decided to fill up the time until dancing class began and then go and apologise to Miss Jones. It was while she was filling up the time that she saw Miranda's locker was ajar and, idly opening the door, saw the attaché case lying in the locker looking very abandoned because there was nothing else in the locker at all.

Holly looked at the attaché case. What a difference it would make if it were hers! How little it would matter to Miranda! Quite likely it would lie there all the term, and Miranda would never notice it. How lovely if Miranda would just lend it! Quite likely Miranda would lend it if she were asked. If a person was asked to lend an attaché case and would have said yes, could there be any harm in borrowing it without asking? When Holly reached this point in her reasoning the attaché case was in her hands.

Holly's eyes were still a little swollen, but her face was flushed with pride when she walked back to her arithmetic class.

"You've been a long time, dear," said Miss Jones. "I was just sending someone to look for you."

Holly looked round the class to be certain that everybody was listening. This was a lovely moment—when they would all envy her instead of thinking her inferior.

"I was talking to my cousin Miranda. She's come round to see me specially. 'Dear Holly,' she said, 'I don't like to see you carrying about a nasty paper parcel while other children have attaché cases; do let me lend you this one of mine.'"

That evening Holly put the attaché case in her locker. Though by now she had almost persuaded herself that Miranda had lent her the case, she had not persuaded herself sufficiently to make herself think that Sorrel and Mark would believe that Miranda had lent it to her. It was sad to think of that lovely attaché case put away in a locker all night, but there was no doubt it was safer there.

The case was not missed for a week. Then Miss Smith asked for it and Sorrel went to fetch it and found it was gone. Anything missing in the Academy had to be reported, and the loss was reported to Winifred who, having examined the locker and found it empty, reported what had happened to Madame.

Madame was puzzled.

"Attaché case? Empty, you say? I expect one of the children borrowed it. Have you asked all Miranda's class?"

"Everybody," said Winifred. "The whole class saw Sorrel receive it and two or three of them saw it put back in the locker the next morning, and Miranda now remembers seeing it there for one day. She says that now she comes to think of it she hasn't seen it since; she didn't happen to want it, so she never noticed it was not there."

"Oh, well," said Madame, "I'll keep the whole school back after lunch and enquire about it. I don't suppose it will be far off."

The children had finished lunch and were pushing back their chairs when Madame came in. When she had been greeted she walked to the top of one of the tables where everybody could hear her.

"One moment, children; I'm sorry to keep you from

your recreation time, but there is a little muddle that
wants clearing up. Last week Miranda's governess, Miss
Smith, brought an attaché case to the Academy with
things in it for Sorrel, and asked Sorrel to put the case,
when she had done with it, in Miranda's locker. This Sorrel did and Miranda saw it there the next day, since when
it seems to have disappeared. Has anyone seen it, moved
it or borrowed it?"

All the children, except those in Holly's class, shook
their heads and looked as uninterested as they felt.
Holly's class was sitting round the junior dining-table with
Miss Sykes in charge. The children were bobbing about
like corks in a rough sea, and a storm of whispers ran
round the table, and one name predominated—"Holly."
And the more the children thought about Holly the more
full of expression this whisper became. "Hol-lee. Ooh!
Hol-lee."

Madame's attention was caught by this bobbing and
whispering. She came over to the junior table.

"You all seem very excited; do you know anything
about the attaché case?" There was a pause. The children
sat still, but their eyes swivelled round to Holly. Madame
looked smilingly at Holly. "Everybody seems to think that
you know something, Holly. Have you seen Miranda's attaché case?"

In the last days Holly had thought the attaché case was
almost hers. She had persuaded herself that if Miranda
knew how badly she wanted it she would give it to her.
When Madame first mentioned the case, so convinced
was she that it had been a real loan she did not even feel
uncomfortable, but then the whispers had started and
they began to penetrate the wall of imagination which she
had built, and suddenly the wall fell down, and there was
nothing left but the awful fact that she had taken something that did not belong to her, and told everybody it

was a loan. The horror of the situation was beyond tears, it just made her feel as if she was full of hot coal. She shut her lips tightly together and stared with a very red face at Madame.

Madame, who had come to make a simple query, saw that something had happened which was not going to be so simple after all. She looked round at the children.

"Holly doesn't seem to be going to answer me. Who else knows about this case?"

Once more all the class began bobbing about like corks and whispering, and this time the name that came to the top was Miss Jones.

Madame hated whisperings and nudges; she felt convinced that a lot of fuss was being made about nothing. She looked round the room with some impatience and caught Miss Jones' eye.

"Would you come here a moment, Miss Jones?"

Poor Miss Jones was feeling miserable. She hated telling tales and had hoped most passionately she would be spared all trouble by Holly explaining what had happened herself. However, where Madame beckoned the staff went. She came over to the table. Madame still had a slightly impatient note in her voice.

"Do you know anything about Miranda's attaché case?"

Trained for mathematics, Miss Jones had an accurate mind. She said, of course, she did not know if the attaché case Holly had brought in was the one that was missing, but she reported how Holly had appeared with an attaché case and had held it up and said, "I was talking to my cousin Miranda. She's come to see me specially, and she said, Dear Holly, I don't like to see you carrying about a nasty paper parcel while the other children have attaché cases; do let me lend you one of mine."

Miss Jones' words fell on a breathless hush. Every face looked shocked except Sorrel's and Mark's. Sorrel and

Mark were looking at the floor, not knowing where else so shamed a family could look. Madame faced Holly.

"Was this attaché case the one that's missing, Holly?" Holly nodded. Madame held out her hand. "Come along, dear, I think this is a matter that you and I should talk over alone."

In her study Madame sat down in an armchair by the fire. Holly, as the door shut, felt trapped and frightened and all her self-control gave way. She lay down on the floor and sobbed so that her whole body shook. Madame let her cry for a little while, and then she patted her shoulder.

"Be quiet, Holly, that's quite enough crying. Suppose, instead of lying on the floor there, you came and sat on my knee and told me all about it."

Even after Holly was on Madame's knee it took her a long time to stop crying, but when she did the whole story came out.

"I never have as nice clothes as the others, and I wouldn't mind that, but I do mind a brown-paper parcel, and when I saw Miranda's attaché case wasn't doing anything I absolutely knew Miranda would lend it to me, and so I took it."

"I see," said Madame gravely. "That must have been a lovely moment when you came into the class and told the children you'd been lent it."

Holly nodded.

"It was the most beautiful moment because, you see, everybody'd been sorry for me because Miriam had been given the scholarship instead of me, and for my cousin Miranda, who's awfully grand, to come all the way to the Academy specially for me, made everyone say 'Isn't Holly lucky?'"

Madame was stroking Holly's curls and looking into the fire. She took a long time before she answered.

"I do see, Holly. I think it's very difficult to distinguish what's really happened and what one thinks has happened, even when one's grown-up, and it's certainly very difficult at your age. I can quite see how all this happened, and I can see how your mind was working, but all the same it mustn't go on working like that, must it? It's most important that you should know clearly what you make up and what you don't. Do Sorrel and Mark want attaché cases, too?"

"Dreadfully."

Madame rang a bell.

It was the duty in wartime when staff was scarce for one of the children to answer Madame's bell. The senior class took turns and were known as the messengers. When the day's messenger appeared Madame sent her to fetch Sorrel and Mark.

Sorrel and Mark were appalled at that summons. To both of them came the idea that because they were the sister and brother of a child who was almost a thief, they were going to be expelled. Outside Madame's door they met and looked at each other with scared eyes. Sorrel gave Mark's tie a nervous twitch and pulled up her socks. Then she knocked.

Madame greeted Sorrel and Mark with a radiant smile. "Come in, children. Mark, open that top left-hand drawer. I've got a new box of candy sent me by Pauline from America. I remember how you loved those American candies the first time you came to see me." When the children had all chosen a sweet she told Sorrel and Mark to sit on the floor. "Well, Holly and I have come to the bottom of this attaché-case business. It seems that she and Mark suffer from the same complaint of letting their imaginations run away with them, but, even though it's not a very bad fault, it is a fault, and it's got to be got rid of. Now, what I suggest is this. I'm going to buy three attaché cases. They'll cost a lot, as you know, and they'll take more money than you've probably got, but we can add to that because presently the Fossils will send you money for your birthdays. On each attaché case I shall have your names stamped so that there'll be no chance of your losing them. Sorrel and Mark will have their attaché cases right away, but Holly will only be shown hers once, and then it will be locked up in a cupboard until the beginning of the summer term." She turned Holly's face towards her. "You can see then whether you can imagine you are carrying your new attaché case when you are not, and whether you can turn your brown-paper parcel into an attaché case. That'll be a very good way of learning where imagination ends and real things begin. Now, take one more sweet each and then, Sorrel, I want you to take the family home. I think an afternoon off will do you all good. You have had enough excitement for one day."

When the door had shut on the children Madame got up and fetched her book of telephone numbers. She opened the book at "C" and laid her finger on the name Cohen.

In spite of Madame being so nice, the children felt pretty wormy inside when they arrived at the Academy next morning, and they felt no better when they got a message to say Winifred wanted to see Sorrel at once.

Holly clutched at Mark.

"Do you think it's something awful?"

Mark looked anxiously at Sorrel.

"It might be, mightn't it?"

Sorrel was feeling extremely doubtful herself, but she managed to smile.

"Well, the best thing is for me to go and find out."

Winifred was working at the bar. She was in the middle of some frappés when Sorrel came in. She stopped with one foot against the calf of the other leg.

"Oh, Sorrel, your Aunt Lindsey has rung up to say that she wants to take you three and Miriam to lunch in a restaurant, and Madame says that's all right and it won't matter if you are half an hour late coming back."

The school were just finishing lunch in the Academy dining-room when Madame came in. This time a kind of shudder ran round. Madame making a speech two days running! Something pretty awful must be going to happen. Probably the Forbes hadn't really gone out to lunch with their aunt, they'd probably been expelled. Madame waited until the children had greeted her, and then she beckoned to them all to come and stand round her.

"I'm going to take you into my confidence, and I trust, without asking for a promise, that you will not repeat to the three Forbes children a word I have said. The attaché case that was missing has, as you know, been found. Holly had it. I need hardly tell you that, of course, it was no great crime she committed. She's a child with a vivid imagination and she persuaded herself that it had been lent. However, that is a fault and it has been dealt with. How, concerns none of you. Why I wanted to talk to you is that I discovered from talking to Holly something in which I think you can all help. The Forbes children have, as you know, no mother, and their father is missing; they live with their grandmother, but, of course, even the best grandmother isn't the same as a mother. The result is that Holly, certainly, and probably the other two as well feel that you children look down on them." There was a gasp from the school. "I know you'll all say to me, 'Of course we don't,' but are you sure? If your mothers make you new frocks out of old clothes and see that your hair-ribbons match and that you've always got clean socks and, incidentally, an attaché case to carry the socks in, have you never, even with a glance, suggested that a child with grubby socks or an unmatching hair ribbon was rather an inferior being?" Madame smiled. "Now, I don't want anything silly. I don't want anyone racing out to buy Holly an attaché case or all of you children making a pet of her, but I think it would be nice if you kept it firmly in your minds that the Forbes children, in some ways, are less lucky than you are, and see that any special piece of luck, like being allowed to give a party, or having a few sweets to hand round, you share with them."

While this talk was going on the children were having a superb and uproarious lunch with Aunt Lindsey. Aunt Lindsey took them to a grand restaurant where a band was playing, and they were very lucky because there was goose upon the menu and they all ate it, and not being used to goose, felt a mixture of pride in having eaten it and rather doubtful in the middle because it was not their usual form of food. It was with dismay they saw Aunt Lindsey look at her watch, and heard her say that the best of everything must come to an end and they were already half an hour late for the Academy.

Climbing the Academy steps each of the children, except, of course, Miriam, felt a sinking inside. People did not mean to look at them differently after yesterday, but they were looking different, there was no doubt of it.

Half the school were down in the changing room when Sorrel and Miriam walked in. One of Sorrel's class ran up to her.

"Hullo, there you are! We thought you'd gone off for another afternoon. You wouldn't think it, but we miss your old mug when you're away."

One of the juniors came up to Holly.

"My mother bought me a Mars bar out of my ration this month. I meant to save you half, but I didn't quite manage that." She fumbled in her attaché case and brought out a dusty, bitten little end of chocolate. "There you are! I won't watch you while you eat it, and then I won't miss it."

215

Chapter 16

AUDITION AT THE B.B.C.

Sorrel's twelfth birthday came at the beginning of the summer term. She woke up to find the sun streaming in and a parcel on the end of her bed. The parcel had been smuggled from the Academy in Mark's attaché case. It was from Pauline. Inside was a big box marked "Candies" and a card. The card said, "I hope this arrives in time for your birthday. I have sent some money for you to buy something, but I think birthdays ought to have parcels." The candies were tied up in the loveliest way. Being used to seeing the sweet ration in a paper bag that was inclined to burst or a flimsy cardboard container, there was pleasure in even unpacking Pauline's parcel. After the two layers of wrapping were off, the box was done up in fine white paper and tied with yards and yards of green and scarlet baby ribbon. The candies had come in a tin and the tin itself was something that had not been seen for years; it was green and had a wreath of pretty little flowers painted on it. When the lid was off there was no utility packing, but wads of tissue paper and under that two paper doilies beautifully cut, the sort that if put away would make part of a present for Hannah on her birthday, for she was sure to think them lovely. The candies themselves were breathtaking, large and squashy, many of them covered with nuts. Sorrel put one in her mouth and then hurriedly put the lid on the box to keep away temptation. It would be so easy to eat the lot, and then she would feel sick, and that would be disastrous on this day of all days.

Lying back in bed chewing, Sorrel thought about Pauline. She had seen her now, for Alice had taken them to cinemas to get to know the faces of Pauline, Posy and, especially, Uncle Henry. Pauline was so lovely in the films that seeing her had at first made her a stranger. She had written twice and Sorrel had written back twice. The first letter from Pauline, especially as she wrote so much about the Academy, had made her feel like a friend, and not much older than herself. Then, seeing her on the screen, she had stopped being an old friend, and had become somebody grand and remote. Then had come Pauline's second letter. Pauline had just received Sorrel's first letter and this time she really had written like a friend. There did not seem to be the smallest thing about the Academy that she was not interested in and nothing was the slightest bit grand about the way she wrote. What fun it must be to be Pauline! Fancy, when Pauline had been twelve she had played "Alice in Wonderland"! What a lovely part to play! She did wish that she could have a chance to play it, but, of course, she was not clever or pretty as Pauline had been. All the same she was going to an audition today. She wished she could tell Pauline about the audition. Winifred said Pauline had never been to an audition at the B.B.C., but Pauline had been to lots of other auditions and she would know just how it felt to wake up in the morning and know you were going to one, a mixture of wormy and excited inside.

Miss Jay had said, "Let's pity the poor Children's Hour staff and try to find something new for your audition. How awful it must be for those who have to listen to hear the same thing over and over and over again."

In the end Miss Jay, assisted by Sorrel, wrote a short

version of "The Princess and the Pea." It was nearly all conversation. The princess spoke and the man and woman peasants, and there was a lovely bit at the end where the princess was supposed to be in bed moaning and groaning about the bruises that were coming up on her because of the pea under the mattresses.

"One ought to have some stuff in dialect," Miss Jay had said, "but you're not very good at dialect. I think, for the second item, you'd better recite some Shakespeare. You shall learn Titania's speech from 'A Midsummer Night's Dream.' You will be able to have the script in your hands, because people do when they're broadcasting, but no pupil from this Academy has ever gone to an audition without being entirely word perfect, and they never will."

Sorrel sat up in bed. In a much bigger and heartier voice than her own she said, "Sounds a wild night;" then she spoke in a deep gruff voice, "Aye, there's a rare storm. The yard's a-swim with water and the river's running down." Then she went back to the hearty voice, but this time it sounded anxious: "You'll not go out again to-night?" Then the man's voice: "No, I have locked the gates, none will wish to go through now till morning."

Sorrel paused there. It always gave her an excited feeling imagining the scene. The doorkeeper's home inside the castle walls, the great gates locked for the night, and the whisper running round everywhere, "Our prince is to be married. Our prince is to be married, and who do you think he is going to marry? Why, the very first princess to knock at the palace gates." When Sorrel thought about all this going on she could hardly wait to knock on the big postern; it was such fun, the part where the princess arrived and, looking small and shabby and dirty, bowed graciously to the two peasants and said kindly, "You may kiss our hand."

Holly and Mark and Hannah came bursting in at Sorrel's door.

"Happy birthday, Sorrel."

"Happy birthday. I've bought you the most lovely present, will you undo mine first?"

Sorrel made room for Holly to get into bed with her. Mark and Hannah sat on the sides. Before she undid her parcels Sorrel opened her box of candy. Hannah made clucking noises.

"Oh, you shouldn't go eating all that rich stuff before breakfast, bound to turn your stomachs."

Nobody paid any attention to Hannah because they knew that she knew that one sweet before breakfast was permissible when it was a birthday or Christmas or Easter day. Sorrel looked at the three parcels on her knee. She undid Holly's first. Inside was a pin-cushion made not very well but with immense pain and toil. Alice had given Holly the stuff, which was part of one of Grandmother's old stage dresses.

"It's to be put away until you have a part," Holly explained, bouncing with excitement. "Now you're twelve, and going to an audition; you're sure to have a part soon."

In Mark's parcel there was a ruler, a hammer and a small bottle of glue.

"That's so that you can mend anything yourself that wants mending," he explained, "or at any rate you can get me to come and mend it, and then you've got the things you need."

From Hannah there were two black bows on little slides.

"As you're to wear your black tunic up at the B.B.C. I thought you might like two new ribbons. Alice says you have your plaits undone at an audition."

219

Alice came in with her parcel, or rather it was not a parcel, it was a little tiny screw of tissue paper.

"It's a little chain to hang that little fish the sailor gave you round your neck when you go to your audition. He said it was for luck, so that's the time to wear it."

Mark sprawled across the bed and looked longingly at Sorrel's box of candies.

"Of course, I know it's Sorrel's birthday, but anyone would think that she was the only one that was going to an audition; nobody seems to remember that I'm going to sing."

Alice gave him an affectionate slap.

"Nobody's under any illusion that you're going to be nervous about it. All I hope is that you don't break the microphone. As a matter of fact, you've not been forgotten, has he, Hannah? Old Hannah here has sat up night after night knitting you some new almond rocks."

Mark recognised almond rocks as socks. He looked suspiciously at Hannah.

"What sort?"

"Grey wool," said Hannah, "two pairs lightweight for the summer."

Alice moved to the door.

"Well, I can't stay here gossiping, I've got our breakfast to take up yet. When you're dressed, Sorrel, your grandmother would like to give you a kiss."

Mark waited until the door had closed behind Alice and then he lowered his voice.

"Of course, one shouldn't criticise one's grandmother, but ever since I've been in this house I've thought it pretty mean; there's never been a present, not at Christmas, not at Easter, not on Holly's and my birthdays, and now not on Sorrel's birthday."

"That's enough, come and get dressed," said Hannah.

"There are some people that don't need to give presents to show their affection."

Mark followed Hannah obediently to the door, but before he reached it he looked back at Sorrel.

"I don't think Grandmother's one of those sort of people, do you?"

The audition was going on all the afternoon. Sorrel and Mark had an appointment at half-past three. They were taken by Miss Jay and Doctor Lente. As a rule only one teacher went to an audition, however many pupils were going, and for two people to go caused rather a sensation in the Academy, especially as one of them was Dr. Lente, who never went to auditions. However, a talent once accepted acquired squatter's rights, as it were, and so the pupils looked wise and said to each other, "That's because of Mark."

They went to the B.B.C. on a bus. Sorrel walked to the bus with a glassy look in her eye, muttering:

> "These are the forgeries of jealousy:
> And never, since the middle summer's spring,
> Met we on hill, in dale, forest, or mead,
> By paved fountain, or by rushy brook,
> Or in the beached margent of the sea,
> To dance our ringlets to the whistling wind,
> But with thy brawls, thou hast disturb'd our sport."

Mark skipped along, swinging his attaché case in which was his music, his head in the clouds, deciding what his voice looked like when it left him and went out over the air to everybody's wireless set. Miss Jay was talking to Dr. Lente about some change in the classroom at the Academy when Mark, without warning, broke in with the result of his thinking.

"It wears long grey trousers made of cloud, its coat is buttoned up with notes, eight of them for the octaves, and the buttonholes are all the sharps and flats. It has a very long grey cloak made of little soft feathers and so long a feather in its hat that no matter how far away anyone's wireless is, the tip, tip, tip of the feather is still in my mouth."

Miss Jay was always willing to talk to Mark.

"Who is this?"

"My voice, coming out of the loud speaker."

Miss Jay ran rapidly over Mark's description to see if there was anything about it that would spoil his singing that afternoon.

"If that feather is in your mouth it mustn't spoil your singing, because I'll tell you something about the man that you don't know. If anything happens to that feather on his hat his heart stops beating and he's dead."

Mark rather liked this version.

"And before anybody knows what's happening there's the dust cart shovelling him away for salvage."

Miss Jay looked at Mark severely.

"Do you know what's going to happen to you if you sing badly? Madame is going to take charge of your attaché case."

"What, for ever?"

Miss Jay looked as if even that were possible, but she followed Madame's instructions.

"No, but perhaps for a great many days; it would all depend on how bad the singing was."

"There's no need for anybody to get in a flap. I'm going to sing very well indeed. I can't think why anybody thought I wasn't."

The B.B.C. looked very imposing with its police outside and sandbagged entrance, and when they got inside past the policeman, and Miss Jay and Dr. Lente were at the reception desk getting passes, even Mark was reduced to respectful silence.

They were taken upstairs by a page boy whom Mark looked at with envy. He did not appear to be much bigger than he was himself. What a gorgeous thing to do no lessons and be a messenger boy in the B.B.C.! That would be even better than going into the Navy.

There were quite a lot of other children in the Children's Hour waiting-room. Three boys who obviously came to sing, a very smartly dressed girl of about fourteen, who had a mother who kept pulling her curls over her shoulders, and a small boy in spectacles with a violin case on his knee. The door opened into the studio and somebody ushered a girl out and said that they would be writing to her. Then they called in the first of the singing boys. His voice came to them faintly through the door singing "I'll walk beside you." The girl with ringlets was sitting beside Sorrel. She gave her a nudge.

"I got here much too early—that's the eighth time someone has sung that song; it must be pretty awful for them up there," she jerked her thumb at the ceiling.

"What is up there?" Sorrel asked.

"The judges. They sit in a room with a glass window looking into the studio; all our voices come to them up there, You can see them peering down at you. I always wonder what they're saying."

"Have you been to an audition before, then?"

"Twice. Once before the war, and once in Bristol; each time I was going to be used my family moved and I couldn't."

"What do you do?" Sorrel asked.

"Well, I think it's a mistake not to give them an all-round view of your work, don't you? I'm doing a speech from Bernard Shaw's 'Saint Joan,' that's just for diction, and then I'm doing a speech of Edelgard's out of 'Chil-

223

dren in Uniform'—it's two separate speeches really, but I'm putting them together—and then I'm doing a little short funny thing in Scotch, and a rather pathetic bit about a child waiting for its father who's down the mine, that's with a Welsh accent. I finish up with a bit of good old North country, which is where I come from. What are you doing?"

Sorrel was appalled. How clever everybody else in the world was! How idiotic everybody in the B.B.C. would think it that she had only got a little bit of 'The Princess and the Pea' and one speech of Titania's!

"I'm just doing some Shakespeare, and a version of one of Hans Andersen's fairy stories. It doesn't seem much, does it?"

"Well, it's no good doing what you can't, is it? It will only put them"—the ringletted girl jerked her finger at the roof again—"off."

The door opened and the boy singer came out and the second one went in. Once more there were muffled sounds of "I'll walk beside you."

The girl sighed.

"You'd think it was catching, like measles or something."

Dr. Lente rolled anguished eyes at the roof.

"It is not suitable, as a song for little boys, and that child has a voice that overtrained is."

It was after the third boy had sung "I'll walk beside you" that Sorrel was called. Miss Jay gave her a smile and sounded as matter-of-fact as she did in the classroom.

"Come along, dear."

In the studio there was a piano on the left-hand side, seats all round the room and in the centre, of course, the most important thing, the microphone. There was a solid stand and across this an adjustable bar, and from one end of the bar the microphone was hanging. A nice girl came up to Sorrel and asked her what she was going to do, and whether she would announce herself or would like to be announced. Sorrel looked desperately at Miss Jay, but Miss Jay was nodding and smiling to what appeared to be the roof. Sorrel, turning round, saw behind her the glass window and the faces looking through that the girl with the curls had told her about. She touched Miss Jay on the arm.

"They want to know if I want to announce myself."

"Certainly," said Miss Jay, "and you'll start with the Shakespeare as arranged."

It was a queer feeling to stand by yourself in the middle of the room and speak to an inanimate thing like a microphone. It was a queer feeling to think that in the room behind the glass window people were not hearing your voice as it sounded in the studio, but as it sounded brought to them over the air. It was altogether so odd that just at first the queerness of everything overawed Sorrel and she could not bring Titania to life.

"I'm reciting Titania's speech from 'A Midsummer Night's Dream,' by William Shakespeare," she said. The lines came out of her mouth, just nicely rehearsed words, but meaning nothing. Then suddenly the studio was not there; she was in a wood, there were silver birches round her like there had been at Martins, and leaves were crackling under her feet and she was speaking in a proud way to Oberon who looked, in her imagination, rather like Uncle Henry looked when she saw him in the films, only, of course, as Oberon he was dressed as a fairy.

> "Therefore the moon, the governess of floods,
> Pale in her anger washes all the air,
> That rheumatic diseases do abound.
> And thorough this distemperature we see
> The seasons alter: hoary-headed frosts

Fall in the fresh lap of the crimson rose;
And on old Hiems' thin and icy crown
An odorous chaplet of sweet summer buds
Is, as in mockery set; the spring, the summer,
The childing autumn, angry winter, change
Their wonted liveries; and the 'mazed world
By their increase, now knows not which is which:
And this same progeny of evils comes
From our debate, from our dissension;
We are their parents and original."

As she spoke the last words Sorrel gave, in imagination, one more proud, angry look at Oberon. Then the leaves were gone and the silver birches and Oberon, and she was back in the studio. Then quite suddenly a voice came out of nowhere, a nice, cheerful, kind woman's voice.

"Thank you very much, Sorrel. That was nice. Now, what else are you going to do for us?"

Sorrel felt silly talking to someone that you could not see, but she answered as politely as possible.

"Please, I was going to tell you about "The Princess and the Pea.'"

"We shall enjoy that," said the voice, "it's one of my favourite stories."

Sorrel folded her hands.

"'The Princess and the Pea,' freely adapted from the story by Hans Christian Andersen."

She had finished. She had been the princess, she had been the peasants. In her mind it had all been real. At the end she felt she should strip off her overall, just as the princess stripped off her nightdress to show her bruises. She paused to give the peasants time to have a good look at her bruises before she let them say in breathless admiration:

"This is indeed a real princess."

The voice spoke again. It was laughing.

"Delightful. We all enjoyed that. You doing anything else for us?"

Sorrel looked at Miss Jay. Miss Jay was talking to the girl who had shown them in, and the girl spoke into the microphone for her.

"No, that's all."

Then the voice said:

"Thank you very much, Sorrel. Good-bye."

Sorrel was not made to go out of the room while Mark sang. She and Miss Jay sat in a corner and listened. Dr. Lente went over to the piano, and in a rather nervous way got out Mark's music. Mark, having been shown where to stand, looked as unconcerned as if he were at home. He sang "Where the bee sucks, there suck I." He sang it beautifully. Evidently the people behind the glass window thought so too. The same voice that had talked to Sorrel said with obvious enthusiasm: "Thank you so much, Mark, that was lovely. Would you sing us something else?"

Mark was charmed.

"I'm going to sing you 'Matthew, Mark, Luke and John,' and then something whose name I absolutely never remember."

"It seems to be a little folk song translated from the Russian," said the girl. "Go on, Mark."

When Mark had finished the voice said, "Thank you very much indeed," and then, "Wait a minute," and then, after a pause, "I'd like to see Dr. Lente before he goes, about fixing Mark into a programme."

Sorrel did not mean to feel jealous and it was not exactly jealousy that she did feel. It is hard when your younger brother is engaged and you are not. Pulling on her coat, she felt flat and sad. There were Dr. Lente and Miss Jay and Mark and the B.B.C. people in the passage

all talking together about Mark broadcasting, and there
was she just one other child who had been to an audition,
and in whom nobody was particularly interested. It was
not even as if singing on the wireless was any good to
Mark, in fact it might be very bad for him; it would be a
terrible thing if he got to like it, as it would take his mind
off his education to be a sailor.

Leaving the B.B.C. seemed a very different thing to
Sorrel from coming into it. Coming in, it had seemed a
grand grey building, but full of excitement; going out, it
was just the place where you had done your best but
somehow it had not come off.

They walked down the road, Mark skipping along in
an unconcerned way, and Dr. Lente and Miss Jay talking
about his singing in the Children's Hour. Sorrel trudged
along beside them trying not to look disgruntled, but
feeling in that mood when you want to drag your feet
and kick at something. Then suddenly Miss Jay turned to
her.

"They were pleased with you, Sorrel. There's a new serial starting in the Children's Hour in a few weeks' time,
and they are planning to give you the part of one of the
children."

Sorrel was so surprised, her breath was taken away.

"Me!"

Miss Jay laughed.

"Yes, you. You did your stuff very well indeed. I gather
it's a very exciting thriller all about catching a spy; you'll
enjoy that." She caught hold of Sorrel's arm, "Won't
you?"

Sorrel beamed at her, marvelling that a world which a
few minutes before had seemed so dismal and grey could
so quickly be sparkling and colourful.

"You bet I will, it will be simply super."

Chapter 17

NEWS FOR SORREL

Perhaps because it was nearly summer or perhaps because Sorrel and Mark were going to broadcast, or perhaps because they began to take an interest in their work, suddenly the Forbes family settled down and found they were quite liking living with Grandmother. Of course, it was a funny life. Now that Grandmother was earning money Alice was trying to improve the appearance of the rooms, but when she had sold the carpets and furniture she had not known there was a time coming when, however much bees and honey you might have, there was no furniture or carpets to buy.

"It's not," she would say, looking at the bare boards in Mark's bedroom, "that we aren't willing to put our hands in our sky rocket, but we're not going to give, even if we had it, a hundred pounds for a bit of carpet that would be expensive at five."

Mark heard what Alice said, but naturally he knew nothing about prices and conditions, and he supposed that Alice was trying to put Grandmother in a good light.

"Even," he said to Hannah, Sorrel and Holly, "if Grandmother had to spend a million pounds I wouldn't think it too much. I'd rather spend a million pounds than make my grandchild sleep in a room that's much too shabby to give to a dog that's got distemper."

Mark, having got something into his head, was not the

sort of boy to let it go again, and he would, as long as he lived in the house, and quite likely always, be angry with Grandmother about his room. All the same, he did not dislike Grandmother. All the children had grown, in a way, fond of her. It was not the sort of fondness that anyone would expect to have for a grandmother. Not that kind of fondness that means you feel you can tell her things because she is tolerant and gentle, as well, of course, as being admirable about Christmas and birthdays. Instead, they had found their grandmother exciting, which is the last thing that you expect to feel about a grandmother. Grandmother, with her moods and fusses, made such a difference in the house even when you never saw her. The first news of her came after Alice had taken up her breakfast.

"We aren't half in one of our moods this morning. Swore the coffee was cold, and then swore I'd done it on purpose when she burnt her mouth drinking it!" "My word! We're in a state. We've had a letter that we think insults us, but we'll read it through later on and see it wasn't meant the way we took it." "Everything in the garden's beautiful this morning, everybody's a darling and nobody can do anything wrong. I wonder how long we'll go on feeling like that."

On the top floor, of course, the need for quietness while getting up had become ingrained in the children. Alice had taken it for granted that they would understand and collaborate.

"Now, for goodness' sake, don't make a noise in the morning. Wake us before we're ready and poor old Alice will be half murdered. We don't sleep very late and the moment we're awake I'll let you know how we're feeling. If we're in a good mood you can scream the place down, but if we've got one of our days then it's never a whisper and down the stairs with your shoes in your hand."

Now that Grandmother was working she was not in a great deal. She, of course, acted every night and the children were out all day, so the only possible meeting days were Sundays, for on Saturday afternoons she played a matinée. On Sundays she often had people to see her and she usually sent for the children, but since Christmas, on the Sundays when she was alone, she always sent for them, and though she was sometimes difficult to understand, she was entertaining and they discovered that, though she never seemed to take much interest in what was happening to them, she obviously talked quite a lot to Madame on the telephone, because she seemed to know exactly how they were getting on.

Another thing which made a change for the better in their lives was the Square garden. In the spring it was beautiful. Of course, there was not much of it, but what there was had been used in the loveliest way. Almond and crab-apple and double-cherry trees flowered everywhere. There was a sloping bank which one day was turned blue by a carpet of blue-bells. There was a whole bed of lilies-of-the-valley, which scented the air for quite a distance round. As well, what the gardener had said was true; the children had come back. The houses in the Square began to be lived in again, not properly lived in, of course, because there was no one to look after them, but one or two floors were opened and, in these, families settled down and nearly all of them seemed to be partly children. The three they had met on Christmas Day became friends. There was a little very pretty fair child whom Holly played with and mothered. She was called Penny, and Holly treated her like a doll. There were babies in perambulators and babies toddling, and lots of the families had dogs and were willing to let other people know their dogs well. When the spring flowers disappeared summer ones began to come out, roses and lupins and delphiniums,

231

and more and more chairs were set out on the lawns on Saturday afternoons and Sundays, and a very friendly atmosphere sprang up. It was lovely, when the children came into the garden, to hear the voices of the other children shout, "Hullo, Sorrel!" "Hullo, Mark!" "Hol-lee, Hol-lee!" and the grown-up people would open their eyes as they passed and smile and say: "How are you today, Sorrel dear?" "How's Mark?" "How are you getting on, Holly?"

At the Academy, life had been quite different ever since the day Holly took the attaché case. Very few of the pupils lived in central London, and so there was no possibility of the children being asked out to tea or anything like that, but Madame's words had taken root and everybody did their best to be extra nice. It was not that they would not have been nice before, because all three of the children were quite popular, only nobody had thought them in need of extra niceness. They had been used to Miranda and had learnt from her that to be a granddaughter of the Warren family was so grand a thing that it put a child in a world apart. When the Forbes children and Miriam arrived, they had quite a lot to live down. After the attaché-case affair and what Madame had said, the children, as it were, started again. All the other pupils let their natural feelings of friendship for them have free play without any intervening wonder as to whether they were putting on side or getting unfair advantages because they were Warrens.

For Sorrel, life had looked up very much since she was engaged to broadcast. Mark's broadcasting was taken as a matter of course. He was one of the small children too young to have a licence and, therefore, not competing for parts; but Sorrel was engaged for one of the children's parts in the new serial after being heard at an audition, and she was given it because she had the right voice for it, and was chosen from amongst hundreds of children. There was a very decided barrier amongst the over-twelves between those who were working and those who were not. There were, of course, quite a number of pupils who were not supposed to be working, who had been sent to the Academy with a view to their being dancers or going on the stage when they grew up. But amongst those who wanted work, to be engaged for a part, whether in a film or on the stage or on the air, was very much something—it gave you a cachet.

Sorrel knew nothing about the negotiations for her part in the serial, because these were conducted for her by the school, and she only knew she had the part when she got the first installment of her script, and was called for rehearsal. The script was given to her by Miss Jay.

"You won't find the whole story here, Sorrel. This is the first week's installment. It seems most exciting as far as it goes; you're to play Nancy."

Sorrel knew that if she was going to broadcast she was probably going to be paid. She had always kept Alice's conversation about bees and honey in the front of her mind. Alice had said she had sold things because trades-people had to be paid. Of course, now that she had met all the family she could see that nobody would ever let Grandmother starve, but equally it would not be fair to expect her to keep them all, and more than anything it would not be fair to let her pay for Mark's school. Not that, as things were at present, Grandmother would dream of paying for Mark's school. She did not even know that Alice had promised to see that he went to a proper school when he was eleven. Of course, by then all those things that Alice had talked about that had to do with probate and lawyers might have been settled, and then the question of Mark's school fees would not arise; but it was certain that, in case there was any lack of bees and honey when the time came, it would be a great help if she had some money to offer, at least for the first term. She was terribly shy of talking about money to Miss Jay, but she felt she must.

"What happens to money that I earn?"

Miss Jay looked amused.

"What do you want to happen to it?"

Sorrel liked and trusted Miss Jay and she decided suddenly to explain about Mark. Miss Jay listened in attentive silence until she had finished.

"I think I can help about that. I can arrange that your money is put for you in the post office; a certain proportion has to be by law in any case. That is one of the terms on which performing licences are issued to children. As for Mark, I don't know what to say. If it is your father's wish that he should be trained as a sailor, I think you should get your uncles and aunts to help. Don't you think they would?"

Sorrel fidgeted with her plaits.

"Well, I don't believe Aunt Lindsey and Aunt Marguerite would, because they're like Grandmother; they just can't believe there could be anybody in the world who wanted to do anything but act. Of course, there's Uncle Francis; I suppose he might help, but he's rather a distant kind of uncle; even when you seem to be talking to him you never feel absolutely sure he's listening." Then her face lit up as a thought struck her. "But I'll tell you who I'm certain would help, and that's Uncle Mose."

"Mose Cohen! Now, of all your family I should have thought that he was the one who would think the stage was the only career."

Sorrel shook her head violently.

"No, he isn't. Uncle Mose, in a way, is a little like Daddy. Daddy always said about anything I asked him, 'Well, let's thrash it out, old lady, and see if we can man-

age it.' Uncle Mose is like that. Of course, he isn't like
Daddy always. Daddy doesn't walk on his hands and he
isn't funny like Uncle Mose, but Daddy sings sea songs
just for cheerfulness, and I think that's why Uncle Mose
puts on funny hats." She looked at Miss Jay with great
conviction. "Yes, that's what I'll do if the worst comes to
the worst; I'll ask Uncle Mose to help."

The rehearsals for the broadcast were held in the same
studio as Sorrel had been to for the audition, only this
time there were a lot of people in the studio and some
bits of furniture, and some cups which she was told
would be used for clinking sounds when they were supposed to be drinking tea. There was a door in a wooden
frame, which was to be shut when anybody was supposed
to be going in or out of a door. There was a plank on
which to make the sound of footsteps, and there was a
doorbell. A young man called Henry, in a Fair Isle jersey
and grey slacks, was producing the play, but as well, of
course, there were the people in charge in that room upstairs with the glass window looking into the studio. From
there came all the music, and green lights for cues and
pauses, and a red light for when the cast were on the air,
and from there, too, came all the effects. At one end of
the studio a little tent had been built, and in this sat the
narrator. Henry explained the tent to Sorrel.

"We get the difference that way of pitch and tone. All
of you are in the story, but he's the man who tells the
between bits and links it all together, and you don't want
to sound as if you were all in the same room."

There were three children in the story. A brother and
sister called Robert and Nancy and a cockney evacuee
called Bill, and they all met at the beginning in a cove on
a beach. The effects upstairs, Sorrel was told, did lovely
things to make the beach come true, seagulls mewing and
water lapping, and the crunch of steps on pebbles. Sorrel

and a fair boy called John, who was playing Robert, and a little red-headed boy called Edward, who was playing Bill, stood round the microphone, their scripts in one hand and their pencils in the other, and read their parts. Henry stopped them at intervals for different things; sometimes they were not excited enough, and sometimes he wanted them to sound as though they were moving about, and what Henry said they wrote down against their lines. Sometimes the woman's voice that Sorrel had heard when she came for her audition broke in. She always talked to Henry as though she were standing next to him.

"We're going to put in some ordinary carrying-on music there, Henry." "We've found some music that we think will do very well for a trotting pony, then you can go back and do it again from where we faded." "That music won't do because it's a walking pony, it's not nearly vivid enough for one that's trotting."

Sorrel and Edward and John, by the time they had gone through their parts twice, began to live them. They met with a thrill of excitement on the beach, and heard from Bill of the queer lights he'd seen on the cliff side, and how he believed it was smugglers, and how he intended to sneak out at night and watch to see what was going on. Sorrel and John then went home to tea with their parents and this was, of course, the place where the cups were clinked, and during tea their father told their mother that he would not after all be able to fish tomorrow because old Bert wanted his boat: there had been lights complained of and the coastguards and wardens would be out having a look.

Robert and Nancy had to ask casually about this and they expected, of course, to hear that the lights had been seen in the cove where they had met Bill; but not at all, it was somewhere quite a long way up the coast. After tea

236

Nancy and Robert had an excited conversation in which Robert made Nancy see how queer and suspicious it was that Bill should see a light in one place and the coast-guards and wardens and people should be sent off to another. It looked as if there were funny goings-on somewhere. It was Nancy's idea that they should take out their ponies and ride over to old Bert's to see if they could get out of him who it was that had complained about lights. It was not until after they had talked to the coastguard that Robert and Nancy were anxious about Bill. There had been very strong complaints about the lights from a lady who was staying in the hotel. She was a stranger in those parts, and the coastguard might have thought she was just one of those women who were full of spy scares, only she had fetched two other visitors in the hotel to come and look at it, and on the face of it, though Bert himself did not think it was much, he thought they ought to go and sort it out. Then came the really exciting thing. A lady walked up the road and the coastguard casually said, "That's the lady who reported the lights." When Robert and Nancy were jogging home again on their ponies they took a short cut and put their ponies to some jumps over some gorse bushes. Nancy got separated from Robert doing this and she had cleared a jump when she saw, to her horror, that she had only just missed jumping on the lady who was staying at the hotel, and who had been sitting behind the gorse bush. The lady, startled, jumped up, and—this was what was so queer—she said: "Ach, Himmel!"

Of course, some of this was to be heard by the listeners as actually happening, and some of it was told by Nancy to Robert, her words falling out over each other in excitement. It was Robert who saw how dangerous this might be for Bill. Just suppose they had run on something, an enemy submarine re-fuelling or anything like that, Bill ought to know; anyway, he ought not to be alone in the cove. He might want help. Sorrel was being Nancy by now and she felt a thrill of fright run through her as she agreed with Robert that the only thing they could do was to go down to the cove and warn Bill to be careful, and since, of course, something really serious might be going on, stay and see what was happening, and, if need be, fetch the police.

There were some other scenes after this and then some effects which were, they were told, an owl hooting and a distant church clock chiming eleven, and then Robert and Nancy crept out of the house and, terrified of every sound, crunched their way across the cove to look for Bill.

Sorrel's broadcast, when she came to the performance of that first episode, was completely eclipsed as far as home interest was concerned by a family storm. Uncle Francis was, as Alice had told the children, putting on "The Tempest." He was, of course, to play Prospero and he had engaged a splendid Caliban, about whom he was excited. In the ordinary way when he did a London season he performed two or three plays as a repertory, but this time he had decided to give all his attention to one production, which should be as beautiful as war conditions would allow. All Shakespearean actors have violent views on different plays and parts. Uncle Francis had always had ideas about "The Tempest." One was that the ideal Ariel would be a child. Now suddenly he had an idea. Miranda should play Ariel. Uncle Francis was the sort of man who expected everybody to do what he wanted. He simply could not believe that anyone would do anything to displease him, and so he thought that when the time came he had only to ask for Miranda to be released from her part in her present play for it to be granted. Unfortunately, he had not waited to ask the

her what he meant to do and that she was to study the
part, but she was not, for the moment, to speak about it.
That had been three months ago, and in those three
months Miranda had lived and dreamed Ariel. Miranda
was Shakespeare mad. She was perfectly prepared to play
in modern comedies, for she knew quite well that good
Shakespeare productions are few and far between, but
her ambition was in the big tragic parts; most of all she
longed some day to play Lady Macbeth. That before she
was fourteen she should have a chance at Ariel was
beyond her wildest dreams. She had often asked her father to give her a part and he had always said he did not
care for precocious children; she must wait until she was
eighteen. When Grandmother had over-persuaded him
and Miranda had been allowed to play Sylvia, on the first
possible occasion when he was playing near London he
had seen her perform at a matinée and had been full of
pride, and that was how he came to think of trusting her
with Ariel.

Uncle Francis did not even write a very pleading letter
to Miranda's management; he simply stated that he was
putting on "The Tempest" at the end of June and he
would like them to release his daughter for the part of
Ariel. The management wrote back courteously but very
firmly, and said they would not consider it under any cir-
cumstances whatsoever; it was then the fur began to fly.
Uncle Francis saw Grandmother, Grandmother saw Aunt
Marguerite and Grandmother interviewed her management. According to Miriam, who was a grand reporter on
an occasion like this, her mother and Aunt Marguerite
never by any chance left the telephone.

"If they stop ringing each other up for one second
Mum screams, 'Oh, of course, I know what Marguerite
must do,' or 'I'm sure I've thought of something.' And

there she is, dial, dial, dial. When Dad comes in at night she tells him all about it and she forgets and leaves the telephone off. It doesn't matter when I'm up because I hear it howl and put it back on its rest, but goodness knows who does it when I'm in bed."

It took ten days, during which Uncle Francis fought passionately and tried everything including the use of lawyers, before it was finally accepted that Miranda was not going to be released. She had made a success, her management wanted her and were keeping her. It was then that Grandmother had her brilliant idea.

"I quite realise that it's not at all the same thing to you, Francis, because naturally you wanted your daughter, but, fortunately, you have a niece who also has Warren blood and who also is very promising." She saw that Uncle Francis was going to argue, so she spoke in her firmest and most settled kind of voice. "Sorrel shall play Ariel."

Chapter 18

ARIEL

It was the day after Sorrel's first broadcast. Hannah, when Sorrel came back from the Academy, told her that she was to sit up in her dressing-gown to see Grandmother when she came back from the theatre. Nothing like that had ever happened before and the children were wild with curiosity to know what Grandmother could want to see Sorrel about.

"I expect she didn't like your broadcast," said Holly. "I expect she was sorry that she borrowed somebody's wireless set and had it in her dressing-room. I can't think why she shouldn't like it because we thought you were awfully good, didn't we, Mark?"

The only wireless set in the house belonged to Alice and lived in the kitchen. Mark and Holly had been allowed to leave the Academy early, for as Sorrel was going to the B.B.C., there would be no one to take them home and Hannah would have to fetch them. By arrangement with Hannah they were back in plenty of time to hear the broadcast. They had sat round the table in the kitchen expecting to be thrilled at hearing Sorrel's voice. Actually they found the story so exciting that they had clean forgotten that Sorrel was Sorrel and thought she was Nancy. Mark tried to explain this.

"It wasn't till this morning that I remembered it had been you, and that was odd because that girl, Nancy, rode a pony and you can't."

If the children had to do stage work, then, from Hannah's point of view, let them appear in the Children's Hour for the B.B.C. At the vicarage her favourite listening had been the Children's Hour. She approved of everything about it, especially the short services. She considered Uncle Mac what she called "a good Christian gentleman," and she was sure no harm could come to Sorrel from mixing with the likes of him. "Of course, what I'd fancy for you," she said, "would be to take a part in one of those Bible stories, but that would mean acting on a Sunday and I couldn't think that right." Then she looked muddled. "Not but what it makes very suitable listening to, so maybe somebody ought to do it. But I don't think it is anything to do with that your grandmother wants, certainly not in a complaining way, for Alice told me on the quiet that it was a bit of good news. Your grandmother sent for me before she went out this afternoon. 'Hannah,' she said, 'I wish to see Sorrel when I come in tonight.' 'What!' I said, 'that'll be after nine, and Sorrel will have been in bed an hour and a half.' Then your grandmother made one of those tittering noises she makes when she's impatient and said, 'I'll see her in her dressing-gown.'"

Because she was sitting up to see Grandmother, Sorrel had a special supper with Hannah in the kitchen. There was a recipe that Hannah had heard given out on the wireless for making a sort of scrambled egg with powdered egg and onion and cheese.

"A bit indigestible," said Hannah, "but it'll have time to settle before you're in bed."

Sorrel was sitting on the kitchen table.

"I do wish I knew what Grandmother wanted. Even though you say it's going to be good news, I can't help feeling as though I was waiting to go into the dentist's."

Hannah never seemed to know when she was telling

something really important. Important things dropped out of her mouth in just the same tone of voice as when she said "That was ever so nice a bit of meat I got from the butcher this week" or "I've been round to see that shoemender again, and he's promised Mark's shoes by Thursday without fail." She was at the stove, stirring the scrambled egg.

"I shouldn't wonder if it was something to do with your school. That Madame that teaches you and that Miss Jay came here this afternoon."

Sorrel shot off her chair and came over to the stove.

"Hannah! And you've known that ever since we came in and you never told us!"

"I didn't know you'd be interested. That Madame looked ever so comic, I thought."

Sorrel paid no attention to Hannah's views on Madame. She caught her arm.

"What did they come about? Didn't you hear anything?"

Hannah was puzzled at Sorrel's eagerness.

"No. I've got more things to do than to wonder why your teachers come round. I've got ever such a lot of washing and mending. Holly's torn a great jagged piece right out of those rompers that she was given for her dancing."

Sorrel went back to the table. If only Alice were in! Alice was never muddled about what was important and what was not. Rows of ideas rushed through her mind. Alice had said it was good news. Of course, Alice was probably right, but just suppose she was wrong. Nobody knew it, but she was not quite clear in her conscience. She had felt that everybody was pleased with her about the broadcast and she had been rather proud this morning; and Miss Jones had said to her during arithmetic, when she had answered a little rudely: "I don't know what's the matter with you, Sorrel. It's not like you to speak like that." Later, when she had asked somebody to bring up something for her from the cloak-room when they went down, one of the girls had said: "You want a lot of waiting on today, don't you? You know, you're not the only person who ever broadcast." Neither what the girl had said nor what Miss Jones had said had until this minute made much impression on her, for she had felt important and thought other people ought to think her important too. Now a fearful doubt crept into her mind. Had Madame and Miss Jay come to see Grandmother in order to say, "If Sorrel gets cocky about anything she does, perhaps we had better not let her take another part?"

Alice came down to fetch Sorrel. Sorrel had, of course, heard Grandmother come in and was waiting at the top of the stairs that led up from the kitchen. Alice gave her an unexpected kiss.

"Run along up. You're to go straight in while I get our supper."

Grandmother was in her drawing-room. She came home from the theatre in a hired car and did not bother to take off her make-up until she got back, so she was looking more like Grandmama on the stage than Grandmother in real life. She was sitting in an armchair. She held out a hand to Sorrel.

"Come here, granddaughter. You have, of course, heard all about Miranda playing Ariel in her father's production. Well, the management won't release her, and so I have told your uncle Francis that he's to try you in the part."

Sorrel felt as if the drawing-room was turning upside down.

"Me! But I couldn't!"

Grandmother, which was unlike her, thought a moment before she answered.

"No actress should say that about any part, but possibly on this occasion you're right. Your uncle Francis is, in my opinion, a pompous ass of an actor, but then I've always thought Prospero was a pompous ass of a man, therefore it's never been any surprise to me that your uncle's considered superb in the part. I, fortunately, have never had the misfortune to see him play it. In the early days of their marriage your aunt Marguerite played the part of Miranda, and that, I knew, could be nothing but a disaster, so I saved myself from suffering and kept away from the theatre." Her voice changed. "All the same, whatever my private opinion may be, your uncle is considered an extremely fine Prospero, and it's been his dream to put on a splendid production of the play. One of the difficulties has been to find a good Caliban. You know the play, I suppose."

"No. I've heard about it lately, of course, because of Miranda, and I know Miranda got her name from that play, but we haven't done it yet at school."

"Well, Prospero, pompous fellow, lived on an island with his tiresome daughter, Miranda. He had magic powers and made creatures his slaves; one of these was Caliban, a strange, sub-human creation, and the other was what Shakespeare calls an airy sprite. That's Ariel. What Shakespeare meant I've no idea, but I can see what your uncle Francis thinks he meant. From Caliban he wants a monstrous, grovelling creature hardly human at all, entirely of the earth; and from Ariel something that's got nothing to do with the earth at all. He sees Ariel as neither a man nor a woman, a creature of light and air and spirit, and to get this effect he thinks he needs a child. That's why he wanted Miranda, who speaks blank verse so exquisitely."

"But I don't!" Sorrel exclaimed. "I'm getting on quite

well, Miss Jay says, but it's only my third term and we didn't learn that kind of elocution at Ferntree School."

"Naturally, I know exactly how far you've got. I saw Madame Fidolia and your Miss Jay this afternoon. Miss Jay said that you have a natural gift for verse speaking, that you have rhythm and that you have a quite nice singing voice, and that's important, because Ariel has a song."

"Oh, goodness!" said Sorrel. "A song, too! He—I mean she—I mean it—doesn't dance as well, does it?"

"Never still for a second," said Grandmother. "Every step a dance, every movement an inspiration. You'll see what your uncle wants when you get to rehearsals." She patted Sorrel's hand. "Don't look so scared, child. Exactly two things can happen to you, and neither would mean the end of the world. You will, of course, be rehearsing on approval, and your uncle may refuse to let you play the part, or you may be allowed to play the part and get quite appalling notices. Appalling notices are unfortunate for anyone, but at the age of twelve they are unlikely to ruin your career. Now, run up to bed, child; you should be transported into the seventh heaven of happiness by what I've told you. What an opportunity!"

Sorrel went down to the kitchen where Alice was cooking Grandmother's supper. Alice grinned at her from the stove.

"That'll teach you, Miss Can't-do-it. I said to Hannah we should see you coming in looking like a wet week."

Sorrel had almost lost her voice.

"But, Alice, you can see I can't do it, can't you?"

Alice had no patience at all with faint hearts.

"Oh, run along up to bed! You've got a chance that hundreds of children would give their eyes to have, and you stand there with eyes like a frightened cow, saying 'Oo-er, Alice, I can't.' You make me sick. You've got Warren blood in you, haven't you? You are your mother's

daughter, aren't you? Well, run along up to bed and before you get into it say fifty times, 'I can do it if I try, I
can, I can, I can.'"

Sorrel's rehearsals were to begin on the following Monday, and since it was term time and she could not be allowed to be free of lessons, it was arranged that Miss
Smith was to teach her with Miranda; the lessons were to
be taught in the wardrobe of the theatre in which Sorrel
was rehearsing. Sorrel dreaded them. Bolstered up by Alice and conscious of Grandmother's scorn if she showed
any fright, she was managing to pretend that she had
some confidence in her acting, but she could not even
pretend she looked forward to doing lessons with Miranda. To begin with, anybody would be sorry for Miranda, who had lived and dreamt of playing this part,
and it was bad enough not to be going to play it; but to
have your younger cousin given it in your stead would
obviously be simply frightful. Then, Miranda was not the
sort of person who liked her life upset for other people.
At the moment, she and Miss Smith were doing lessons
comfortably in her own schoolroom, and now, instead,
she was expected to turn out after breakfast and go
round to a theatre to do lessons in a wardrobe for the
convenience of the cousin who had taken her part. Whatever way you looked at it the arrangement was a pretty
mean one for anybody, and it would be an extraordinarily nice girl who could be pleasant about it. Miranda
might be a lot of things, but "nice" was not a word you
would ever use about her. Sorrel shuddered whenever
she thought of lessons on Monday.

Sorrel was not the only one who was shuddering. On
the Thursday, Alice came back from the theatre with a
message from Miss Smith. Would Alice bring Sorrel to
the Saturday matinée so that they could discuss what
books and things she would need for Monday.

Miss Jay was taking an enormous interest in Sorrel's part. From the time Sorrel had been given it there was less than a week to the first rehearsal, so there was no time with everything else she had to do to learn the whole part, but Miss Jay took her through as much of it as she could, explaining any word that she did not understand, but being careful not to teach her any inflexions.

"I know your Uncle Francis is a great authority on this play and I don't want to let you get ideas before he starts in on you. All I want is to be certain that you're word perfect in each scene as you study it, and don't say any word like a parrot, but know its meaning."

Sorrel confided in Miss Jay her fear of lessons with Miranda. She did not, of course, put it that way. She said:

"Do you think I must do lessons in the wardrobe? If I absolutely promised to come here every minute I could and worked before breakfast and when I got home at night, wouldn't that do?"

Miss Jay laughed.

"I sympathise with you, but I can't help you. The law is the law and you've got to do lessons. It'd be a shocking thing when you go down to the L.C.C. on Monday for your licence if it was turned down because you're not having sufficient education. That's why Miss Smith's taking you; they've approved Miss Smith to teach Miranda, and they can trust her to see that your lessons are not neglected for your stage work."

"Well," said Sorrel, "I don't care what anybody says, but I think it's going to be awful for everybody. If I was Miranda I'd simply hate it if I had to go out to do my lessons to suit her, and, being Miranda, she'll hate it even more than I would."

Miss Jay reopened Sorrel's copy of "The Tempest."

"I quite see your point, but, really, what you two little girls like and don't like can't be considered. If you are to play the part it's the only solution and, as a matter of fact, it will be very good for you. If you're ever to be the actress that I hope you're going to be, you'll have to learn to assert yourself." She looked up from the Shakespeare. "You do want to be an actress, don't you?"

Sorrel was surprised at the fervour with which she answered. She had not known until that moment how fearfully she did want to be one.

"More than anything in the world."

"Good, because in my opinion, and, mind you, it's only an opinion, you've got as great a chance of becoming a good one as any pupil I've taught since Pauline Fossil." She turned back to the book. "Now then, we'll take that scene again; I'll give you the cue.

'Come away, servant, come! I am ready now.
Approach, my Ariel; come!'"

Because Sorrel was going to the matinée with Grandmother, Holly and Mark were allowed to invite Miriam to tea. Miriam came flying to Sorrel the moment the children reached the Academy on Saturday morning.

"I've had another letter from Posy. She says I don't tell her any of the sorts of things she really wants to know, and she's asked me rows and rows and rows of questions, and I do most awfully want to answer. I haven't got a class after twelve o'clock, but Mark and Holly have. Could you possibly write to Posy for me then, if I told you what to say? You write beautifully, and I write so terribly slowly, and all the things I think don't get time to be put down by my pencil."

Sorrel had come to the Academy that morning for a special class with Miss Jay, but she would be finished by twelve o'clock. She had meant to spend the rest of the time, while she was waiting for Holly and Mark, learning

249

Ariel's next scene, but Miriam was so full of hope that she simply had not the heart to say no.

At twelve o'clock Sorrel sat at her desk and Miriam leant over her shoulder. Miriam laid Posy's last letter in front of her.

"You read it and you'll see what a terrible lot of things she wants to know."

Sorrel smoothed the sheets of paper.

> DEAR MIRIAM,
>
> Have you started centre practice? When you get to the bourrées, especially the bourrées changé, ask Madame to show you what she showed me, or perhaps she has already. It's that point coupé jetté bourrées changé bit that she makes so clear. I do wish I could talk to you instead of writing a letter, and then I'd know how far you are and if Madame has shown you any of her things. You ask in your last letter about the American ballets. Of course, there are some, and I hear they are just wonderful, but my contracts have not let me get away and nothing has been here lately. I asked you in my last letter to tell me about "Hamlet" "Comus" and "The Birds." How is Helpmann's choreography? Do you like it? I hear that he is very keen on line and so is Manoff. They say there's been a new ballet this year called "The Quest," about Una and the Red Cross Knight. Pauline and Garnie say I ought to know about them, but I always hated English literature, and if it's Spenser I wouldn't be interested. Please go and see it before you write again and tell me all about it. Pauline says will you please tell Sorrel that she's working in a new picture, and she won't be writing for a week or two

250

because she is on location. Nana says she hopes that you wear enough when you're dancing, as England's so damp, and from the sound of you you probably suffer with your liver. That's because Madame described you as a pale little thing with dark hair. That's how Petrova looked and Nana always thought she had a liver. Please give my love to Madame and tell her that I'ye added a little bit to my message that my feet say each morning. When you're ready to work on your points, I'll send a combination to you which you can send to me every morning at your practice, and I will send it back to you. I won't send it yet because it's not so good demi-point, and too advanced anyway.

> *Love,*
> POSY.
> xxxxxxxxx

Sorrel tore a clean sheet of paper out of the middle of an exercise book and wrote Miriam's address and the date on the top right-hand corner.

"Well?"

Miriam practised little steps while she dictated.

DEAR POSY,

I do a little centre practise, but Madame says that you forget that I'm not quite nine, and you didn't do her things nearly as young as that. Would you please write in littler words next time. I take your letters to Madame and we read them together, but though Madame explains them they are still very difficult.

Now I will tell you about the ballets. I have seen "Hamlet," "Comus" and "The Birds." I think "Hamlet" is queer, but Madame says it will be easier when I have read the play. Hamlet is dead at the beginning and dead at the end, and all the middle is what he dreams when he's dying, Madame says. It is a beautiful ballet for line; there is a queen in it who has ladies of the Court to attend on her, and always they're grouped round an entrance which is centre stage left. There is one bit I like very much, when all of them hold golden cups.

"Comus" is a lovely ballet. Margot Fonteyn dances the lady and she has some beautiful foot work to do, but what I liked best was the attendant spirit danced by somebody called Margaret Dale. Madame says, will you please tell Monsieur Manoff that this is a part that Vera Nemchinova should have danced. She says that Monsieur Manoff agrees with her about that dancer. All the same, Madame agrees with me that Margaret Dale is beautiful in this rôle, but I think in three years I will dance it better than she does. "The Birds" I have only seen once; there is a part of a nightingale danced beautifully by Beryl Grey. I went with Madame to see this ballet, and she said that it was good for me to watch Beryl Grey. I have not seen "The Quest." Dad has been on tour for E.N.S.A. and he's now rehearsing for a revue and Mum does not like ballet. Dad will take me when he has time, and I will write to you all about it. I shall be starting point work this autumn. Madame says that you always had precision; why haven't I?

Love,
MIRIAM.
XXXXXXXXX

P.S.—Holly sends her love and says she still hasn't got much beyond dancing a baby polka, so you wouldn't have wanted to give her your scholarship. Holly dances the baby polka as Dr. Lente would do it, and as Miss Jay would do it, and sometimes, when she is very bad, as Madame would do it. She makes us laugh and laugh.

Sorrel, whose hand was getting tired, folded the letter. "Well, I won't have any more P.S.'s, that's quite enough. It's lucky I've taken so many lessons on the history of the ballet or I would never be able to spell those words and names. I never knew Holly did imitations."

Miriam was always immensely serious about people's work.

"She does, but nobody's seen her yet. She does talking imitations, too. I told Mum and she said that your mother was a mimic and she was awfully funny, but she was never allowed to do it properly because Grandmother and Grandfather wanted her to be a serious actress."

Sorrel handed the letter to Miriam.

"You won't lose it, will you, after I've taken all the trouble to write it?"

Miriam looked surprised.

"Of course not. I'm taking it this very second for Madame to read and she'll send it away."

Miriam dashed out of the door and Sorrel looked after her. Miriam was always a puzzle to her, she was so purposeful, so unafraid of anybody, so certain where she was going. If Miriam could speak blank verse at all, which she would never try to do, she would not be afraid of acting Ariel. If she was going to play the part at all, she would know she could do it. Why, oh why, was she, Sorrel, not like that?

Sorrel arrived at the theatre that afternoon well before the curtain was up. Alice sent her to Miranda's dressing-room.

"It's no good you coming in with us, we get in a state if people hang round when we're making up. I've had a word with the stage manager, and when Miss Smith's done with you you can come down on the stage and watch the play. Wait till we're on the stage and then knock on our dressing-room door and call me. I'll take you down."

Miranda was making up when Sorrel went in. Miss Smith was sitting by the dressing-table doing "The Times" crossword puzzle, and in a corner of the room sat a little fair girl knitting. Sorrel had wondered what on earth to say to Miranda. Miranda saved her the trouble of wondering. In answer to Sorrel's knock Miss Smith said "Come in," and Miranda, streaking grease paint onto her face, muttered in a furious voice:

"They can let you come into my dressing-room if they want to, and they can make us do lessons together, but I won't speak to you, ever."

Miss Smith was in an armchair; she patted its arm.

"Come and help me with my puzzle, Sorrel. Mary's trying very hard to get a vest finished for her baby brother, but we'll ask her to help us with words if we get stuck."

Miranda rubbed her grease paint smooth.

"Well, I hope you don't all chatter; if you do and I dry up on the stage, it'll be your fault."

It was terribly awkward. Miss Smith went on with the crossword puzzle as though nothing were wrong and tried to pretend that Sorrel was helping, which she was not. Occasionally she asked Mary to help, but Mary obviously was not the sort of person who was good at crossword puzzles, because when she was asked for something with nine letters she suggested words with three or four. The call boy came round and said, "Overture and beginners, please," and Miss Smith got up and took Miranda's first-act dress off a coat hanger, and Miranda put it on, and then Miss Smith fetched her bonnet, looked for her gloves and gave her those, and still Miranda said nothing. At last the call boy knocked on the door and said, "Miss Brain, please," and Miranda, with her nose in the air, stalked out and slammed the door.

When the door was shut, Miss Smith tidied Miranda's dressing-table.

"I don't have to go down with her for this entrance, Alice looks after her. I'm sorry she's being so difficult, Sorrel; it's not your fault."

Mary laid down her knitting. She was a round-faced little girl with fair hair cut in a fringe; she looked the sort of child who would never say anything but "Yes, please," but now her voice was angry.

"I think Miranda's being perfectly hateful."

Miss Smith went on calmly tidying the dressing-table.

"Miranda isn't really angry with Sorrel. She's so terribly disappointed, poor child, she doesn't know what she's doing."

"All the same, she needn't take it out of Sorrel," said Mary stubbornly.

Miss Smith smiled at Sorrel.

"You mustn't let it make any difference to you, just go quietly on as if nothing has happened. Now, tell me about your lessons. You were in the same class as Miranda, weren't you? But Miranda seems a little bit behind you from the reports from the Academy, especially in mathematics and literature."

Sorrel, to the best of her ability, explained to Miss Smith exactly where they had got to that term, but she knew she was not sounding very intelligent. Miranda was being even worse than she had expected. How awful to

255

have to rehearse with Uncle Francis, who would probably be angry with her because she was not as good as Miranda, and as well go up to the wardrobe and do lessons with Miranda, who would not speak to her.

If Miss Smith thought Sorrel's answers not very intelligent she showed no signs of it; instead, she unpacked a paper bag and held out a sponge sandwich.

"Look, this is the sponge sandwich I promised you with a cream centre, or what pretends to be cream. We'll have tea after the act and then you can go down on the stage and watch the rest of the play, dear. I'll just pop along the passage and put on the kettle."

Mary waited until the door had shut behind Miss Smith. Then she winked at Sorrel.

"I may be mean, but I couldn't be more pleased really; I know she's your cousin and all that, but if you ask me, a disappointment won't do her any harm."

Sorrel rather liked the look of Mary.

"I feel that too in a way, only the awful thing is that she really would have been good as Ariel."

"Do you think you won't be?"

Sorrel fidgeted with her plaits.

"When somebody like Grandmother or Alice or Miss Jay at the Academy has just that minute been talking to me I know I will, but when I'm alone, like in my bed or my bath, then I'm not a bit sure."

Mary held out the vest to see how it was getting on.

"I know just how you feel; it's how I felt when I thought Miranda was going to play Ariel. You see, if she had, I expect I'd have played Sylvia. I kept kidding myself I'd be as good as she was, but inside I knew I wouldn't. It's that bit in the second act when she has to get all dramatic. I do my best at it, but you ought to see the stage manager's face at the understudy rehearsals. As a matter of fact, though I wouldn't tell them at home, I was not a bit certain that if Miranda gave up the part they wouldn't get somebody else and leave me as understudy."

"Don't you want to be an actress?"

"No. I started as a dancer, but my legs got too fat; then I understudied Wendy in "Peter Pan" with this management. I'm reliable, that's a thing understudies have to be, you know: always punctual, never ill and always know my words. If I could be certain the people I understudy would never be off I wouldn't mind understudying until I grow up."

Sorrel was quite incapable of believing there could be a person who felt like that.

"But it's so dull. Just sit in a dressing-room and knit."

"Oh, well," said Mary contentedly, "it's not so bad, and I take my money home every Friday and that's a great help; and it's not as if I was going to do it always, because as soon as I'm old enough I'm going to be a hospital nurse." They could hear Miss Smith coming up the passage. Mary lowered her voice. "But, mind you, anyone who understudies Miranda and has to share her dressing-room earns their money."

They had a funny tea. Sorrel, in spite of the goodness of the sponge sandwich, could only nibble at it and look at Miranda out of the corner of her eye. Miranda had her cup of tea and a piece of sandwich at the dressing-table and spoke to nobody. Mary, who was obviously quite accustomed to this sort of atmosphere, ate three slices of sandwich and clearly enjoyed every mouthful. Miss Smith kept talking and did not seem to mind because nobody answered. Sorrel was glad when overture and beginners were called for the next act.

Alice waited until Grandmother was safely on the stage, and then she took Sorrel's hand and led her through the pass door and down to the stage manager. He was following the play in the prompt book. Alice gave him a nudge.

"Here's the other granddaughter; you'll have no trouble with this one."

Sorrel found it fascinating to watch the play from the stage. In three or four steps she could be on the stage herself and in front of the audience; it was like being half in one world and half in another. For the first time for days she forgot all about Ariel. It was such fun seeing Grandmother and Miranda and all the other actors and actresses within touching distance, as it were. From where she stood it sometimes seemed as if the people on the stage were speaking to her and when Grandmama said that Sylvia ought to be whipped, she felt a shiver run down her spine.

Miranda, when she went off to be whipped, came down to the prompt side to await her end-of-act call. Sorrel moved nearer to the stage manager. After all, it was no good looking or smiling at a person who would not speak to you. Miranda was always surprising.

"I don't suppose Dad will let you play Ariel; you're only rehearsing on approval, you know."

They had, of course, to talk in whispers, and even that was a risk with the stage manager so close to them. Sorrel came right up to Miranda so that she could speak in her ear.

"Perhaps he won't, but I'm going to try very hard to be good enough. I don't see why you should be hateful about it, it's not my fault that you aren't playing it."

Miranda looked at her in surprise.

"Goodness, you have changed!" She said nothing more for a moment, then she drew Sorrel to her again. "I don't believe you're the sort to tell tales about people. What I'm trying to do is to get everybody so sorry for me that they'll let me play it after all."

Sorrel thought that was pretty cool.

"What about me?"

"I don't care a bit what happens to you; I'm always going to think about me and nothing but me, that's the way to get on." The act was coming to an end. Miranda straightened her frock preparatory to taking her call. "There's just one comfort I've got: if Daddy does allow you to play the part, you'll be simply awful in it."

The curtain came down and Miranda ran on with the rest of the cast. She stood in the centre of the stage holding Grandmother's hand, smiling and bowing. The audience whispered to each other: "Isn't that child sweet?"

Chapter 19

REHEARSALS

Miss Smith took Sorrel on Monday morning to the Education Officers' Department of the London County Council, which was in the County Hall by Westminster Bridge. Fortunately, the children's father had brought their birth certificates amongst his papers when they left Guernsey. Miss Smith said this saved a lot of trouble, as births were difficult things to prove without certificates. Grandmother could only have got a copy from Guernsey, seeing it was occupied by the Germans, through the International Red Cross, which would have taken months and months. Grandmother had already had an application for a licence sent for, and this had been filled in by her on behalf of Sorrel, and by the manager of the theatre where "The Tempest" would be produced on behalf of the theatre management. The application had then been sent back from the County Hall and Grandmother had a letter telling her to send Sorrel to the County Hall with the particulars of her birth, as she was to be examined by the medical officer and interviewed on behalf of somebody in the Education Department. Sorrel thought all this a lot of nonsense because she was perfectly well, had been to a dentist since she came to London so all her teeth were in order, and she knew she was all right at her lessons. Miss Smith said that the London County Council rules for children in the entertainment industry were

260

good and prevented people from allowing children to earn money under bad conditions.

"There's absolutely nothing to be frightened of, Sorrel dear; just answer each question you're asked, that's all you've got to do."

Sorrel found this was perfectly true. The doctor was like any other doctor that she had ever seen, and just as friendly. He prodded her all over and sounded her heart, and told Miss Smith that she was undersized, but a tough little specimen, and though she was thin he could not find a thing the matter and supposed she was the thin kind. The education man was just as nice; he scarcely asked Sorrel any questions because he knew Miss Smith. He was, however, very interested to hear that Sorrel was going to play Ariel, and said that playing a part like that was an education in itself. Sorrel thought that was quite likely true, but wished all the same that she was playing Alice for her first part, like Pauline had done. Alice never had to say things like:

> "All hail, great master! Grave sir, hail!
> I come to answer thy best pleasure;"

The education man pulled one of her plaits.

"You look very solemn; aren't you pleased to play Ariel?"

Sorrel, having been told by Miss Smith to answer any question that was put to her, was perfectly frank.

"I can see it's a big opportunity, everybody says so; but, you see, I haven't been training very long, and until we came to live with Grandmother last year I never thought of being an actress. Actually, now I want to be one very much, only—if I could have chosen—I wouldn't have started with Ariel, and I wouldn't have been rehearsed by my uncle Francis. He's a very nice man, only, of course, he's a relation and that makes a difference."

261

"He's a very fine Prospero," said the education officer, "but the man for my money is your uncle Henry—there's an actor! What he wants to be messing about on the pictures for, I don't know. What a Hamlet!" He gave Sorrel's arm a pat. "If we're going to have a child Ariel, I should think you'll be very good. You've got some lovely stuff to say."

"The most sensible line I've learnt so far," said Sorrel, "is saying 'Grave sir.' Now that describes my uncle Francis exactly."

Miss Smith took Sorrel's hand.

"Well, if you've passed her we must be getting back; she's got her first rehearsal at twelve o'clock."

Uncle Francis at rehearsals was very like Uncle Francis playing a charade. He was grand, and serious, and very aloof. For a whole week he was like that, quite calm and never raised his voice. To her great surprise, Sorrel enjoyed herself. She never saw much of the play or of the actors, because her scenes were taken together as far as possible, so that when she was not wanted she was sent back to her lessons. Then suddenly, on the Monday at the beginning of the second week's rehearsals, Uncle Francis changed. He had said on the Saturday that no one would have a book on the Monday, and Sorrel, who knew her part by now, had not minded a bit, but on Monday she found that having no book meant a lot of other things as well. Uncle Francis made a speech. He explained what the play meant; he spoke in his big booming voice and used long, grand words, and though Sorrel put on an interested face, she scarcely understood a word he was talking about. At the end Uncle Francis said:

"That is what we have got to get over, and I want pace and, of course, full value to the prose. Clear, everybody?"

Everybody scuttled off the stage except the people who were playing the shipmaster, the boatswain and the mariners, and the stage manager called out "thunder over" and then the rehearsal began.

Sorrel was standing beside the girl who was playing Miranda. Her name was Rose Dean. Rose smiled.

"It starts with a storm, you know; you'll see some terrific goings-on in the effects department later on, thunder and lightning, wind and goodness knows what. There's a boat, you know, being wrecked on the island."

Sorrel, of course, by now knew the story perfectly, for Miss Jay, as well as taking her through all her scenes, had explained it to her in a simple way. Sorrel was glad to hear about the thunderstorm and hoped, although it came before her entrance, to be allowed to come down to the side of the stage and watch it.

In the previous week Sorrel had learnt where she came on for her various entrances, and when Uncle Francis said "Approach, my Ariel; Come!" she was ready, and she ran as she had been taught to do and knelt at his feet, then raised her head to speak.

Uncle Francis let her get to the end of her first speech without interruption, then he told her to stand up.

"That, my child, is said like a little girl at an elocution class. Tell me, what do you think Ariel is like?"

Asked directly like that, Sorrel forgot the listening cast and forgot to be shy of Uncle Francis. Except for her weekly rehearsals and broadcasts for the B.B.C. and the afternoon when she had watched Grandmother's play, she had hardly thought of anything else, and a picture of Ariel had grown in her mind.

"It's something not real at all, like the wind; you've caught it, and it does everything you ask but all the time is simply longing to be up in the air again where it belongs."

Uncle Francis took her chin in his hand.

"Is that your idea or Miranda's?"

263

Sorrel was surprised at the question.

"Mine. Miranda never said anything about Ariel. We didn't know she was supposed to play it till she wasn't going to."

Uncle Francis's voice became more caramel even than usual.

"It." He turned to the cast who were sitting round the stage. "You notice she uses the word 'it.' My conception entirely."

Sorrel had no idea what the word "conception" meant, and only hoped that it was intended nicely.

"Is it a he or a she?" she asked.

"Neither," boomed Uncle Francis. "It. And how do you suppose you look?"

Sorrel had no idea. Miss Jay had said there were innumerable ways of dressing Ariel; the last time she had seen the play Ariel wore a tunic of rainbow silk. Sorrel thought that would be gorgeous.

"Rainbow silk?"

Uncle Francis roared.

"Rainbow silk! Rainbow silk! And what else did you plan? A wreath of roses round your hair? No, my child. Ariel is a strange shape, almost terrifying in the way nature is terrifying."

Sorrel, though very disappointed about the rainbow silk, tried not to show it.

"Do you mean with a long nose and big ears?"

Uncle Francis looked for the moment as if he were going to burst. At the same moment the cast began to laugh. Uncle Francis wavered between bursting and laughing. The laugh had almost won when he turned to the stage manager.

"Are the designs there?"

The stage manager fumbled amongst some sketches and then brought a bit of paper to Uncle Francis.

264

"Here's the rough."

Uncle Francis showed the picture to Sorrel.

It was of a strange creature with weird hair going backwards with little curls on the end of each hair. It was wearing a very tiny piece of stuff and at the back it had stiff wings rather like a beetle's. It was so unlike what Sorrel had pictured that for a moment she could only stare at it, and while she stared she tried to think of something polite to say.

"It's very unusual."

"Your face and arms and legs are faintly blue," said Uncle Francis. "The wig and the dress and the wings are silver."

Sorrel went on staring at the picture. Blue! At last she said, because she could not think of anything else and that was what she was truly thinking:

"'Their heads are green and their hands are blue, and they went to sea in a sieve.'"

"Now," said Uncle Francis, dismissing Sorrel's quotation as if it had never been made, "you will go off and make that entrance again, and don't forget there's nothing real about you; magic, my child, magic, magic, magic!"

Sorrel, running to the side of the stage, thought to herself:

"It's all very well for Uncle Francis to talk like that, but it's very difficult to feel magic and blue all over and dressed in silver when you're wearing a school tunic, which you've outgrown, of a school you left last year."

Sorrel was given the part of Ariel. Not, of course, just like that. There were desperate days when both she and Uncle Francis were in despair; and almost worse days when he did not look despairing but grieved. Yet somehow the days of rehearsing on approval came to an end, and she knew they had come to an end because Miss

265

Smith was told to take her to Garrick Street to have her wig fitted, and to see Mrs. Plum, the wardrobe mistress, about her dress.

The situation with Miranda, of course, got worse as Sorrel's rehearsing of the part got better. Miranda had hoped to hear her father tell her mother how shocking Sorrel was. She had hoped to hear her mother on the telephone telling Aunt Lindsey how shocking Sorrel was, and she knew that from there, for that was how things went in the family, Aunt Lindsey would ring up Grandmother and then everybody would know how shocking Sorrel was. Instead she heard the very things she most hated to hear. Her father would discuss Sorrel at meals.

"That child has a quality. She is inexperienced, of course, almost amateur, but she has a miraculous gift for getting about the stage quickly, and being always in the right place, almost without appearing to move. Then, of course, that queer little voice of hers. Quite definitely she has something."

"How does she sing the song?" Aunt Marguerite asked.

Uncle Francis very consciously acted when he was acting and, in spite of being pleased with Sorrel, he thought there must be something wrong with a performance which came naturally and easily.

"Just sings it, true and clear like a boy. Sometimes I say to myself that I'd like it this way, or that way, and in the end I leave it. It seems very right as it is. Extraordinary!"

Miranda's anger with Sorrel and her wish to hear her criticised were not really jealousy. She was jealous of her for having the luck to play the part, but never once did it cross her mind that Sorrel might be as good an Ariel as she would have been. Miranda knew that her speaking of Shakespeare was outstanding, and that she had only to appear in a good part for her gift to be admitted. She had heard Sorrel speak Shakespeare and she knew she was not in the same class as herself. Her jealousy was entirely professional. Somebody else was getting the chance that should have been hers. She really minded so much that she got pale and quite ill looking, and when she found that her father and mother were looking at her anxiously, she added to the effect of illness by acting being much worse than she was. She had her reward at last. One evening when she came in from the theatre her father called her to him. He stroked her hair. He spoke in his most caramel voice.

"Your management have consented to allow you to play Ariel at a few matinées. Will that bring back the roses into your cheeks, little daughter?"

Miranda was enchanted. She felt sure she could trust her father to see that some influential people were in to see her play, and apart from that she would at least have the occasional pleasure of acting the part in the way she knew it should be acted. "Poor Sorrel," she thought, "I'll show them what's what."

Miranda arrived in the wardrobe for her lessons the next morning with shining eyes. Miss Smith was talking to Mrs. Plum about Sorrel's dress, so Miranda drew Sorrel into a corner.

"Have you heard? I'm going to play Ariel at some of the matinées."

Sorrel remembered the conversation she had with Miranda on the side of the stage.

"So you've won."

Miranda shrugged her shoulders.

"As far as I could. If my management won't release me, they won't, though I think it's pretty mean of them. Even a few matinées are better than nothing. I'll always get my way, Sorrel, because I know what I want. You'll see."

What with Sorrel's rehearsals and broadcasts and her lessons, she did not know that anything else was going on in the world, but, of course, quite a lot was. Mark sang in a children's revue on the air and got immediately, or rather the B.B.C. got, the most enormous fan mail, particularly from old ladies and clergy and inmates of hospitals and nursing homes, all of whom said Mark's voice had done them good. Mark was not himself very interested in the broadcast except that after it he had two letters from boys who had been at school with him at Wilton House. They both said they had heard him sing, and one said it had made the matron's cat sick and the other that the headmaster's wireless had broken in half, but, as well, they told him all about what was going on, about cricket and school rows, and how somebody or other had cheeked somebody else. Mark, drifting along at the Academy, had accepted life as it was, partly because it was new, partly because he had enjoyed being a Polar bear, and partly because there did not seem to be anything else, but getting these two letters made Wilton House come vividly back. He saw the cricket pitch, and he could remember the feel of the short, dry grass round it while he and a friend lay watching a match and eating cherries. He remembered lots of other things, too, and though, of course, he had not really liked a lot of it at the time, he liked all of it when seen in his memory. He was not caring for the summer term at the Academy; it was hot in London and nobody played any proper games. He never had cared for his dancing classes, and now he pictured what the boys at Wilton House would say if they could see him in a bathing dress and white socks and sandals dancing every day.

When Mark had come home from his broadcast he had been quite pleased when Hannah had said: "You ought to be in a church choir singing 'Oh, for the wings of a dove,' like the boy I heard once in a cathedral." And the next morning he had been charmed when Grandmother had said: "I heard you yesterday, grandson. It was beautiful." And he had been entirely satisfied with Alice when she had said: "We weren't half proud of ourselves last night, my old china." He knew that china was short for china plate, and that Alice was calling him mate. It was a friendly term with her and it showed that she was thinking affectionately about a person. He was pleased too when the Academy staff said he had been good, and really delighted when Dr. Lente patted him on the head and said, "That a delight was." But when he got his two letters and heard about the cat being sick and the wireless broken in half, he knew that was the real way to think about singing, and how he would feel himself if he heard any of the boys at Wilton House caterwauling over the air. Because she had always been the leader of the family since their father went away, Mark went first to Sorrel.

"I do wish I needn't go to that awful Academy. I do wish I could go back to Wilton House."

He was standing at Sorrel's bedroom door. Sorrel was crouched on the floor practising how, by moving her shoulder blades, she could keep her wings continually on the move. She gave Mark only half her attention.

"So do I, but I shouldn't think you could; but you'll go somewhere different in the autumn."

Mark glared at her back view.

"Ever since you started to act in that awful old Shakespeare you don't pay any attention to what anybody says."

Sorrel gave her shoulder blades another twitch.

"Mark, just look at my shoulders; am I moving them just a little, so that I'll make my wings tremble, or am I jerking them up and down?"

Mark shot his chin into the air.

"I couldn't care less."

There seemed only one other person after Sorrel who would understand about Wilton House, and that was

Hannah. He heard Hannah before he saw her. She was singing while she ironed and her voice came rolling down the stairs.

> "Do no sinful action,
>   Speak no angry word;
>   We ought to spend our points today."

Mark leant against the table on which Hannah was ironing.

"I do wish I could go back to Wilton House. It's where I ought to be."

Hannah felt the iron against her cheek.

"You never spoke a truer word."

"Well, can I?"

"Now, don't be silly, Mark dear. You run out and play in the garden; pity to waste this nice sunny evening."

"But why can't I?"

Hannah shook her head.

"There's things beyond yours or my understanding, Mark, and what I say is, what you don't understand, take on trust."

Disconsolately, Mark hung over the banisters and slid down. How hateful everybody was! Why could not he go to Wilton House? Surely somebody besides himself must see what a sensible idea it was. The word "sensible" brought somebody to mind. He and Petrova had kept up a short but entirely sensible correspondence and every week or two Petrova sent him entirely sensible presents, things that anybody would want; a proper little model aeroplane made by a mechanic she knew, and a whole set of spanners, and one of the best pocket-knives he had ever seen. Grandmother, he knew, was at the theatre. He slipped into her drawing-room, opened her desk, found a sheet of paper and a pencil and, breathing hard through his nose, because he hated writing, he wrote Petrova a letter.

Holly and Miriam were sent with Hannah to Sorrel's dress rehearsal. Mark was asked, too, but nothing would induce him to go.

"If Sorrel is going to act in that awful Shakespeare she can act by herself; I don't want to see her."

As a matter of fact, neither Hannah nor Holly nor Miriam enjoyed the play very much; in fact, in one place Holly went to sleep. Hannah was so appalled by Sorrel's clothes and general appearance that she made Holly nudge her each time Sorrel came on so that she could shut her eyes, and that, of course, is not a very good way to enjoy a play.

Miriam was quite happy until some dancers appeared during the song "Come unto these yellow sands," then she sat up as if someone had stuck a pin into her.

"Oh, my goodness! What an arrangement! Have you seen their feet!"

Before the dance was over she could not bear looking at it any longer, and she swung round in her seat and put her legs through the back so that they were in the row behind, and buried her head in her arms. Fortunately there was no one to see this rudeness or Miriam would have got into trouble, for both her father and mother were very strict about theatre manners.

When Sorrel came in that evening after the rehearsal, Hannah did not even try to be polite.

"Shocking! What Mr. Bill would say if he could see you, I don't know. No more on than some poor savage. I was so upset my stomach hasn't settled yet."

Holly was frank.

"Well, of course, I think it's a dull play, but I thought you were most awfully good. You were just like that bit of silver stuff we had in a puzzle, that had to break up into five pieces to make up into buttons for a man's coat. I wouldn't have been able to listen to Uncle Francis, only, of course, he was so like Grandmother was on Christmas Day, but the worst thing was that Miranda. I'll show you."

Rose Dean was a good actress in ingénue parts, but she was not well cast for Miranda, and she had been so bullied by Uncle Francis that she was in a state of nervous twitter. Holly, not, of course, using the right words, gave an imitation of her that was so funny that Sorrel forgot for several minutes that tomorrow was the first night. Then Hannah came, still looking very disapproving, and fetched Holly off to bed and Sorrel was left alone, and suddenly it seemed as if something was spinning in her middle. She clasped her inside with both hands and said out loud, although there was no one to listen:

"Oh, goodness! I do wish tomorrow was over."

Chapter 20

PLANS

Sorrel's performance of Ariel caused quite a lot of interest. It is difficult for anyone to be a success in a part of Shakespeare's because there are so many people who love all Shakespeare's work and have strong ideas how his parts should be played. There were a large number of people to be just angry because Ariel was played by a child, and that, of course, was not Sorrel's fault, and would have happened just the same had Miranda played the part. There were just a few who wrote about "little Miss Forbes tripping and posturing," but they were the sort of people who hated the sort of Ariel that Uncle Francis imagined. As well there were a large number who wrote nicely: "Silvery-voiced little Sorrel Forbes." "Little Miss Forbes spoke Ariel's lines in a way that is a lesson to far more experienced actors." "Sorrel Forbes, as Ariel, gave a quicksilver performance, and her childish pipe, together with her weird blue make-up, gave an ethereal effect which was curiously moving."

Sorrel herself had thought that once the first night was over, everything would be lovely, that she would have all the fun and excitement of playing Ariel and nothing more to worry about. Acting for Uncle Francis was not a bit like that. Almost every performance every actor did something he did not like, and when the curtain came down he saw the company on the stage and gave them

what he called "my little notes." He had little notes for
Sorrel all the time, and generally a great many of them,
because, as she played all her scenes with him he could
not help hearing and seeing anything he did not like.

Except for the little notes there was quite a lot about
playing Ariel that Sorrel did love. There were moments
when she really forgot she was Sorrel and felt that she
was Ariel. Particularly she felt this at the end when she
ran in and lay quivering at Prospero's feet when he said
she could be free. Uncle Francis had taught her to raise
herself up in one ecstatic movement when he said this,
and Sorrel had found it easy to do. She knew that everybody ought to like an uncle, but she could not really
make herself fond of Uncle Francis, and when she listened to Uncle Francis being Prospero she thought how
awful it would be to be under his spell. He did not mean
to be what Hannah called "a make-trouble," but he was
the sort of man who could not have anyone around him
without thinking of things that they ought to be doing.
Ariel, who wanted to fly away, must have felt simply
bursting with pleasure on the word "free," and Sorrel felt
bursting with pleasure, and even, through her blue paint,
looked as though she did.

One of the things that Sorrel learnt was about getting
fond of a part. She had first discovered this when the
serial finished in the Children's Hour at the B.B.C. She
simply hated to think she would not be Nancy anymore, it
seemed odd to think she would not be; it was like killing
somebody almost. Now, though it was nervous work acting with Uncle Francis, she had got to love Ariel and to
feel she was Ariel, and it was with dismay that she heard
Miranda was to play at the next Wednesday matinée.

From the moment that Miranda was going to play the
Wednesday matinée, in a queer way the position between
Miranda and Sorrel changed. Miranda grew gay and ex-

cited, Sorrel silent. It was not that Sorrel wanted to be mean; it was only fair that Miranda should play Ariel a few times. But Ariel was her part; she hated somebody else doing it, and she particularly hated somebody else wearing her dress and wig.

Sorrel had not known what was the proper thing to do when somebody else was playing your part, whether you went to the theatre or not, but Miss Jay settled that.

"I've two seats for us in the dress circle, Sorrel. I'm very anxious you should see Miranda's performance."

Miranda had been quite right when she said that her father would not let her performance pass without having some interesting people in to see her. She had made a success, and she was Uncle Francis's daughter, and she was a Warren. Though Sorrel had done very nicely as Ariel, she had done nicely because of the very simple, almost childlike way that Uncle Francis wanted the part played. Miranda had done well as Sylvia as an actress, and people had talked about her as the latest sprig off the Warren tree. Sorrel was a sprig, but there was not as much fuss about it.

Sorrel found it interesting seeing the play from the front of the house. It was fun knowing all the actors, and the comedy scenes were much funnier from the front, and the scene where the goddesses appeared was really beautiful. Miranda looked so like she did as Ariel that it was quite odd. The wig and the blue paint would make any two children look alike, but there was any amount of difference in the way Miranda played the part. Different inflexions on different words, a different way of moving, different everything.

In the first interval Sorrel was very careful not to say anything to Miss Jay to show she wanted to know how good she thought Miranda was. Then two men in the row behind them began to talk.

"Francis's idea of Ariel and mine are worlds apart, anyway, but at least in the wisp of a child who normally plays the part he had what he wanted. This Ariel is a girl, and not only a girl, but a girl with a pronounced personality and bursting with talent. I would stake anything I had that this young woman has an enormous career in front of her in the great parts, in the great way; but if you want to see Francis's conception of Ariel see the other child."

The two men went out then to get some tea. Miss Jay turned to Sorrel.

"Did you hear what that man said?" Sorrel nodded. "Did you understand it?"

Sorrel nodded again.

"I think so, except about Miranda being a girl. We're both girls."

"Miranda's older than her age and you're younger than yours; but that part's not important, it's what he said about the playing of the part that is. Miranda's brilliant—and yet as Ariel you give the better performance, and that you'll find all the way through your stage career. It's getting inside the part that matters, and I think you've got inside the part as your uncle wanted it, and Miranda hasn't."

"But he said he would bet Miranda would be a great actress."

The attendant brought their tea. Miss Jay took the tray and balanced it on her knee.

"So she will. Great like Edith Evans, perhaps, if she works; but you won't have that sort of career, and you wouldn't aim at it."

"No," Sorrel agreed. "What I would like would be to act something like Pauline Fossil. I would most awfully like something like that."

Miss Jay poured out Sorrel's tea and passed her the cup.

276

"Well, we must see if we can manage it, and perhaps in a few years' time somebody else of twelve will say to me, 'What I would like is to be able to act like Sorrel Forbes.' Wouldn't that be fun?"

Mark had put on the envelope to Petrova, "Strictly Private and Conferdenshul." When Petrova's letter came to him she had written the same thing on her envelope, only she had spelt confidential right. Like all Petrova's letters, it was to the point.

DEAR MARK,

Of course you must go to Wilton House. I have written to Madame and she says that what you want to be is a sailor, like your father, but she thinks that it is difficult to arrange because at the moment your grandmother's looking after you and she wants you to go on the stage. She has suggested that Pauline have a talk about it with your uncle Henry, and I have cabled Pauline and asked her to do this. Madame says that your uncle Henry is the right person because your grandmother does anything he says.

Gum says he would like to adopt you until your father comes home. We will see about this when we hear from your Uncle Henry.

Yours,

PETROVA.

P.S.—I am sending you a screwdriver. It's always useful to have a good one.

Holly and Miriam were great friends, and almost every week Aunt Lindsey would come round on Saturday and fetch Holly to spend the afternoon. One day, at the end of July, she called for Holly to spend not only Saturday but the whole weekend. To Holly, spending the weekend

with Miriam was all fun. It was anything but fun to
Hannah.

"And your pyjamas that threadbare I'm ashamed to
pack them. And no bedroom slippers, and only your
house shoes to wear. But there, humility's good for us,
they say; but my cheeks won't stop flaming the whole
weekend, every time I think of your aunt's face when she
opens your attaché case."

It was a lovely weekend. Aunt Lindsey took them to the
Zoo and to tea in a shop; but the best thing of all was that
on the Saturday night Uncle Mose came home. Uncle
Mose had been doing a two months' tour of the Middle
East, and he was not expected back for another week; but
somehow he wangled his way on to an aeroplane instead
of a boat; and there he was with a little red fez on the side
of his head, sticking his face round the door and grinning
at Miriam and Holly and rubbing his hands and saying,
"Vell, vell, vell!" He brought back some presents; nothing
big, as they had to go in his pockets, but the most exciting
were two bananas. Miriam could hardly remember what a
banana looked like, and Holly only just. They decided to
eat the bananas, but to save the skins to take to the Academy to show off. They ate the bananas on Sunday; and
afterwards Holly, carried away by the excitement of having a banana, gave an imitation of how all the staff at the
Academy would react to seeing a banana. Holly's imitations were becoming quite a feature of the Academy. Of
course, the staff were not supposed to know about them,
because she was nearly always being funny about the
staff. The students loved them, and whenever there was a
dull moment someone was sure to say, "Holly, do Dr.
Lente teaching a class to sing"; or "Holly, do Madame
making a speech"; or "Holly, do Miss Sykes trying to give
a literature lesson and pretending she hasn't got hiccups."

Aunt Lindsey and Miriam laughed a great deal at

278

Holly's imitations of the reception of the banana skins;
but though Uncle Mose laughed, he had a look on his
face as though he was being serious as well. When Holly
had finished he said:

"Let's see some more of your imitations, young woman.
What else do you do?"

Miriam was exceedingly proud of Holly and bounced
with excitement.

"Do Dr. Lente at music; that's much the funniest."

Holly did Dr. Lente and then Madame, and then Miss
Sykes; and, finally, she wound up with Uncle Francis
being Prospero. This last took all the thoughtfulness out
of Uncle Mose's face and made him roar. When he had
stopped laughing, he beckoned Holly to him and put her
between his knees.

"So you're going to be a comedienne, are you?"

Aunt Lindsey had laughed so much, the stuff on her
eyelashes had run down her cheeks. She mopped her
face.

"Addie was a mimic, you know, Mose. We always said
she ought to have gone in for it."

Uncle Mose gave Holly a kiss.

"I take a great interest in your career, young lady. We
always wanted a comedienne in the family, didn't we, Miriam?"

Miriam took a deep breath and dashed forward and
pushed Holly aside and sat on her father's knee.

"I've thought of something. Let Holly be a comedienne
instead of me. I mean, I never was going to be a comedienne; but let's stop making me train all round to see
which way I shape. Let me do nothing but dance. Please,
Dad, please."

Uncle Mose raised his eyebrows in a question mark
over Miriam's head and looked at Aunt Lindsey, and
Aunt Lindsey gave him a funny sort of smile.

"I never did think it was going to be any other way, Mose; but it's funny we should have a dancer."

Uncle Mose was a man who came to decisions and stuck to them. He put Miriam off his knee and got up and stretched himself.

"Well, I'm going for a walk. Who's coming with me?"

Miriam flung herself at him again.

"But you can't just leave it like that; you must see Madame about me."

Uncle Mose gave her hair an affectionate pull.

"And who said I wasn't going to? As a matter of fact, I'm going to see Madame tomorrow, but not only about your future, young woman, but about the future of my niece, Holly."

Chapter 21

THE END OF THE STORY

Uncle Henry cabled to Grandmother and told her that he wished Mark to be sent to a boarding school, preferably the one in which his father had placed him, and that he would be responsible for the school fees. Grandmother sent for Mark the moment she received it.

"Read this, grandson." Mark read the cable and beamed at her. "And why is it necessary for you to go to your uncle Henry when you want something, instead of coming to me?"

Mark was quite unmoved by her tone.

"As a matter of fact, if you want to know, I didn't. I wrote to Petrova and she cabled to Pauline, and Pauline talked to Uncle Henry."

"Of course, it's absolute nonsense," said Grandmother, "your uncle saying that he will pay the school fees; he's never paid for anything in his life."

Mark looked proud.

"I've arranged for that too. I have been adopted by somebody called Gum."

Grandmother snorted.

"I've never heard of such behaviour. Here I take you into my beautiful home and bring you up in the lap of luxury and have you educated at the very best stage school the world can provide, and this is how you repay me."

Grandmother was lying on her chaise-longue and Mark was standing beside it. Now he made room for himself to sit.

"I think this room is very nice, but I don't myself care for the rest of the house. I never have. If Sorrel hadn't lent me the fourteen bears out of her bedroom, my bedroom wouldn't seem like home at all. I don't exactly know what the lap of luxury is; but if that's what we've got, I still would rather be at Wilton House. And though I think the Academy is all right for girls, it isn't all right for boys at all. I haven't played cricket once this term. I'm made to dance in white socks, and I simply hate it."

Grandmother fixed him firmly with her eye.

"And what about that beautiful voice? Is that to be squandered at a horrid little boys' school?"

Mark's eyes were every bit as firm as Grandmother's.

"As a matter of fact, if you want to know, we sang a concert of Gilbert and Sullivan at Wilton House, and that's very important sort of singing; and our singing master was just as good as Dr. Lente."

Grandmother threw off the silk shawl that was over her knees, and pushed Mark to one side and trailed across the drawing room.

"Ambition! Ambition! 'Cromwell, I charge thee, fling away ambition: by that sin fell the angels!'"

Mark was determined not to let Grandmother recite to him. He caught her by the hand and led her back to her chaise-longue and tucked her shawl round her, and opened the cigarette box and handed her a cigarette and lit it for her.

Grandmother puffed for a little while in silence. Then her eyes twinkled.

"Go to your horrid little boys' school. I've one great comfort, Mark. What an atrocious nuisance you will be to the Royal Navy." She made an imperious gesture. "Go away, grandson. Go away!"

As a matter of fact, Mark did not go to Wilton House that autumn. The headmaster was terribly sorry; he would have liked to have him back, but the school was full and he could not take him until after Christmas. Mark was not very upset about this because Madame was putting on some more concerts for the soldiers, which would include at Christmas a little version of "Dick Whittington," in which Mark was to be the Cat.

To Sorrel it seemed a long, dreary autumn term. "The Tempest" came to an end and she was not asked to do another broadcast; and though she had "m'audition" ready, including a dance in which she got on her points, nobody seemed to want to see or hear her do it. She had even got an audition frock ready, for Hannah had decided that she must have a new frock, and the silk one was only suitable for parties and first nights. It had, as a matter of fact, not been worn since the first night of Grandmother's play, because, owing to everybody being so busy and Miranda being so difficult, Miss Smith had not arranged a party for Miranda's fourteenth birthday at which party frocks would be worn. Hannah had been very reasonable about the utility frock and had not made any fuss when Sorrel had chosen coral colour, only saying that with the winter coming on they could do with a bit of brightness. There had been a party of a sort given by Uncle Mose and Aunt Lindsey for Mark's eleventh birthday; but that had been noisy games like "murder," and not suitable for silk with yellow flowers on it. One way and another, Sorrel felt terribly flat; and because she felt flat she was a prey to miserable thoughts, and the most miserable of all was that there was no news of their father. News was coming through now about other prisoners in the hands of the Japanese, but nobody ever wrote and said they had seen or heard anything of their father. Sorrel tried terribly hard to go on hoping; but little by little a horrid, snake-like fear was settling down inside her.

The autumn was depressing for everybody because the weather was so nasty.

Alice said: "When the fog gets into my old north and south and I can't see anything in front of my meat pies, I feel a bit off and I don't care who knows it."

In spite of the special matinées for the forces, the term dragged and dragged. Almost every day groups of children were waiting in the hall in their best clothes, and everybody called out "Good luck!" "Good luck!" but Sorrel was never among them. Mark and Holly felt this shame as keenly as Sorrel did. They took a truculent attitude about it. Mark said:

"I wouldn't want to act in an old pantomime, anyway; and that's all they're going to the audition for."

Holly said:

"It's just because they've all done dancing longer than you, and that makes a difference. And who wants to dance, anyway?"

But they were ashamed, no matter how hard they pretended they were not, and felt that the Forbes family had been let down.

Then one morning early, just before the end of the term, the telephone bell rang. Alice ran up the stairs beaming from ear to ear.

"Put Sorrel into that new frock, Hannah. Her Miss Jay has just rung up. She's to go for an audition. Somebody's ill in some show and they want a child to take her part."

Sorrel was the only child going to an audition that morning. She felt very self-conscious as she stood in the hall waiting to be inspected, though she knew she had nothing to be ashamed of in her coral-coloured frock with Holly's coral bows in her hair. Mark and Holly were so proud of her that they made a point of seeing that everybody in the Academy had a look at her and wished her good luck. Mark raced round, raking out anyone who might possibly have missed her.

"Go and see Sorrel, she's going to an audition. She looks all right, she ought to get it."

Sorrel came back from the audition, her face radiant. Someone was putting on the pantomime "The Babes in the Wood"; there was an epidemic of influenza, and the girl babe had been very ill and would not be well enough to play this Christmas, and Sorrel had got her part. The part was written in verse and quite easy to learn; but, as well, there was a song and there should have been a good deal of dancing; but, fortunately, the boy babe danced very well, so Sorrel's dancing could be simplified, and she had learnt quite enough by now to manage what was required of her. As they went home on the night of the audition, Mark summed up their general pleasure.

"There's Sorrel with a big part in pantomime, and me being the Cat in 'Dick Whittington' and going to Wilton House next term, and there's Holly playing the Dame in 'Dick Whittington,' and she's the youngest pupil in the Academy that ever played a Dame, and, as well, it's almost Christmas. I should say we were pretty lucky."

Christmas was much more difficult than it had been last year. Even though the children, what with presents and pocket-money, and, in Sorrel's case, earnings, had far more money to spend, presents were absolutely hopeless; there were hardly any of them in the shops, and those that were even bearable cost over a pound.

Sorrel bought books for everybody; books were as scarce as everything else if you wanted a special book, but if you went with an open mind, prepared to take anything that was suitable, you could get some good things. There was a book on aeroplanes for Mark and a book on costume for Holly; and a very grand hymn book for Hannah, with tunes as well as hymns in it; and a novel for Alice. Alice liked reading something that she could cry over. This book had a picture of a girl's head on the cover and on the inside of the cover it said, "This book will make you laugh and will make you cry, but you will not be able to put it down."

Mark gave another set of useful presents—nails, tin-tacks, wire, everything for mending. Holly gave every-body notepaper. Now that Sorrel and Mark wrote reg-ularly to one of the Fossils a lot of notepaper was used, and there never seemed to be any. Alice wrote to friends in the theatre when she had time. Hannah was always writing to people she had known in Martins, so note-paper and envelopes was obviously a good choice. Plants were even more expensive than they had been last Christ-mas; so, instead, they bought flowers. These cost enough, Alice said, to make the hair on a saint curl; but the chil-dren said Christmas was Christmas and should be prop-erly kept. They bought flowers not only for Grandmother but for Aunt Marguerite and Aunt Lindsey as well. No-body gave a present to Miriam, though they would have liked to, because nobody wanted to give one to Miranda, and it might look pointed.

On Christmas Eve, Sorrel went up to bed at the same time as Mark and Holly, so that they could all have the thrill of hanging out their stockings at the same moment.

"That's the gorgeousness of Christmas," said Mark. "I know the stockings can't simply bulge like they used to, but it doesn't make any difference to how you feel inside when you hang it up. I absolutely know this is going to be the loveliest Christmas we ever had."

Christmas morning started as usual: Holly sitting beside Sorrel in the bed, and Mark on the eiderdown at the other end, and Hannah sitting on the side of the bed, and Alice standing at the door as audience. The only unusual thing about this Christmas morning was that Hannah seemed queer. She kept saying she felt all of a jump, and she made three false starts before she began her carol. At last, however, they got her started:

"The first Noel, as the angels do say,
  Was to certain poor shepherds in fields where they lay,
  In fields where they lay, a-keeping their sheep,
  On a cold winter's night that was freezing so deep."

All the children took enormous breaths to blow into their instruments when the door opened and who should come in but Uncle Mose. He looked messy for him, and he needed a shave, but he was his usual gay self. He rubbed his hands.

"Vell, vell, vell! Happy Christmas, everybody."

The children hugged him and asked what on earth he was doing there at that time in the morning. He rubbed Mark's hair the wrong way and played with Holly's curls.

"I've travelled all night because a present for you three had gone astray. It went down to Martins by mistake and I've been to fetch it back to get it to you in time for Christmas morning."

They all spoke at once.

"What is it?"

"Where is it?"

"Is it for all of us?"

"You shall play it in," said Uncle Mose. "Come on, start again."

The children hummed down their trumpets and Mark beat with a free hand on a drum, and Hannah kept time on a triangle.

"Noel, Noel, Noel . . ." And then they all stopped because someone was singing, a big, cheerful voice coming up the stairs. The door opened, and there was their father!

Such a lot of talking went on. Luckily, their father had been able to gossip to Uncle Mose on the train or he would never have sorted out the jumble about "The Babes in the Wood," Wilton House, the dame in the pantomime and the Fossils; but as he knew it already, he was able to sit on the bed amongst them and tell them with absolute truth that he was proud of them all and thought every arrangement was splendid. He told them a little about himself, how he had been wounded and hidden in a native's hut, and finally escaped across India, and how they were meant to have had a cable and he did not know why they had not.

While their father was talking, Hannah and Alice went away. Uncle Mose was following when he popped his head back through the door.

"See you tonight, everybody. What's the betting this is the best Christmas night this house has ever had?"